AN EDUCATION IN LONGING

AN EDUCATION IN LONGING

A Novel

Charlotte Stein

An Imprint of HarperCollins*Publishers*

HarperCollins books may be purchased for educational, business, or sales promotional use. For information, please email the Special Markets Department at SPsales@harpercollins.com.

hc.com

FIRST EDITION

Interior text design by Diahann Sturge-Campbell

Smoke rose © say_hope/Stock.Adobe.com

Library of Congress Cataloging-in-Publication Data has been applied for.

ISBN 978-0-06-342386-2

26 27 28 29 CPI 10 9 8 7 6 5 4 3 2

For you, Mum

Prologue

Mina knew the rule was that people could only see Harrowhall if they had magic in them. Yet when their creaking Ford Fiesta crested the hill everyone called the Test, and her dad parked in a good spot to view the valley where the university hid, she couldn't bring herself to look.

She stared out of the side window instead, at another family who were doing the same thing as them. The mum all dressed up, out of the car right away. The dad snapping pictures of his lithe, long-limbed daughter posing in a way that said she'd expected this to happen.

And the daughter was probably right to. Families with money—they had all kinds of ways to tell if their kids would blossom into magic wielders and go on to learn how to use their abilities at universities like this one.

Expensive assessments, by rogue witches.

Illegal blood tests, by unlicensed alchemists.

Mina had heard of them all, even through the meager grapevine a girl like her could access. But the prices had always been too high for her family to afford. All she had was the feeling of not quite belonging, for most of her life. And a hope that she finally would was burning a hole through her body.

Just for once, she thought.

Then looked through the gap between the front seats. Quick, like ripping off a blood sticky bandage. Every bit of her expecting to bleed in a big frightening rush, and then unable to fully process when something else happened instead. She simply stared at the squashed-down view she'd allowed herself.

The hint of a spire, so sharp it seemed to pierce the sky. Some sense of higgledy-piggledy bricks stained by years of soot from chimneys she couldn't quite see. A single narrow window like a dragon's eye, winking in the dying light; a spiral of smoke tinged with a strange violet hue.

It made her breath catch in her throat to see it. For a second, she couldn't move or speak—not even when her mother tried to commiserate. *Never mind love*, she said. *We still think you're something special.* Then her dad reached back to pat her hand and offer her a tissue.

He only stopped when she sat forward in her seat.

Fumbling and greedy about it, every bit of her trying to get at more of that beautiful place. To seize more of it, now that she knew it could be hers. She was about to walk those halls, and live among real witches and wizards, and learn those magical lessons. And that meant it was okay now to let herself enjoy the view.

But as she went to drink it in, the view was abruptly obscured. One second there was that beautiful, sprawling building surrounded by trees and rolling greenery and grounds too extensive to follow.

The next, there was *him*.

Just him, strolling up to their car in a way that quickly devoured everything she most wanted to see. She watched his broad shoulders swallow the hedge maze by the fountain, and the lake that looped around the easternmost wing. Then his height stole the turrets, the towers, the most fairy-tale parts.

Until finally he stood there, filling the glass.

Face almost turned into a silhouette by the sun behind him. Most of him nothing more than an impression—of messy, thick, dark hair; beautiful bones; blazing eyes. Every bit of him seemingly oblivious to her and her family. Like some monstrous cat that finds you so unthreatening it barely registers your presence.

It only cares if it wants to eat you.

But he already had something for that.

She saw it more clearly than the rest of him—a fat, gleaming apple, red as a ruby, resting in his hand. He tossed it up, as she watched, and caught it again. Then he took a bite, big enough that it verged on disturbing. She caught a glimpse of a lot of teeth and a deep curve carved into the flesh. Past the core, almost all the way through to the other side.

Followed by slow, lazy-looking chewing. *Rude, incredibly rude*, she thought.

But her parents didn't seem to notice. Her mother said, "Oh, Jeff, I think she can see it," and her father said, "You're bloody right, Marjorie. I know that look." While she sat there, seeing nothing but gleaming teeth and a hollowed-out apple.

And the words he mouthed after swallowing that enormous bite.

Clear as anything somehow, despite how little she could see of his face.

You will never, ever belong here.

Then as her face burned, he turned his back to them. He walked back down the hill to the beautiful place he had come from, with everybody he *did* think was worthy to be with him. A boy wearing something that looked bespoke, another with the most amazingly styled hair.

And the girl from the car next to theirs.

Beautiful and perfect, in all the ways she knew she would never be.

Chapter One

Mina decided that the best thing to do was avoid the guy who thought she didn't belong. But unfortunately for her, the guy who thought she didn't belong did not want to be avoided.

She saw him the moment she arrived, as she struggled up to the enormous gates with two suitcases and several bags in her hands and under her arms. He was just beyond the wrought iron spirals and spikes, directing students to where they needed to be. Face obscured still, but that shape unmistakable.

His shoulders looked like an enormous yoke, of the sort someone might use to carry a preposterous amount of milk. And then his body arrowed down to a narrow waist, narrow hips, impossibly long legs.

He had to be well over six foot.

Maybe even close to seven, she thought, and wished she hadn't. It made her drop one of her bags. She had to chase it down the hill to her left, instead of going through into the grounds. And by the time she'd retrieved it—her best and only boots now muddy and her face pink with the effort—they were almost closing the gates.

Those tangled swirling metal arches started swinging inward of their own accord, as she clambered back to where she'd been. She only snuck through by turning sideways and sort of scrambling. And just as she thought she'd managed, she felt her skirt snag on a curl of wrought iron. There was the sound of something ripping; she tried to stop.

But it was too late.

She walked up the endlessly long cobblestone driveway with the hem hanging in tatters. People stared, someone turning to a friend to whisper. And every one of them looked so different to her. None of them had slightly crooked incisors. Or hair too wavy and unmanageable to style into anything decent. Or thighs and waists and chests thicker than a sheet of paper.

Their clothes weren't drab, secondhand, torn.

They all wore what looked like a uniform—but obviously wasn't.

It was just the right style, the sort only rich people knew. Shirts that looked thick and yet also near transparent, jeans that seemed like they were made of something other than denim, chunky sandals that appeared ugly to her untrained eye but probably weren't. And beads everywhere—around necks in loops, on arms almost up to the elbow, strung about waists like belts.

Beautiful, she thought.

But not as beautiful as what she was supposed to be paying attention to.

There it was. The source of all her dreams and nightmares. Harrowhall, in all its glory. So tall she couldn't see the top of the many towers from where she stood. So wide it seemed to touch the tangled forests that surrounded it on either side. And all of it put together so haphazardly you could hardly believe the place stayed standing.

It was like looking at a monster made of stones in the middle of sinking into a slump. She almost felt afraid to stay standing there. *Any second now and the whole place is going to collapse on top of your defenseless body*, a little fearful voice in her head said. But that fearful voice couldn't win.

There were too many other incredible things to take in.

Like the shadows that didn't seem to belong to anything, beneath windows that winked out when she looked at them twice. Or the lettering above the archway, sometimes in a language she could read and sometimes in one she couldn't. Some sort of Underneath thing, she assumed, but couldn't be sure.

The guidebook they had sent her hadn't really explained any of that sort of business in detail. It didn't name the creatures that lived in that shadowy place, or give an alphabet she could learn. A lot of things were just left for her to guess or fumble her way through. Like some of the doors she could see, set way too high up for anyone to safely use. Mystifying to her, at first.

But then she realized.

She thought of that whistling sound even ordinary people could hear, in the dead of night. The way she used to rush up to the roof of their block of flats, just to try to catch a glimpse of what that whistling meant. Once she had even thought she'd seen something through the darkness—some hint of a broomstick, a flutter of material, the gleam of dark eyes looking back at her.

But nothing like she would get here.

Here someone could fly out of one of those doors right now. She even tensed, breath held, heart beating like a bird in her chest, thinking they just might. And only let that glorious idea go when someone pushed past her. She watched them disappear through the great red doors beyond the archway, half hurt, wanting to say something to them. But they spoke before she could. "The Brawl is in ten bloody minutes," they spat over their shoulder, and the words dropped down inside her.

Mostly because she knew what he had to be talking about. Placement, he was talking about placement—that was the thing they were all doing in ten minutes' time. She even got her guide out and frantically flicked through it to make sure. And found it, in chapter 1. *At the start of every new year, each student is assessed and placed accordingly, in either novice, intermediary, or advanced classes, within their respective years. However, it should be noted that a particularly talented new student may find themselves taking the place of a student of long-standing, in some advanced classes, and vice versa for any long-standing student who falls short of the faith the school has previously put in them,* she read, the words as polite as she remembered.

But less polite seeming, now that she'd heard someone call it that.

A fight, he had called it; it was a fight of some kind. And one that also prompted the guide to say something else. A single line detached from the previous paragraph, which she now traced with one slightly shaky finger.

Many unfortunately find the rigors of placement a trifle too much.

Death, they mean you can die doing whatever the challenge might be, she thought, and for the first time in her life actually considered running away from this place, instead of toward. Even though, of course, she had already known the risks involved. She was aware that sometimes students didn't come back from Harrowhall. It was the reason for the liability waivers, and the memory erasures, and the constant refrain of sacrificing for the greater good of humanity.

It just felt a little different now she was here.

And someone was already out to get her. *People probably kill each other for places in the advanced classes,* her mind whispered, as she stepped up to the door and stared into the strange empty darkness beyond. Everything silent, so silent, despite all the people she'd seen pour into the building.

Until she took a steeling breath and stepped inside, and the riot of sounds hit her. As if you could only hear it all when you chose to be a part of it. And after you had, there was no going back. She was in the maelstrom of bustling, rushing bodies now. The cries of "I think you go this way," and the crowing of those who already knew just what to do. Like she was in some sort of fancy train station at rush hour.

It even looked the way fancy train stations did.

The floor was something that seemed like marble and here most likely was. A million heels and heavy shoes clicked and clattered over it, before disappearing into a warren of dim passageways branching off from the central space. And the central space was round, and domed, and dominated by a staircase.

She followed it up with her eyes, until it too dissolved into whatever was up there. More halls, she imagined. More doorways to who knew what. *It is very easy to take a wrong turn in Harrowhall*, she remembered reading, and vowed to move slowly. To take careful steps and always pay attention to where she was going.

But that mass of seething bodies had other ideas.

She took one step, and they just swept her along, like some great flesh and fashionably clothed river, until she was somehow past the staircase and down the left-hand hallway. Then someone knocked her suitcase out of her hand, as careless as only the incredibly rich could be, and she stooped to retrieve it. She buried herself among people's backs and bags, reaching for the handle. Almost suffocated for a second, sure it was going to get kicked away.

But she managed to snag it.

She straightened, pleased with herself.

And it was then that she saw him again.

He was just there, in the center of the hall. Impossible to miss—and not just because he stood a head taller than almost everybody else. There was also the fact that all around him, absolutely everyone bustled and ran and doubled back. They called out names and tossed cases, jostled and pushed and darted down halls.

While he remained so unnervingly still it seemed impossible. She couldn't make out an expression on his face, or a hint of him breathing. Like he had been turned to stone by some spell she didn't yet know. She even took a step toward him, thinking maybe he wasn't a threat.

Then his gaze flicked down, switchblade quick.

And suddenly their eyes were locked. Tightly, to the point where she couldn't immediately pull herself away. She tried to, and it was like running through treacle, through mud, through glue. She couldn't get any traction. She was stuck fast and getting more so by the moment. *Maybe this is the assessment*, she found herself thinking frantically. *Trying to extricate yourself from the gaze of horrible men.*

Though of course she knew it wasn't just his horribleness that held her.

It was finally seeing his hideously handsome face. Because now that there was nothing to obscure her view of him, she couldn't pretend he might possibly be anything else. There was no more hope for something plain or made repulsive by centuries of inbreeding, courtesy of a probable upper class family.

Every part of his face was perfect.

Eyes the color of spilled ink, wide set enough to almost be unsettling, turned down at the corners like something from a painting by Rossetti. Then there were those brows, thick and dark and just a little untidy, toward the middle, stark against that pale skin. The bone structure hinted at before but so clear to her now. That jaw like something carved from stone, those cheekbones broad and high.

Almost everything heavy, heavy, heavy.

Until you got to that dimple. The one that looked as if a ghost had pressed a finger over his lips and left a faint imprint behind. Part of it above his mean mouth, just underneath his firm nose. Part of it below, down the middle of that strong chin. And every bit of that image so oddly familiar she got a little flash of something.

Like a memory, of being laid down in long grass. Sunlight making patterns on tanned skin. For some reason, her nails were painted blue—they looked dark against the pink of someone's lips, as she hovered one finger over an indentation very like his. Almost *exactly* like his.

Though she couldn't remember who it could have possibly belonged to. She didn't know any handsome men, didn't like them, didn't trust them. And even if she had, she couldn't recall doing anything of the kind.

She was an indoor girl. A lover of evening, midnight, the witching hour. Of curling up in wintertime with a mug of something dark and sweet, a book open in her lap. She would have never laid out like that, in heat so fierce she could almost feel it now. She could almost taste it, almost smell it.

And it was this that helped her finally wrench away.

It was just too real, too weird. Like he was doing something to her mind somehow. *Here that's completely possible*, she told herself, then stumbled through a sudden break in the crowd, without thinking. She pushed against the seething river of bodies, intent on nothing but getting away. No thought of where she was going, just escape, escape, escape. There was one of the passageways—she took it gladly. She kept going until she was far from his cruel gaze.

Too far, really.

She looked back the way she had come, but somehow that Grand Central Station mess was no longer there. There was just a pinprick of darkness at the end of an endless hall. And the hall itself was no less disturbing. Portraits lined the wall in front of her and the wall at her back. Heavy, dark portraits of men with pale, somber faces and steely disapproving eyes.

Like older versions of the boy who thought she didn't belong.

Which explained a lot. He was probably a legacy, who'd never had to crest that hill and pray. Most likely he lived in one of those gated magical communities and policed those boundaries like a wolf. Always lying in wait for trespassers, always ready to pounce when they set foot where they didn't belong.

They turn a corner, and there he would be.

Though, god, it was a shock when that exact thing happened. She got to the end of the hall and tried to turn in a direction she hoped would bring her back to the entrance, and there he was. Somehow, there he was.

"That's not possible, you were just—" she started to say and pointed back toward the entrance. But his expression told her the mistake she'd made immediately. His lip curled, his eyes suddenly lit with a kind of amused contempt. Like he couldn't believe she was thinking something that preposterous. How could she not understand that this wasn't an ordinary place, with pedestrian things like passageways that went in normal directions? *You may find that the laws of physics are not strictly obeyed at Harrowhall*, the welcome guide had said.

And here was the proof.

Or was it more like proof of the kind of magic he could do? She saw what he had at his hip. Attached to his belt with a loop of leather. Simple looking, for someone like him—just plain, dark wood tapering down to an almost sharp-seeming point. But unmistakable all the same.

A wand. He had a whole actual wand.

One that he could just use anytime he liked.

She even thought he might, right then and there, on her. His hand hung very close to it, open and just a little tense. *Like a gunslinger*, she thought, waiting to draw and shoot her dead.

And it would shoot her dead, too.

She had absolutely *nothing* to defend herself with. No wand of her own—students didn't even get one until they had mastered the basic forms. And she was nowhere near mastering anything at all. Sometimes she had strange dreams, and when she woke things had shifted around. But nothing concrete. Certainly, nothing that could hurt him. And he plainly knew it. It was all over his smug face. It was in the way he stood there, blocking her path. "Are you going to let me past?" she stuttered out finally.

Then watched his lips peel back over those unsettlingly large teeth.

Like some approximation of a smile.

"Maybe you should just try," he said, accent exactly as she

could have predicted. Every word seemingly dragged from low down in his throat, and so clear and clean it made her think of cut glass, the good crystal, crisp air.

Old money, she thought automatically.

And it made her bristle. Her face heated; she went to go around him in a blundering rush. But he stepped to his left when she stepped to her right, and she almost ran right into him. She got a wave of his scent, like winter air when you open a window. Something seemed to brush the back of her hand, the flat of her thigh.

However, when she looked, she could see she had never actually gotten close enough to touch him. It was just the space between them, so strangely heavy it rubbed against her. It left her wanting to scratch, to shake it off. She thought of spiders running across her skin and dropped a bag.

Then two more followed when she went to pick it up.

She scrambled for them, on her hands and knees now, and was sure she heard him laughing. But when she glanced up, red-faced and sweaty and full of things she wanted to spit at him, the look on his face stopped her dead. His eyes had darkened to the deepest black she could imagine, entirely lightless and empty. And there was a kind of strain about his features, a tension—as if he was trying to force himself not to do something.

And she suspected this something was very wicked indeed.

It made her heart jump in her chest, just seeing a hint of it. Every angry word fell back down her throat so abruptly she had to swallow to stop them choking her. Then somehow, she found herself scrambling back across the floor. Heels digging into what was probably marble, hands behind her, frantically sliding.

While he stood there, calm and still and cruel-eyed.

Almost impassive in a way that somehow felt more terrifying. She could only stand ten seconds of it before she turned, and stumbled to her feet, and ran back the way she came. And she only stopped when she realized:

She had left her suitcases behind.

Chapter Two

She expected him to do something terrible to her belongings. After all, that was what bullies usually did. Michael Matheson had once hung her PE shorts from the falling-down eaves of their high school roof. Her life was littered with boys throwing her books, her homework, her bags into places she couldn't reach them.

She couldn't imagine this would be different. She'd get to the assessment hall and find her underwear hung across it like a banner. Or arranged on the floor to spell something out. She would almost make it through and find the words *fat ass* blocking her path. Then end up being decapitated by some lobbed spell, because the sight of it had thrown her.

But when she finally made it, there was nothing of the kind.

There was just a great drafty room, divided into four lines of extremely nervous-looking students. And he didn't even seem to be among them—though she knew he was definitely supposed to be. At Harrowhall, it didn't matter how many years you'd been attending, or what kind of advanced level you'd made it to, or how many perks you had attained prior to right now.

You faced the assessment, all the same.

And you risked losing every bit of privilege you'd managed to grab, she thought, as she took in all the greedy gazes, lighting on anyone who looked particularly weak. Which, of course, only made the whole thing scarier. Her heart was a trapped rabbit in her chest when she finally forced herself to join one of the lines. Sweat prickled beneath her arms and over the nape of her neck. And her head swam with everything she'd tried to memorize from the guide.

Cupped, closed, clenched, she murmured to herself over and over.

Though she wasn't entirely sure what good that would do. There was no guarantee that knowing the names of the basic forms would make magic happen. All she knew for sure was that so far, there was nothing. Nothing when she'd tentatively tried in her bedroom at home. Nothing now, as she fumbled through each move.

Furtively, because nobody around her seemed to be doing the same. In fact, the girl behind her—as pretty as Mina was plain, doe-eyed and skin glowing a deep brown, hair as lustrous as black ink from a pot—looked positively mystified by what she was doing. Her lips parted, as if to ask. But then she seemed to draw back, embarrassed. As if it was wrong to even inquire about it, somehow.

It made Mina nervous enough that she had to find out. "Are new students not supposed to practice?" she asked as quietly as she could. But the girl's frown only deepened. And she shook her head.

"I don't even know what it is you're practicing."

"It was in the guidebook. The chapter on basic forms."

"Oh. I see. We couldn't afford anything like that."

"But we didn't buy it. It was sent to me. I thought it was sent to everyone."

The girl didn't say anything to that. She didn't need to, however. Mina could tell what her expression meant. It was half angry and half resigned, as if she knew full well how brutally unfair that was but also hadn't expected anything better from a place like this. It was run and ruled for rich white people.

Honestly, it seemed like a miracle that she even had a guidebook.

But she didn't intend to keep its secrets to herself. She glanced around to see if anyone was watching for illegal sharing between the sort of students who didn't quite fit the aesthetic, and then lowered her voice even further. "Okay, look. You have no reason at all to trust me. For all you know, I'm a rival trying to sabotage you for a place in some advanced class. But we don't have time for me to prove otherwise, so you can either take this advice or not. The five basic forms are these: cupped, closed, clenched, reached, and opened. You start with cupped—cupped hands, like this." She made the shape the diagram had shown her. Two curves through the air, as perfectly symmetrical as she could make them, and ending with something that looked like she was gathering water to drink. "That's to draw the magic to you. And then right after that move, fast into closed. Arms together, hands together like you're praying. Or you can do clenched too, with your fists. Those are the ones that are supposed to be good at creating something to defend you. Does that make sense?"

No, she thought despairingly.

But the girl's expression said something else.

She watched Mina put her arms together, hands clasped, and a spark seemed to light her eyes. Like she'd seen something she recognized on some deep level. Or maybe knew, in that moment, that

Mina wasn't trying to trick her. *It's my earnestness,* Mina thought. And for once in her life, she didn't regret it.

There was no punishment waiting for her because of it.

The girl grabbed her hands instead. "Thank you," she said in a tone Mina recognized all too well. It was the same one she would have used upon realizing someone was actually doing right by her.

Instead of the usual.

"Don't thank me. It's only fair," she said. Then before she could offer her name, the girl lurched forward. Someone pushed her from behind, she pushed into Mina, and finally Mina stumbled, half turning, and almost crashed into the professor waiting at the front. The bored-looking one, with the clipboard and the pen that definitely wasn't fueled by anything ordinary.

No ink flowed from the tip.

Only a kind of silvery light.

"Name?" he asked. Because apparently this was it.

"Mina Morrow," she replied, the words barely out before he started in on the same spiel she could hear all the other register takers spinning out.

"Wands and other magical aids go in the lockers provided; none are permitted during the assessment. Flying spells are prohibited, and attempts at performing them will be punished. Other than that, there is only one rule: Make it as close to the center of the maze as you can before the clock strikes midnight, to secure your place in any of the classes. Good luck," he said in the flat drone of someone who had been forced to say it a thousand times.

Then he pushed her through the door behind him before she could ask any of the million and one questions she had. *If you don't get there in time, do you get expelled?* she thought frantically, as she stumbled from a well-lit hall into whatever was out there. And after that, she had no time to think at all. She barely even managed to register the grass under her feet, or the towering walls of a hedge maze on either side of her, or the fact that there was an inexplicably night sky somewhere above them.

Cool air and cold darkness slapped her in the face, and a second later it was followed by heat. A searing, blazing heat that actually seemed to singe her hair as it flew past her face. She smelled burning. Her cheek was suddenly hot.

But it was only in the aftermath that she grasped what had happened. She shot a look down the narrow alley behind her, and saw the blazing glow of it as it disappeared into darkness. A fireball. Someone had hurled a whole goddamn fireball at her head.

And if she didn't move fast, they were definitely going to do it again.

She glanced back at the direction it had come from and saw them there, at the end of this shadowy lane. Hands already cupped to try a second time. Confidently, too. Like they'd done this a million times before. Like they'd been coming here for years or understood everything about the place before they'd even walked in the door, and finally they were going to get access to the elite classes they belonged in. That they were *entitled* to. *How is this fair?* she found herself thinking for the thirtieth time. Though this one definitely had a keener edge than all the others. Now she wasn't just sitting in her bedroom, reading that new students were assessed alongside old. She wasn't just thinking about what an advantage people would have if they could pay for the information early or came from families who already understood and taught and practiced all this.

She was about to be murdered by that deranged level of inequality.

Unless, of course, she did something about it.

The only question was: *What?*

She glanced behind her and saw nothing but a dead end. In front, the next turn out of this lane looked to be a good thirty feet away. This guy was going to reduce her to cinders before she covered half that. And there was nothing to use as protection just lying about. No bin lids, no big rocks, no tree branches to use like a cricket bat.

The only thing she had was magic.

But she shook when she tried cupping her hands.

The curves through the air came out juddering, awkward, not as symmetrical as they needed to be. The sides of her hands met in the middle offset. One slid awkwardly over the other. And after this first failure, she made the mistake of looking up, down that narrow lane, to her tormentor.

She could see him grinning now.

All teeth, in the electrically bright light that was gathering in his palms.

It made her even clumsier. For a second she couldn't even remember what she was supposed to do. She stood there, paralyzed, hearing the word *cupped* in her head but not the action that went with it. Then she finally tried, and it was too frantic. It was too fast. Her hands smashed together, hard enough that it hurt. A little sound of pain escaped her, even as she went to do it again. And again. And again.

Like someone trying to make a flame spurt out of a faulty lighter. Worse than that, really, because she wasn't getting so much as a spark. There was nothing happening, nothing at all—as if there'd been some mistake. She didn't have any magic in her after all. She was ordinary, and now she was going to die for it, courtesy of a fireball so big and bright she could see it without even looking up.

It lit the whole of this dark lane. It bloomed through her eyelids when she squeezed them tight shut. She could almost feel the heat before he hurled it, yet still she kept at that busted lighter. That match that wouldn't strike. Right to the last second, right to the point of him jeering as he went to throw.

And that was when she heard it. Above her, someone hissing through the dark and the quiet. "Hey, hey, hey," she made out. And she looked, and there the speaker was. The girl from the line, all liquid eyes and one reaching hand. "Grab it," the girl said the second Mina saw her. She even shook it frantically. Stretched down further, like she'd never been more desperate for anything to happen in her life.

It made Mina get hold before she'd even had a chance to doubt.

Though she didn't expect it to work. The girl hadn't looked particularly strong. Thin and barely an inch taller than Mina's five foot three. Yet somehow the moment their hands connected, her feet left the floor. She scrambled, searching for purchase, finding it and then not, finding it, then not. Then that light suddenly boiled bright, and she felt heat blooming against her lower legs, and she yanked them up. She tucked them to her stomach and pulled with her arms.

And suddenly she was on top of a great bristle of twigs and leaves.

On her back, breathing hard, unable to believe what had just happened.

But there was proof it had. She could feel it on the backs of her legs. And when she finally caught her breath enough to twist around and look, she could see it, too. Two perfectly shaped ovals burned through her woolen tights. Then in the center of each, a lot of suddenly too-pink skin. Like she'd been very weirdly sunburned.

Though she didn't understand how she could make out that part in the darkness. Until she looked up at the girl crouching over her, and saw what she had in her hand. A little ball of magic light, sputtering a little but never to the point of going out. And it seemed to be getting stronger, too. More sure.

"Yeah," the girl said, half a grin visible in the glow. "That's because of you."

But Mina didn't have time to be happy about that. Or relieved. The asshole who had just almost burned her legs off was now apparently trying to aim lightning up at them. And though he wasn't succeeding, the crackle and spit of it wasn't doing the hedge beneath them any good. The acrid scent of burning leaves filled the air. Embers glowed too close to her hand.

She had to scuttle away over something that wasn't meant to be scuttled over. Twigs bit into her palms, hard enough to hurt. And when she went to get on her knees, her hand sunk into a gap between the branches, right up to the elbow. She almost face-planted—and probably would have, if it were not for the girl.

The one who got a hand under her left arm and heaved.

The one whose name she didn't even know.

"I'm Mina," she gasped out, as they stumbled and fumbled their way down the top of the hedge to some dark and entirely deserted corner. *No one wants to linger where they might end up in last place*, she thought, once they were huddled there, hugging themselves, burned and breathless, but still in one piece enough for the girl to answer her.

"Anaya," she said, and Mina felt a hand clasp hers. For a shake, it seemed like. Though her new friend held on long past the usual point for a greeting. Like she needed the comfort of it.

But who could have blamed her?

They had just almost been murdered. And now they stood with nothing but strange black behind them, like the world simply cut off beyond the hedge. And in front, the view was even more disturbing. Pure carnage, of a kind that sent a jolt through Anaya the moment she took it in.

Mina felt it through their still linked hands.

She squeezed that hand back, as the Brawl hit her, too. Someone somewhere was screaming that their eyes were on the wrong way. In the distance, what looked like a set of horns were peeking just over the top of the hedge. Then this horned thing moved, and when they did, the ground shook.

Like they belonged to some mammoth thing.

"A minotaur," Anaya whispered, seemingly awed and terrified at the same time. And Mina understood that. It was one thing to read in the guidebook that mythical and supernatural creatures could be encountered here. It was quite another to see them. To know that they could possibly be summoned or maybe transformed into, and then kill you.

And there was more than that, so much more.

Tears in the sky above various places around the maze that disgorged hungry, searching tentacles. Followed by multiple hapless students obviously trying to seal them back up. They saw one jagged mouth zip closed, and the great gooey tendril that had emerged got cleanly snapped in two. It tumbled down into one of the lanes where they couldn't see.

But they could hear.

Screams followed.

As if it hadn't quite died. As if it was still squirming away down there, squeezing people to death. Or sliding over them, leaving a trail of burning acid. While they quite obviously tried to fight. Great gouts of rainbow-streaked flames flew up from between those hedges. In fact, great gouts of rainbow-streaked flames flew up from just about everywhere.

One of them hit a shield someone made out of thin air, two lanes over from them, and then careened so close they both ducked. They watched it paint the sky purple behind them, breaths held.

And all of it was only half visible to them.

Only something they could guess at.

Because everybody was on the ground.

"Why don't they try to escape each other up here, too?" she found herself asking. Faintly, almost like she was talking to herself.

But Anaya answered all the same. "I don't really know. I think maybe . . . maybe it's not that easy to. Honestly, I don't even know how I managed. It was like one second I was on the ground. And the next I was up here. With absolutely no explanation as to how. Or how I managed to get you up, either."

"Maybe you used some kind of teleportation magic."

"But all these experts can't? That seems really unlikely."

"You could be a prodigy."

"It was hard enough lighting this to see my way, once I was up." Anaya held it aloft as she spoke. That faint blue-tinged ball of light, incredible to Mina in more ways than she could count. But she had to concede the point. "So maybe one of them hit you by accident. Like a blowback from something they only intended for themselves. I mean, look at this mess," she said, pointing to something they could more clearly see. Someone had turned themselves into a giant spider for some reason, and the person behind them now had a pincer where a hand should be.

"Well, whatever did it, we probably shouldn't waste it," Anaya said in the middle of trying to calm her frightened breathing. "We could get pretty far, pretty safely like this. Enough to not get expelled, anyway. And seeing all of this, being not expelled is pretty much all I'm going for."

"Same. I mean, god, can you imagine what the third-year advance classes are like?" Her new friend shuddered, as if picturing it.

And Mina had a good idea what it was she had in her head.

"You probably step into one and find Cthulhu waiting for you."

"Or else some asshole just murders you immediately for daring to turn up."

"You mean like the asshole who was staring at you in the entrance hall?" Anaya asked, and when she did, Mina felt those liquid eyes on the side of her face. Staring through the darkness, waiting for an answer.

Though when she dared to look back, the expression she found was not unkind. It was something else, something softer, something that made her want to confess what had happened in the hall of headmasters. That coldness, that feeling that he might do something very bad indeed.

She had to force herself to keep it light. "That wasn't anything," she said, but Anaya didn't back down.

"It was enough that other people noticed. I heard a bunch of students wondering if he found you so fascinating because you were secretly something other than human."

"I don't even know what something else I could be."

"A succubus, they guessed. Come to suck out his soul."

"That's insane. That isn't a thing. I'm as human as anybody."

"You don't have to convince me. Your hand is the hottest, sweatiest thing I've ever held. If anything, I'm worried you're *too* alive," Anaya said, kindly enough that Mina couldn't help laughing. Even with the thought of him in her head and all this going on, she laughed.

And got a laugh back.

Half hysterical, like her own.

But it was there. It was enough.

"Feel calm and strong enough to go for a little bit farther?" she asked.

"I do now," Anaya replied. Then they just went. Aisha in front, Mina behind, both still linked by that too-long handshake. Each step more like wading than anything else, and wobbly as hell. But they managed. They got to the end of the first lane still in one piece.

Then it was just a matter of jumping to the next.

A couple of feet.

Fairly doable, Mina thought. Though she wasn't relishing a landing on the other side. Or particularly happy about what she could see when she made the mistake of looking down. That was a severed arm, sprawled across the grass. And said severed arm *was still moving.* It crawled slowly but steadily toward a hunched dark shape, by a corner across the way.

So of course she could guess what the hunched dark shape was.

Her stomach turned at the thought. She had to look away, at

Anaya, as she got ready to jump. A little clumsy run up, and then what looked like the easiest leap in the world, and she was over.

No big deal, Mina thought, as she took a few steps back and then ran, just like Anaya had. Exactly like that, it seemed like. Yet something happened the moment her foot left the safety of the hedge. Shapes seemed to disappear into darkness. Darkness became suddenly solid. And somehow there was way too much empty air in front of her. She passed right through the place she was supposed to land and kept right on going, down, down, down, legs flailing, hands snatching at twigs and leaves, body spiraling as she went.

She actually twisted all the way around in the air.

Though that turned out to be a good thing, of sorts. She didn't face-plant right into the grass and end up with a bloodied nose, at least. She just got a flash of pain from that bone at the base of her back, and a thump to the head, and some of the wind kicked out of her.

But even that passed pretty quickly. She managed to take a breath after a second. Another second after that and she could sit up, slowly. The base of her spine protested and one of her arms groaned, but she got there. Now all that was left was taking stock of her situation. Because the maze had shifted mid-leap pretty obviously. And that was most likely the reason people didn't clamber around on top. But where exactly had it put her?

A moment away from Anaya? Or a mile?

More toward the beginning, or less?

She couldn't tell at first through the gloom.

It took until something lit up the sky, somewhere above her head, for her to work it out. She got a flash of open space around her, square in shape instead of a narrow lane. Then stone beneath her, like she'd somehow landed on a sort of table. Moss riddled and ancient looking, but sturdy. She hauled herself up using the edge of it, no problem at all.

The maze must have really shifted, she thought, as she looked around, a little dazedly. But she wasn't sure that explained why she was here. Because now it was dawning on her where *here* actually was. Not somewhere useless, not an inch from the start, not a millisecond from being expelled.

She was in the middle of the fucking maze.

She knew she was. The little square the hedges had formed just screamed it; the stone plinth almost hummed with the energy of it. A fool could have guessed this—even before she saw the person who was in here with her. Standing at the only way into this little area, back to her.

But obvious, all the same.

Those shoulders.

That hair like midnight.

And good *god*, the things he was doing. A million movies and books and best guesses could never have prepared her for what magic looked like, in the hands of a master. Even the things she and Anaya had seen—they didn't compare. He curled his arm over his head, wand gripped in his hand, the tip of it trembling with tension. Like a conductor, urging his orchestra to even greater heights.

Then from the end came a kind of shimmering wave. It rose up, from the ground to somewhere above the hedge walls. And she got to see in great and glorious detail what rose up with it—*people*. Students. They simply lifted in the air like they were made of nothing. They floated and flailed impossibly.

But flight isn't allowed, she found herself thinking.

It took her a second to realize that flight wasn't the thing happening here. That he hadn't gifted them with the ability to swim around in the air. No, no—it was *gravity* he had affected. *He had turned gravity upside down*. And now they all batted against some invisible boundary, most likely put there in anticipation of outlandish spells just like this.

Though somehow, she doubted many were capable of it.

Few here seemed anything like his equal. Someone tried to sneak in by making their body some sort of porous thing—able to pass through one of the hedge walls, to the side she and this bastard was on. But the bastard caught it. He made a series of movements with his free hand, so fast she couldn't even make out what they were. A fist maybe, followed by two fingers straight up, and then something else, something tricky.

And suddenly the sneak had turned to stone.

He stood there, in the corner—a statue of himself.

While the first set of victims screamed from the sky. "Let us down, Harker," they yelled. "Come on, mate, just leave it out." And she processed two things when they did. His name, as horrible and snooty as she'd imagined. Then hot on its heels, the fact that these people, these people who he had just sent into the sky and turned to stone—they were his *friends*. They knew him; they were pally with him.

But he was ruthless with them regardless.

Apparently, the top spot was for him, and him alone.

And here she was, accidentally occupying it. *This is a mistake*, she wanted to say. *I don't know how this happened*, she wanted to say. But she knew he wouldn't listen, that none of that would hold any weight with him. So instead, she slid toward the edge of the stone table she was still sprawled on. Slowly, slowly, slowly, breath held, no clue in her head where she was going to escape to but doing her best to do it anyway. If she could just get down onto the grass, she told herself, as she squirmed one foot over the edge and down. Toes straining for the ground inside that shitty patent leather shoe she shouldn't have worn, hands tight on the stone to stop herself sliding all at once, body trembling like a plucked wire.

She had almost made it, when something scratched the back of her shin.

She felt it bite into her skin and couldn't help her sound of pain and surprise when it did. Just a small one, and she managed to cut it off immediately with her hand over her mouth. But it was enough, she could tell. His back clearly stiffened the second it happened. That raised wand lowered, slow, slow.

While she stood there frozen, quivering, awaiting her doom.

Barely able to breathe. Barely able to think. Almost wanting to plead.

And still, it was a jolting horror when he suddenly turned. Whip quick, wand ready, face so hungry for whoever was trying to steal his prize. He looked like a demon in the slanting moonlight. So when he took a menacing step toward her, she did the only thing she could.

She hauled herself up onto the plinth. Then she scooted back across it, too fast for her frantic hands. One of them gave as she went; she wound up sprawled on her back. Her head clunked against the stone, hard enough to briefly daze her.

But she still felt that hand on her ankle.

Like she had imagined him doing in the hall of headmasters—only somehow even scarier. It tugged, and she slid so fast and so easily across the surface it stole her breath. For a second she thought, *God, I'm just going to fly right off the end and directly into his mouth*. And just as she was coming to terms with that terrible thought, he simply launched himself up. All in one move, like a great cat pouncing on its prey.

Before landing like an enormous cage over her completely defenseless body. His hands slapped the stone on either side of her head, hard enough that the crack hurt her ears. She tried to immediately move her legs and encountered what had to be his thighs on either side of her.

It was bad; it was really bad.

But having to look up into his face was worse.

His black eyes glittered, as deathless and cold as they had been when she'd first been at his feet. And now they practically crawled over her face, the messy cloud of her dark hair, the hands she had somehow bunched into the beige blouse she shouldn't have worn. He saw it, and a flicker of distaste crossed those classically handsome features.

Though strangely, they looked a little less classically handsome up this close. She could see now that he had a slight gap between his two front teeth. That his scything cheeks were a little softer than she had first thought. That his mouth was too curlicue, his eyebrows too messy.

They almost met in the middle.

Yet somehow, none of those things seemed to make him ugly.

They just made her flash on the boy in the long grass again. That face different, but the resemblance was there. It made her flinch, when whoever was laid with him whispered some soft words. *You are so pretty*, she said, in a voice that felt even more familiar than he did.

She had to bat it away.

Clearly, he was just fucking with her mind somehow.

"Get off me," she spat, with all the anger and frustration she hadn't been able to aim at him in the hall. She even somehow managed to shove at his chest—for all the good it did her. It was like striking stone. The impact hurt the wrist she'd already pranged, painful enough that she clutched at it.

Much to his amusement.

"You made it all the way to the heart of this terrible labyrinth, and that's all you have? A little love tap? I'm afraid you're going to have to do better than that if you want to keep cheating your way through the ranks," he sneered.

As if that was going to make her give in.

"I didn't cheat, you asshole. It just happened."

"Of course it did, of course."

"The maze moved."

"So it just favored you, for no reason."

"You think I want to be here, trapped underneath *you*?"

Something dark flickered across his face—anger maybe.

Though it didn't linger long enough to say for sure. That smug smile widened, and he leaned down to speak a little closer to her ear. "Well, let me see what I can do to make you more comfortable," he said, so low and soft it felt like a caress against the side of her face. She flinched away and almost went to shove him again.

But when she did, something happened.

Something went through her—a sort of silvery sensation. Like her blood had suddenly turned into mercury. And for just a moment, just the smallest little fraction of a second, she thought she saw a light. There, in the hands she had reached up to him. It gleamed between their bodies, clear enough that it seemed like he saw it, too.

He glanced down, something like surprise on his face.

And he acted fast. He shifted so he could use his wand. To defend himself, she thought, or attack her maybe. However, just as she braced for him turning her guts inside out, she saw him aim at the stone, at the side of her. He drew a swift line, between his arm, and his leg, and her head, and her body.

Puzzling, at first.

Harmless seeming almost, despite the brightness of that line, the heat of it. And then he slashed another one above her head, and she got what was happening all in a rush of horror. He was drawing a rectangular hole. He was drawing a rectangular hole for her to fall into. In a second, the stone was going to give way beneath her and dump her god knows where.

The Underneath, she thought automatically.

Then she didn't even stop to think. She just tried to shove past the bar of his arms, his legs. She scrunched up and pushed herself into that gap between both, fighting to get through. But just as she got hold of the edge of the stone plinth, just as she started to haul herself to freedom, half of her body just fucking *dropped*.

Suddenly her legs were dangling, instead of laying flat on something solid. They flailed behind her, like a puppet with half its strings cut. And that tenuous grip on the stone simply wasn't enough to keep her stable.

So she did the only thing she could.

She grabbed a fistful of his sweater with her free hand. And when she lost her grip on the stone, she held on tight to him. *Bizarrely tight*, she thought—until she saw what her clenched fist looked like. There was that light all around it. That little spark still there. It meant he couldn't get free, when he tried to grab her hand and shove it away. Like she'd glued herself to him somehow, strongly enough that there was no real escape.

She was shocked to hear him gasp. To see the look on his face as she tumbled all the way through—a flash of outrage, followed by scalding hot fury, clear enough that she knew exactly what it meant even before it happened.

She'd dragged him with her.

He was following her down, down, down, into whatever nightmare he'd condemned her to. Flailing as he went, as if he were no more graceful than her. And all the while, she held on. She didn't know why, but she did. When they landed, she still had a fistful of his sweater.

So of course he did it on top of her.

She got that enormous shoulder jamming right into her left breast. His heavy thigh smacked her hard enough across the stomach that she knew she'd have bruises tomorrow. And his face landed so close to hers she could have called it a kiss. She felt the burr of his stubble, the hint of something softer than bone and muscle.

Lips, she thought, as she tried to get away.

She shoved and squirmed frantically, every part of her so horrified and disgusted she didn't even care that she was probably plunging deeper into some godforsaken part of the Underneath. Let the monsters down there eat her—it was a better fate than being close to him. Or letting him see how burning red her face suddenly was.

Only once she had made it a safe distance, she could see there weren't any monsters at all. She wasn't hemmed in on all sides by the weirdness she had both feared and longed for all her life. They were still surrounded by hedges. They could have been a foot from where they'd started out, if it hadn't been for one minor detail.

There was a set of gates here. Big gates flanked by the same sorts of people who'd taken her name, at the start.

And then it sank in.

"You sent me to the *beginning*?" she gasped, too furious and flabbergasted to even think of holding her tongue. "What did I do to you to deserve being expelled?"

But he just laughed. He laughed in this bitter sort of way, as he slowly started to climb to his feet. Shook his head, like he couldn't believe she was such a fool. Then finally, he met her gaze, as the sound of a clock striking midnight rang out over the maze. "The punishment for barely making it beyond the gates isn't expulsion, you annoying creature," he said in this weary way. "Though you might wish it was, once you attend your first boring basics for beginners lecture and realize what you have dragged there with you."

A monster, she thought automatically.

Pulled from the depths somehow, when she wasn't looking.

And of course, in one way she was absolutely right. Because he looked human, he looked ordinary, he could have passed for a person in all the ways that mattered. But as she looked up at him—head full of the words he'd just said and what they most likely meant, what they told her about how much closer he would now be than he would have ever as some advance class–attending champion—she understood completely: He was as monstrous as anything with fur and fangs and fifteen arms, in almost every single possible way.

Chapter Three

It took her a lot of effort to drag herself up the path to the dormitory. And not just because she was battered, and bruised, and her burned legs were stinging. Not just because she was exhausted, right down to her bones, and every muscle in her moaned whenever she moved. Or that she had only been able to wave at Anaya from afar as everybody was given their dorm assignments.

No, it was mostly him.

And the thought of how much more horrible he was going to be after this.

Now she wasn't just a thing that didn't belong. She had actively thwarted him. She had dragged him back to the beginning with her. He was almost certainly going to be forced into some of her classes, thanks to this stunt. And all these horrid thoughts made her actually hesitate on the path that led to the place she was going to be staying.

The Narrows, her assignment papers said.

Ominous sounding, she had thought when she had read it. And even more ominous with all this weighing on her. Brawls, and burns, and the thought of being murdered for ripping away some of the privileges a man like that enjoyed. Better, she thought, to turn back now, before this probably evil building finished the job he had started.

But then she saw it, between the trees.

A gray, teetering structure, five stories high and as thin as a knife. Thinner than that even. She took a step to the left, and somehow the whole thing seemed to disappear. Then she stepped back, and there it was. A perfectly normal building, housing at least a hundred students.

She could see some of them, in fact.

Candlelight danced in a few of the windows, illuminating all kinds of activity within. A boy was unpacking his things; another was talking animatedly to someone she couldn't see. Then a little up and to the left, she saw the silhouette of a girl sitting on her windowsill. Single braid over her shoulder, head bowed, book in her lap.

Everything about it so beautiful it made her breath catch.

And she just couldn't let him rob her of that.

She started walking toward it before the rest of her had even had a say. And she climbed the spiral staircase inside the same way—in a daze of dreaming about what that might be like. That kind of peace, that kind of time to just quietly read, in some gloriously dim and haunted-seeming setting.

Like something out of a gothic novel, she thought, as she got to the room they'd listed and slid the ornate key they'd given her into the similarly old-fashioned lock. Then she shoved at the oddly narrow door to her room and burst in, and there before her was everything she had never had in her whole life.

It was a room of her own, bigger than any in the tiny, cramped council flat she had called home. And it was filled with things she had only ever dreamed of before now. There was a dresser, with a whole oval mirror, on one side. A wardrobe—big enough that she could imagine Narnia waiting for her just beyond its doors—

next to a bookshelf absolutely crammed with books, overflowing with books, oh, it was more books than she had ever had at her fingertips in her whole life. She had to physically force herself not to bury her face in them immediately.

And not just because she had other things to explore first.

She was also absolutely filthy. She held up a hand and saw there were still grass stains all over it. When she turned her head, her hair left a trail of twigs and leaves. Her whole body felt stiff with dried sweat and almost stained in all the places he'd touched it.

She had to sort herself out before she lived her bookish gothic dreams.

And she started by flicking through the sheaf of parchment on the dresser. A little welcome packet, with things in it like instructions on how to use the tiny bathrooms that came with each room. There was a sink but no taps. You dipped your hands in, and water was just supposed to appear.

None of which she believed, until she poked one finger at the ceramic bowl and suddenly it was wet. She jolted back, astonished—and even more so when she realized the water had a scent. It smelled like wildflowers and summer grass, sweet and heady, and when she drew a handful of it to her filthy face, it formed a lather.

She managed to soap herself with hardly anything at all, so eager she didn't stop at her face. She stripped off in that tiny teeth-like-tiled bathroom, then scrubbed until the last remnant of this hellish day was gone. Or at least, she scrubbed most of her. Her shins were too sore to be treated so roughly—they gleamed pink and raw, even in the splinter of moonlight that filtered in from the tiny window above the sink, and required more care.

She had to just dab them with damp toilet paper.

Though it wasn't really toilet paper at all. It was a cut glass bowl filled with tiny little sheets of what felt like silk. She almost didn't use them, they seemed so soft and luxurious. It felt like a waste until she tried it, and somehow the sting eased almost immediately—as if they had some healing property she didn't know about. And sure enough, when she looked in the welcome packet under first aid, it listed this weird tissue.

Many materials in the magical world are adaptable to a number of circumstances, she read, and marveled—not for the first time—at the way these people lived. At all the amazing conveniences right at their fingertips, so much a given that the welcome packet barely really touched on them. It was perfunctory about it, matter-of-fact, almost bored.

Here is where you will find your personal items, she read, under the word *storage* in bold black. And before she could even form a skeptical frown, she unearthed exactly that. All her clothes folded and hung in drawers and in the wardrobe. Even though she'd last seen them in the hall of headmasters, abandoned in a fright.

Do they just magic their way here automatically? she wanted to ask someone desperately. But it wasn't until she got to page 4—school communications—that she realized she could. She read about it in between shivering and shoving on her nightgown and almost screamed with delight.

She even knew who she was going to message immediately.

Anaya, can you hear me? she scribbled on a torn-off piece of one of her notepads. Then she pushed it into the top drawer of the dresser, as the welcome pack instructed, and shut it closed around that ghostly white scrap of paper. Breath held, half of her sure the pack had to be lying.

Until there came a thump.

And a rattle.

And she opened the drawer up in a fumbled rush, and there it was.

A reply from her new friend. *Can you believe this??* it said. With a big thick underline to make the excitement extra obvious. *Have you seen the mirror? It shows you what you'd look like with different haircuts and outfits on. Please talk me out of giving myself a pixie cut, because I think it might be lying about how good I'll look.*

And after that, she simply had to test it out.

She sat at the dresser and thought of herself with a fringe. And it only bloody gave her one. She stared for a good thirty seconds, caught between how incredible this was and how horrible she looked. Before she remembered that Anaya was waiting for a reply.

Do not do what the mirror says. I think it might be mad, she scribbled, then sent it through the magical postbox drawer. And a second later, she got a reply. So fast, so full of eagerness, in a way that wasn't just delightful because it was so unspeakably magical. There was also the little pang she got when she read Anaya's next words.

I'm so glad I've got someone to share all of this with. Do you know there is no heating? Everything is just a perfect temperature, all on its own. My Baba would be having a fit now over the thermostat if we had the house this lovely and hot, she had written, as if it was just that easy to find a friend and talk with them about things.

Familiar things, too.

She knew what it was to have to watch what you were doing. To have little money and wear three sweaters instead of having the heating on. *I'm so glad I have you, too,* she wrote back, and for the first time in her life, it didn't feel nerve-racking to say something like that. Someone else had talked that way first.

Somehow here, in this cold and aloof and moneyed place, she had found an ally. A partner in a crime. Someone as valuable and soft as that bastard was worthless and cruel. It helped her breathe out. To settle in the same way the sight of the girl at the window, reading, had. In a way that still did, once Anaya had said good night, and she was left alone with a candle that lit itself, on a holder with a handle like something from a novel by one of the Brontë sisters, and an armload of books that she carefully selected, for maximum immersion into this strange new world.

The Complete Compendium of Creatures, she chose immediately. And then: *A Guide to the Underneath, Rules for Navigating in Between Places, The Complete History of Harrowhall.* In fact, there were several histories of various schools there. She noticed a few American volumes, a Canadian one.

Though they weren't quite as wide-ranging as she would have liked. *Here is not going to be the place to find out what exactly happened with the three unseen wars, and the overthrow of colonial rule, and the stalemate schism,* she thought, as she searched and came up empty. *Most likely living in England means you'll never know how badly they were outgunned, simply because other countries grasped magic quicker. All that matters is it made us a narrower, rule-obsessed place, and you need to know those rules if you want to survive here.*

All of which was disheartening.

But still fascinating in its own way. She clambered across her new big, lovely bed, thinking of all the secrets between what was said that she might be able to unearth, all the things they would probably dance around in official accounts. She'd always been good at figuring out what was between the lines, layered in subtext, left unspoken. She had needed to be, in order to navigate the world as an introverted fat girl, as someone forgotten and left to the edges of everything.

As someone clever but often thought of as not.

He thinks you're not, she thought, as she eagerly turned to the first page of her first magical book. Then hot on its heels: *And that will be his downfall, that will be the way you protect yourself. That will be how you live deliciously, in this dark place. By doing this.*

Though it was deep into the early hours before she found anything useful. Her eyes were drooping; the candle had almost burned to nothing. She glanced up briefly to get the crick out of her neck and saw the darkness outside shifting to a cool, cold gray. Then just before she drifted off, she saw it.

The Underneath feeds all magic.

And it is your clearest thoughts that forge the connection.

Chapter Four

She knew she wasn't fully asleep anymore. But it didn't feel as if she was awake, either. Everything felt soft-focus and sort of distant, as if she were watching it through a camera. The candle flickering down to nothing on the windowsill in front of her wasn't the one she'd left burning. That arm dangling over the brass frame of the bed didn't actually belong to her.

And there wasn't really a man in the corner of her room.

She was dreaming; she was just dreaming. All she had to do was give it a second, and he would dissolve down to nothing. But somehow a second went by, and he was still there. Another second, and he seemed even more solid than he had before. She made out broad shoulders, a hulking body.

Then just as she was thinking that was madness, he moved.

Some part of his body shifted, still in shadow enough that she couldn't make out what the part actually was. She couldn't tell what was happening, until something seemed to abruptly glow in the darkness. A deep orange ember, bright enough that it illuminated a small circle around itself.

Then she saw teeth.

Fingers.

A hand.

And she knew. Whatever was there had just kissed a cigarette to his lips. He had taken a drag, slow and deliberate. Now he was exhaling smoke in a steady plume that she couldn't quite see.

But could definitely smell.

It was too sweet to be tobacco, too strange to be anything of this world. Even though she knew it shouldn't be. *The use of Underneath ingredients as intoxicants is strictly prohibited and may result in expulsion*, she had read. But obviously whoever this was didn't care. He took another drag as she watched, even lazier than the first one. And this time he didn't let the cigarette leave his lips.

He clamped it there, as if he was about to do something he needed both hands for. Though somehow, she didn't really imagine he would do anything at all. Dream creatures had to stay where they were, after all. They couldn't really harm you; they couldn't really do anything to you.

Unless of course you had done something the welcome pack told you not to.

Never fall asleep anywhere except your bed, she remembered laughing over. Because of course, it had seemed funny then; it had seemed ridiculous. *As if I'm going to drift off in a library seething with ghosts or a lecture hall that might at any moment slip into another dimension*, she had scoffed.

But she couldn't scoff now.

She was still sitting in the window seat.

And she felt pretty sure the window seat counted as somewhere else.

In fact, she knew it must. Because as she sat there, frozen, the thing in her room lifted one impossibly long leg and simply stepped over the frame and onto her bed. As if it was no more than a footstool or a doorstep. Then it just started walking across the mattress toward her, in that same slow, effortless way.

As if it knew she couldn't move.

She couldn't even scream.

The Complete Compendium of Creatures had told her to make loud noises if something otherworldly approached her. But even though this thing definitely fit that definition—even though it looked like a shadow and moved like one, too—she couldn't get out a single sound.

And now it was upon her.

It stood over her, so tall she had to tilt her head back to look up at its no doubt terrible visage. But not for long, no, not for long because after an endless and terrible moment, it started to lean down. Its hands—tipped with claws, oh god, it had claws—reached for her. *This won't hurt,* she thought she heard it say. Though she knew it lied. The coldness of its hand burned before it even laid it on her.

And then it did, and finally it happened.

She screamed.

Chapter Five

She woke with a start, sure that she would see a nightmare around her. The walls of that demon's terrible dungeon, she imagined. All slippery, moss-covered stones scored by the nails of any number of victims. Or maybe the man himself, smiling at her with a mouth that took up most of whatever face he had.

But somehow, all she actually saw was sunlight, streaming through the curtains. The sheets pulled up around her ears. Her books stacked neatly on the bedside cabinet. *You went to bed like normal and just dreamed you drifted off in the window seat*, her mind informed her.

And that seemed reasonable.

Or reasonable enough that she could focus on other things.

Like the fact that it was somehow forty minutes past nine, when her first lecture was, according to her assignment sheet, at ten. It was at ten, and she was still half asleep and in her nightdress. So she flung herself through peeing and washing and dressing in a mad scramble, then bolted out the door. Down the spiral steps, into the low gray sunlight beyond, up to the main building, and then left and left again.

She got there with seconds to spare.

Though it didn't look it once she was inside the dim and dusty-looking hall. Fifty sets of eyes all swiveled to her, like she had turned up in the middle of a lecture by the not actually present professor. And they stayed on her, as she made her slow, red-faced way up the steps that bisected the rows of seats. She saw someone lean and whisper something to her glamorous-looking friend. Another person laughed, loudly enough that others joined in.

But she couldn't hurry and sit down.

There weren't any seats left. Not even next to Anaya, who was crammed between two massive brickheaded rugby playing–looking lads, one of whom she was clearly fuming at. Mina could even see why—he'd obviously just sat on the bag she'd tried to save a seat with. Anaya tried to give him a shove, and there was a hint of the yellow backpack Mina had seen on her friend the day before.

She had to gesture at Anaya not to do anything silly on her behalf, like get beaten up by someone with ears like fists. Then she put on an amused, brave sort of face to really drive the reassurance home. *Everything is fine,* she told herself.

Even though her situation was actually pretty dire. Every single row seemed full—until she got to the final one, and glimpsed a space with something like relief, and took a step toward it. Then the people obscuring it sat down, and she saw who she would be sitting beside if she took it.

The bane of her existence.

Just slouched there, bold as brass and so casual it was infuriating. His hair looked hardly brushed. The sweater he was wearing had a hole in it. He had gum in his mouth and seemed barely bothered about chewing it. And she could already tell that he had no means to take notes.

No bag, no pad in front of him, no pen in his hand.

Much to her irritation. She had spent a good amount of the

stipend she had been awarded on the twelve spares in her satchel. There was so much paper and so many notebooks in there that her shoulder was aching already from carrying them all. And here he was with absolutely nothing. Like he wanted to make it absolutely clear how little he needed this, how above it he was.

I should be in a class far ahead of this, his entire attitude said. Then he spotted her, and it said something more. *I should be far ahead of you,* it seemed like. In fact, for just a second, she thought he was going to shift a bag or a coat and dump it into that spare seat. As if he was saving it for someone better and cooler and more polished—even though of course he couldn't possibly be. Everyone was here already. If he did it, he would be doing it just to spite her.

Though was it really spite if you kind of hoped he would?

As if I want to be close to you, she thought, so heatedly it seemed like something he should feel. But if he did, he gave no sign of it. He just stared at her, like he had in Grand Central Station, like he had in the hall of past headmasters, like he had in the maze. A little sullen, a little amused, a lot like a challenge.

Go on, I dare you, girl who doesn't belong, it looked like to her.

So she answered in her head: *I will, bastard who wants to break all my dreams.* Then she stumbled and fumbled and fought her way past his probable friends, and shoved herself into the seat. Breathless and even messier than she had been when she started this day. But she had done it.

And of course, she regretted it instantly.

Sitting down that fast and frenziedly meant she hadn't thought about where any of her limbs were going. So now her hand was on the armrest of her seat, quite by chance. And his hand was in the same position, on his armrest. And both were far too close together. She could have clenched her fist and grazed the cuff of his sweater.

Though it wasn't the cuff she was concerned about.

It was how far up he had shoved it. How much forearm he had exposed, and how thick that forearm looked, and oh, the amount of *hair* all over it. She didn't even have to see it. She could actually feel it whenever she so much as took a breath. The shift of her body stirred her arm, and there it was.

The brush of that fur against her own frighteningly bare skin.

None of which she could cover up. She couldn't abruptly tug her sleeves that far down—he would notice she was doing it. She just had to pretend nothing at all was happening. That none of this bothered her. Even as she felt each individual hair almost bristle against the back of her hand.

It made her think of spider legs, of things scurrying over her.

She ached to rub wherever he was almost touching.

And that wasn't even the only terrible thing about sitting so close to him. No, god, no—there was also that winter air scent. The one that was now so strong it seemed to fill her body every time she took a breath. She could almost taste it on her tongue, like melted ice, like frost on glass. Strange sounding, she knew, but at the same time it made some kind of sense.

Because for some reason, he seemed to have almost no body heat at all.

He shifted, and instead of getting a bloom of warmth from him, she got a wave of cold. Like she was sitting next to the opposite of molten lava—freezing instead of fiery, yet somehow no less searing for it. It branded the side of her face, the back of her hand, her arm. It made her want to move away even more than the brush of his hair had.

But before she could, she felt *him* shift.

He leaned toward her, so close it made her go rigid.

"Happy now, about doing this to me?" he asked, so close to her ear and so amused sounding she could tell what it meant. He knew she was uncomfortable. He knew this was hell for her. And now he wanted to make sure she suffered for her perceived crimes.

Even though the crimes weren't hers at all.

They were his, and the sheer injustice of that made her spit fire before she could stop herself. "You did this to yourself. If you hadn't been so eager to punt me from this place, you'd be in whatever snooty advanced classes you wanted to be now. Instead of being stuck here with someone you loathe in a lecture you've probably been through before," she hissed under her breath. Though it was loud enough that the guy on the other side of her shifted nervously. And a girl in front almost looked back.

At which point she realized:

None of these people were his friends. He had no friends in a basic class like this. Everybody here was afraid of him to almost as great a degree as she was. Greater, really, because none of them were squabbling with him. It was just her, signing her own death warrant.

"I was doing you a favor, sending you back to the beginning," he said, even more heatedly than he had those first words. Yet somehow, she still didn't stop. She kept her face forward, but she answered him in kind.

"Is that what you tell yourself to help you sleep at night?"

"No, I count how many ways I could ruin you, and that sends me straight off."

"Well, this conversation is going to have you out like a light, then."

"If this cuts you that deep, god knows how you're going to cope here."

"I wouldn't have to just cope if people like you would let people like me be."

"What exactly do you mean, 'people like me'? Who is the *me* in this scenario?"

"People who look wrong and act wrong. People who don't know the proper way to dress or the right way to talk or the exact etiquette needed to get anywhere in life. People who have nothing," she said, so frustrated and furious that the last word came out far too breathless, far too scorched by emotion.

It made her seem vulnerable, she could tell, and vulnerability was the last thing she wanted to reveal to him. It was like baring her throat for a thing with fangs. He was probably going to say something so vicious now that she'd never recover.

Yet somehow, instead, silence followed.

A long silence of the sort that built and built until she had to break it. She had to see what was happening. Her head was too full of all the terrible things he could have been doing to not. She imagined a fireball aimed at her head, and turned jerkily, breath caught in her throat, heart hammering.

But there was nothing.

Just him staring at her with this strange, almost flummoxed expression on his face. As if she'd said something so wounding he couldn't quite recover. He just had to sit there, bleeding, instead of firing back. Even though she knew that couldn't be the case. It wasn't possible to stab someone with their own scorn.

And even if it was, she didn't have the skills or the weapons to do it.

She had no skills here or weapons at all, full stop. It was the reason she looked away from him and at Professor Hargreaves the second she swept into the room, as brisk as a January morning, all hard angles and sharp bones. To gain knowledge, to hear something of use. To drink in every drop of possible armor that this professor could impart.

Despite how hard looking away was.

All she could feel or focus on was his gaze, burning into the side of her face, as a woman who should have captivated her took to the lectern at the front. She was all in black, and thin as a witch's finger, and so immaculately coiffed it almost looked as if someone had set a swirling iron-gray helmet on her head instead of a hairdo. And then there were those eyes—like flint frozen inside a glacier. You could practically feel the icy sting of them, every time they slid over you.

Yet still she squirmed over the asshole sitting next to her. Still she missed the start of the professor's introduction, because her concentration was elsewhere.

It was maddening.

She only managed to listen when Hargreaves got to the good stuff. The magic stuff that made a bunch of other students sit up straighter, too. She saw one girl open her notebook, ready to take down every word this iron lady said. And only then realized that she hadn't even gotten out her own.

She'd been so distracted she had left it in her bag.

She had to scramble for it, with the professor's voice going on over the top.

"Now," she thought she heard her say, "can anyone tell me what the five basic forms are?" But by the time she sat back up, breathless and flushed with her fists full of pens and paper, someone had already answered.

And Hargreaves was on to the next thing.

"Indeed, that is the most important thing to remember," she said. While Mina sat there, boiling under the heat of the freezing sun sat next to her, wondering what on earth the most important thing had been. Then just as she was ready, pen poised in her hand, eyes on the professor as she turned her back to write on the actual honest-to-goodness blackboard, something nudged her hand.

A slip of plain paper pinched from her own bag. Neatly folded in four around the writing she could just about see—like a dark ghost through the layers. All of it familiar from the thousand times this had happened to her in high school. But so absurd to experience here that she doubted her own instincts.

Surely, she thought, he wouldn't.

Surely, he was above something like this.

And she opened it, all in a fumble, and found exactly what she should have fully accepted would be there. *I know I am utterly fascinating, but if you want to stay alive, you had better start paying attention to something other than me,* it read in script so lovely it was almost a work of art. Though of course she couldn't appreciate those densely packed curls on every curving letter, or the swaying slide of each *L* into whatever letter came next. She couldn't wonder why someone so brutal could make something so pretty. She was too busy crumpling the nasty note up into her fist, as if she could make it not be a thing somehow. She wasn't supposed to endure this kind of torment here. Here was meant to be brutal and frightening and full of pitfalls, true—but not those ones.

Not sad, mundane, petty little things like passing mean notes.

She wanted to spit at him for it, and only managed to not because the room had suddenly gone silent. Hargreaves was regarding them all gravely, and it seemed as if everybody could feel the change in the air. Then the woman spoke, and Mina could hear it, too. Something in her voice—a certain new vigor. As if she was getting to the portion of proceedings that she actually enjoyed.

And not in a way that was going to be good for them.

"Now, one of the most important things most of you here today—the new students, not the lazy, useless, arrogant ones who've found their way to this basics class because of their own foolishness—must do is begin the process of sorting the mythical from the not. Because the likelihood is, being in a class such as this, that you were not born into magical communities, and therefore may not possess the necessary knowledge to determine the difference between stories you were told, and facts that exist. And even if you are aware of what is fact, there may be various details and intricacies that you are simply not privy to, in the world outside Harrowhall. So I like to begin by asking you all to identify whether any creature or being I mention belongs in either the real column, or otherwise," she said, and as she did, she slashed four lines onto the blackboard with a piece of chalk. Simple, really. Until she added, "And of course, should you guess incorrectly, there will be consequences. If the creature is real and you tell me they are not, they will appear and try to kill you. If the creature is not real and you tell me they are, the sucking void of their nonexistence will attempt to drag you in and eat your soul. Good luck, one and all. If you do die, try to do so with the minimum of fuss."

After which, there was quite a bit of laughter. It rolled over the lecture hall in a fairly brash wave, at first. But when Hargreaves didn't join in or break, it began to slowly dwindle down to nothing. A few nervous titters were all that was left, by the end, and even they dissolved under that unrelenting stare. It swept over the room, clearly waiting for silence.

And in the middle of it, Anaya caught her eye. She mouthed something, expression tense and eyes shot through with the same kind of unsettled light Mina had seen in the maze. *Can you shield yet?* Mina thought she said.

But she couldn't answer.

Harker's smirking face was in the way.

Say no and he would know it. Show fear and he would see it. And all while he didn't seem the least bit bothered. "Oh, this old trick," he groaned, as if he'd seen it a million times before. As if it was nothing, really. Instead of something that made some jug-eared lad in the fourth row bluster and stutter when Hargreaves said the word *werewolf* and then pointed at him.

It took the lad an age to get a "no" out.

Then he held his breath. His eyes darted left and right, searching for signs of said creatures suddenly appearing. He even looked up, as if they might somehow spring from the ceiling. And only when nothing seemed to appear did he let out a relieved breath. It was almost a low whistle, and it ended on a chuckle.

Lots of people chuckled, in fact. *As if such a thing was really going to happen*, that ripple of noise said. But that just made it more shocking when a great ripping sound shot through the hall, on the end of it. A wrenching, terrible thing, that made Mina think of bodies being split in two.

Even though the lad was still in one piece. He scrambled up out of his seat, without a scratch on him, and seemed to run for the door for reasons that were not yet clear to her. But then he tripped, hard enough that she winced and looked away, before his face could smack into the lecture hall floor. And as her head turned, she saw it. Not a thing from the ceiling, or the walls, or out of the end of Hargreaves's wand. From below, it came. Like all the stories said about the Underneath—only worse, more frightening, weirder.

It was a hairy, clawed hand shoved right through the seat he'd just been sitting in. It must have sprouted up right between his legs, she thought, like an intensely weird and brutal plant. Then as he'd fled, it had obviously grabbed hold of his ankle, and now here he was, sprawled on the floor, nose bleeding, words babbling out of him. "No, please, I didn't mean to get it wrong," he said.

But Hargreaves only watched as impassively as a person waiting for a bus, when the wrong one goes by. It made her heart pound to see that face—more than the hairy hand did, more than the way it was grabbing him, more than the sound of him screaming, more than everyone around him trying to get out of the way.

Because in the maze, it had been possible to pretend that professors were watching and waiting to step in if things got too terrible. But here it wasn't. Here she just had to watch as something bristling with tooth and claw dragged him into the hole it had come from, one slow agonizing inch at a time.

First his feet went.

Then his legs.

And finally all that was left were his hands, scrabbling at the tufted, torn edges of the seat the monster had burst through. The last thing Mina saw were the whites of his knuckles, his splintering nails. A single person reaching for him, the way she wanted to, before fear made them snap their hand back, and shake it as if it were covered in bugs.

For all Mina knew, it *was.*

Nightmare bugs from the depths of the Underneath.

Brought here by a deranged Q&A with a deadly end.

And this was just the *theory* classes. The Autumn term was supposed to be simple history, the basics of gathering magic and what it could be applied to, possible career paths. But instead there were apparently quizzes with deadly consequences. Questions that could lead you astray.

Christ only knew what was going to happen when it got to the Spring term, and intensive practical classes started. She'd read a little about it—that the first thing they did after Christmas was see if you'd managed to learn how to fly. But now she was starting to think that the description after it hadn't been a joke. That they really did just push you out of a fifth-floor door, and if you hadn't cobbled together the skills to do it, you plummeted to your death.

Horrible, she thought.

Though she was at least grateful that she knew it, now.

That she'd had some sort of idea about all of this, before.

It was extremely clear that no one else did. That none of them had done any reading at all.

She suspected that was the reason they looked caught between being frozen, and throwing up. Like they'd all thought they were relatively safe after the Brawl, and were very quickly learning that this was not the case. *Everything* here was harrowing, absolutely everything, and it didn't pause because you didn't know. It didn't pause because you hadn't studied.

A fact that seemed to take hold of them, next. Some of them sank back into their seats, in the tortured silence that followed, and tried to find their books. She saw the title on one—a tome she'd read most of the night before, *The Complete Compendium of Creatures*. And she was glad she had, because no sooner had a girl opened it, then Hargreaves jerked her wand in her direction, and the book slapped back closed.

Fast, too. So fast it almost took off the ends of the girl's fingers.

"I do not recall saying you might use study aids. Now, next: wraiths," Hargreaves said. And a ripple of pure panic went through the room. Someone stood as if to leave, but Hargreaves stopped them with one whipcrack of a look. They shrank under its glare.

Then she made them say it. Yes to wraiths. Or no?

At which point, Mina almost stood herself and shouted it out. She knew what beings like that were. She understood what they could do. And she could stop this with a word; she was sure she could. In fact, the answer was on the tip of her tongue when she felt it.

Suddenly around her upper arm, tight and cold as an iron cuff created in some icy wasteland, and so forceful she barely made it an inch from her seat. She didn't even manage a breath.

He stopped it with his other hand.

Right.

Over.

Her mouth.

"You think if you try to save them, it'll work? You think this place recognizes things like justice and heroism? She'll have you butchered instead, and me with you for having the bad fortune to be sitting at your side," he hissed, so close to her ear she felt his wintry breath trail over the side of her face, a cruel caress.

Though that wasn't what turned her guts to soup.

It was the taste of him. The taste of his skin. He'd shoved his hand over her mouth so fast and firm she hadn't had a chance to close it. And now her tongue was touching the soft plume of his palm. Sweet as syrup from something overripe, that sense informed her.

And she hated it for that.

She hated all of this.

It didn't even help that the girl got it right, and no wraith howled its way into the lecture hall. Or that when he finally let her go, he almost seemed to be trembling, too. As if he'd been afraid, on some level, the same as she had. No, no, the only thing that she could think of was that she would never get that out of her head now.

He was the worst person in the world.

Her mortal enemy until the day she died.

And now she had to always know that he tasted like sin.

Chapter Six

She decided the best course of action was to get really fucking excellent at fighting things with magic. And not just because three students were now missing after her first class, and the one who had returned after being grabbed by a gargoyle was simply not the same as he had been.

There was also her mortal enemy, making everything worse.

He had ended Hargreaves's lecture by somehow transporting her out of the hall and into a tree outside. It had taken Anaya half an hour to help her down, and both of them had been late to their next lecture on the history of the Underneath. Professor Cobble had been a good deal warmer and friendlier than Hargreaves—*like a human sparrow*, Anaya had whispered—but he had still been displeased.

They had spent most of the lecture being pecked by invisible crows.

She still felt sore hours later.

And so it had to be done. She had to make him afraid of her. To figure out his weaknesses and use them against him. But of course the problem was: doing something like that wasn't exactly easy at Harrowhall. There was no student database you could just look up. No outside internet you could use to unearth who anybody was.

The place was a closed circuit.

All she managed to really uncover was his full name and what he was mostly popular for, and even that happened quite by accident. She went the wrong way and wound up passing a trophy cabinet, and when she glanced inside, she saw it. A picture of him in the captain's position of some kind of sports team. Then below, it said who the captain was.

Harker St. James.

The perfect moniker for a man like him.

Posh and pretty and cold sounding, and easily shortened to something cool. *Hark*, they probably cheered, on the sidelines of whatever match he was playing. *Hark*, his teammates most likely called, across a field for whatever sport he played. The one they called Gauntlet, she imagined—because that seemed to be the favorite topic of discussion in the university paper she'd picked up from the shop the other day.

The very, very expensive shop, on the edge of campus, that everybody called Boddies.

But was actually called Bodlin's. Bodlin's, filled with everything you could want, but nothing you could afford. Wands were out of reach, pens you could fill with magic cost a fortune, even candles and practice kits and scarves emblazoned with the name of the university team were too much. But she had managed to get the *Harrowhall Gazette*, and read about the bloodbath the game against a school called Omundson had been.

Apparently, the aim of the game was to prevent the opposing team from getting anything magical through a sort of hoop, by any means necessary. And he'd lopped off someone's arm with a teleportation spell, before they could get the winning point. *I sup-*

pose it's a small mercy that he didn't do that to me, she had found herself thinking, after reading. Though of course she couldn't be comforted by that for long. There was still time, after all.

And now she had yet another example of how ruthless and brutal he could be. *I am a goner*, she thought, as she dashed down the right staircase to the dining hall. Or at least, the dining hall was what Anaya had called it in the note she'd sent to Mina's drawer. But when Mina got there, she discovered that those two words didn't really cover it.

It looked more like an exclusive club, made for expensive cigar smokers. She found Anaya ensconced in a huge leather chair, leaning over a polished mahogany table with claw feet. And her own huge seat was just as good. It felt like sinking into velvet butter. She groaned over it, loudly enough that Anaya laughed.

"Wait until you see what happens with the food," she said, as she handed Mina a menu. Or what Mina *thought* was a menu. But there wasn't actually anything on it. It was just a thick rectangle of cream card, with the name of this particular dining hall at the top. *North Side*, it said and then below, in curlicue script: *Please make your selections.*

"I don't understan—" she went to say, but before the words were out, a gentleman in what looked like full black tie arrived, with a silver trolley. He set two salvers in front of them both, and sets of silverware, and just as she looked up to ask, he removed both silver domes to reveal what was beneath.

Two plates of food.

And the one in front of her was exactly what she would have asked for, if someone had bothered. As if the menu just knew what she wanted and supplied it. It gave her two fried eggs with sunshine bright yolks, a slice of ham thick as a paving slab and still sizzling, a side of neatly cubed potatoes clearly fried in something more savory than vegetable oil. The whole thing smelled divine—far better than anything she could have paid for.

But that was fine. This, at least, was covered under the terms of her enrollment.

And that meant she was going to eat better than she ever had in her life.

She even picked up a fork to do just that. She let it hover over the egg.

Yet somehow, she just couldn't bring herself to stab the yolk. To spear a potato. To pick up some of that ham. Her guts seemed to roil at the very thought, and she had to set her cutlery back down. She sat back, telling herself it was just an ordinary lapse in appetite. That it was just early for breakfast. That she would feel hungry in a second.

But deep down, she knew it wasn't anything of the kind.

She knew it was him.

It was the way he turned her stomach.

The stress and fear he struck into her, and how it robbed her of simple pleasures.

Though of course she couldn't let Anaya know that. She couldn't allow Anaya to be dragged into any of it. Sweet Anaya, who was actually doing okay, and just wanted to enjoy her dinner. No, no, she needed to put on a show of dinner eating.

Only somehow, Anaya took one look at her fussing with her cutlery, and seemed to just . . . know.

"If you're thinking of how to get that asshole off your back, all I know is do not use poison to do it," she said, as she used some frankly delicious-looking roti to scoop an unhinged smelling portion of dal makhani into her mouth. Then just as Mina was about to ask what she meant, she swallowed and continued. "Apparently, someone tried to do that last year to take his captain's spot on the Gauntlet team, and it did nothing to him. He shrugged it off like they'd fed him a spoonful of sugar."

"And I'm guessing he wasn't pleased once he did."

"Well, the person who did it did not come to class the next day."

"Did they come to class ever, after that?"

"They did not."

She sank back in her chair. Picked up her fork again, and poked at the egg she didn't want to waste. "This place is psychotic. And I mean I knew it was because of the memory erasures and the liability waivers and stuff from the books. But even by those standards—"

"Yeah. I heard two people talking before you got here. Did you know that last year, so many people died at the end of first-year flying exam that there was a government investigation? Of course, it's impossible for the government to find Harrowhall guilty of anything. But still. The fact that they even managed to *try*."

"We live in a really fucked-up society."

"Yeah, I thought all the baseline inequality was bad enough."

"Right. Here it's superpowered. And yet somehow still grindingly dull and predictable." Mina sighed and set her fork down. The egg was now mush anyway. "You know he tried to pass me a note in the lecture hall? Like a bog-standard bully. I thought it was going to be a drawing of me with a giant butt."

"Is that something that's actually happened to you before?"

Their eyes met over their plates. The silence spinning out, despite how not silent everything was really. The dining hall was getting busy now. Plates clattered, chairs scraped back and forth, people yelled for their friends to join them. Just like she'd always imagined doing when she got here, and somehow fit in.

At least I do with you, she thought at Anaya.

And somehow Anaya seemed to understand, because she reached a hand across the table. She put it over Mina's. "We have each other now," she said. "When we pass notes, it's the good kind. The best kind. The kind I used to hope I would have with someone but never quite managed."

"Shall we write each other's names on our pencil cases?"

"I already have. Mina and Anaya, besties forever."

She went to laugh at that. Yet somehow, a laugh wasn't what came out. It sounded more like a sigh of delight. And it came with such a strange and unfamiliar feeling. A flood of warmth, a flicker of something in the back of her mind. Like with Harker—a sense that she was seeing Anaya but someone else at the same time.

Jyoti, her mind whispered.

But the name flitted away before she could fathom it. After a second, she couldn't even remember what it was—and even if she had been able to, a crash over at the end of the hall soon had her knocked out of it. Harker whipping his wand around, it looked like. A table was currently trying to eat whoever had pissed him off.

Next time, that'll be me, she thought, and focused back on the problem at hand.

"He must have a weakness. Some way to make him stop whatever it is he's trying to do to me," she said, and Anaya looked thoughtful for a moment.

Before she delivered her answer.

"Maybe you should start with *why* he's doing it."

"Because I messed things up for him. I got him demoted essentially."

"Yeah, but he was already obsessed with you before that."

Mina shrugged. "Maybe I was just an easy target, then."

"I don't know about that. I mean you're here talking about murdering him."

"It isn't murder I have in mind."

"Then what?" Anaya asked, one eyebrow raised.

As if what Mina was thinking involved a caper of some kind.

And of course, Anaya would have been down for it, clearly.

It was the reason she shook her head. "I just want him to leave me alone."

"So then what you need is a leave-me-alone spell."

"I can't even make any spell at all. Never mind one that sounds made up. And somehow, I doubt I'm going to learn, because the last lecture I was in with him I couldn't hear the professor over the sound of my own thundering heart."

"Yeah, but lectures aren't the only way to work out how to curse someone."

"So what? I just go to the library and look it up?" She made a scoffing sound on the end of her sentence. But Anaya just stared at her in this long and very pointed sort of way, until finally, it clicked. "Oh my *god*, I should totally go to the library and look it up. Why didn't I think of going to the library and looking it up?"

"You're not in your right mind. A homicidal magic wielder is trying to wear your intestines as a hat," Anaya said, half laughing. But half serious, too. It made Mina's stomach flip a little bit, to see that worry in her dark eyes.

So she tried to brush it off.

"I don't think you get to call yourself a magic wielder until you graduate."

"Somehow that doesn't seem like the thing you should be focusing on."

She sighed. "Because the other part makes me want to barf."

"Pity. This food is *outrageous*. Honestly, I'd give them credit if I didn't suspect any authenticity is coming from whatever this dining room spell is ripping right out of my head," Anaya said—almost offhandedly

But it made Mina shiver, just a little.

This place took, no question about that. And in ways you barely understood until the taking was already done. The only question was: How much could she take from it, before she had nothing left?

Chapter Seven

The library was enormous, of course. Though even by the standard she imagined, it was pretty staggering. It made her gasp, when she stepped through a pair of double doors that looked like nothing at all. They suggested something normal—but beyond was anything but. It was too big for the building it sat inside. Like an optical illusion, like something from a sci-fi show.

It took her five minutes to get from the entrance to the main desk. Then another ten to find the section she needed, after the iron-haired lady sitting behind the counter directed her to where it would be. Her legs were tired and her stomach was growling by the time she got there. She was genuinely starting to worry about getting lost and then starving to death.

But god, it was worth it for the books.

Oh, the books upon books upon books.

Their spines glittered in the dusty lowlight. They tempted her, from shelves that towered over her head and seemed to teeter under the pressure of them all. She found herself looking at the mosaic-patterned floors, head full of that story of a building sinking because the architect hadn't accounted for the weight of the books.

She would have gladly sunk with it.

She would have let herself be buried by all this paper and ink.

She barely paused for breath when she got to the right section. She grabbed ten books without even paying much attention to the titles. Clutched them to her, all higgledy-piggledy, one of them falling as she maneuvered to the table set between the stacks. She snagged it as she sat down, and set it next to the biggest haul she'd ever managed in her life.

The closest before this was the time she'd visited her cousins in Essex, and they had a library nearby. But that had been tattered paperbacks, full of secondhand tales of whatever people thought actual magic was like.

This was the real deal.

These were tomes bound in leather and filled to the brim with things she had only been able to guess at before. Like the fact that several natural disasters had indeed been averted by magic—the slide of the Handermore shelf into the Atlantic, the flood that threatened California, the asteroid that almost took out Melbourne. Hints at other things, in places on the other side of the various schisms.

All spells, all kept under the shroud of secrecy that countries held over their magic use.

Or beneath a code of silence enforced against a population.

If you find you want to share with anyone not under the auspices of the magical authorities, or speak of magic to anyone ordinary, you will find you cannot, she read, in a chapter of a book called *Great Deeds of the Twentieth Century. Your words will get lost in your mouth, your messages will dissolve to nothing, your screens will turn to static.*

And from what she could see, that was how most things seemed to work. You could learn if you were allowed here. You could make yourself great and perform feats within certain set parameters. But you could never share beyond what was set by the authorities. *Those who decide that a fancy bandstand in Windermere should be saved from collapse but a tower block shouldn't*, she thought, as she scoured the pages for something less bitter and more useful.

And she found it.

It was in the third book she devoured, midway through a chapter on defeating creatures that your professor could allow through a rip in the fabric of reality to randomly murder you. *Werebeasts can be repelled by common stinging nettles if harvested in areas where the veil between the Underneath and the real world has grown thin*, she had written breathlessly, in the notepad she'd already filled with all kinds of hints and tips and facts.

And then there it was.

If a denizen of the Underneath has attached itself to you, you may find your mind affected. Concentration can prove abruptly difficult, memory is often affected, in extreme cases the divide between reality and dreams could begin to erode, she read, and felt a great rush of adrenaline go through her as she did. Suddenly her heart was thudding, heavily enough to almost hurt. Her mouth went dry; hair prickled where she hadn't even realized hair was.

And not just because that seemed to describe her exact situation.

There was also what it said at the end of the paragraph.

Even the most advanced student will struggle to fend off certain creatures. Then even more troubling: *The help of faculty should be enlisted.* Because the problem was—what could she say? What could she report? He didn't outwardly look like something that came from that shadowy place. And if he did, somehow, nobody seemed to know it. Nobody seemed suspicious.

Even though there were other things that fit.

The poison, she thought. The poison should have made people wonder.

But it hadn't.

And that meant one thing and one thing alone. *He's popular and important enough that they don't want to face it, they don't want to hear it, if you say anything they'll hate you, not him*, her mind whispered, in a way she couldn't really argue with. So now she had to reckon with the fact that she was in even more danger than she had first thought. Tell and she'd be in trouble on two fronts. Keep it to herself, and she was going to have to fight something potentially unfightable.

Despite the fact that she could barely fight at all.

She'd only managed magic that one single time in the maze, and had no clue why that was the case. What she had done differently then, to what she had tried at other times. It had felt just as clumsy as it had when the fireball had almost hit her. Just as clumsy as it did now, as she brought her hands together.

Clumsier even.

Of course it had been clumsier. She had done it with him between her legs. With his face above hers, expression so full of fury and loathing it had made her hands shake. It had made them fumbly and frantic. They hadn't locked together perfectly; she knew they hadn't.

But the spark had happened all the same.

So what had been different? *When I want it to happen, I just picture the top of the maze, the darkness, the way it made me feel when it bloomed in my hand*, Anaya had said to her, as they tried to get her out of that damned tree. So she closed her eyes and attempted just that. Tried to think of every detail, every nuance, every feeling. The shadow slanting across his face, cutting it cleanly in two. His hand on the stone by her head, close enough that she had felt his thumb brush her cheek.

Or had it been the charged air between his skin and hers?

She didn't know. She only understood the sensation that seemed to flood her, when she closed her eyes and thought of it. When she slowed her breathing and considered his face. Something seemed to part or open inside her, and through it flowed that strange kind of warmth. That silvery feeling, like her veins were filling up with mercury. Then she opened her eyes, and oh.

There was a glowing flower in her cupped hands.

Beautiful, glorious—she could have wept to see it.

She probably would have done so, in fact.

If it were not for the shadow that suddenly slanted across the sweetness she had conjured. And the voice, deep and sardonic, cutting into the focus she had only just managed. "Well, what do we have here?" he said.

And of course it was him, of course it was.

Who else was it going to be, ruining her moment?

Yet still, somehow, it shocked her. She stood so fast and so violently it knocked the table. Two books spilled onto the floor, heavily enough that the bang they made echoed up to the rafters. She heard what sounded like birds up there flutter in the aftermath. Someone somewhere shushed loudly.

But they needn't have.

The only sound that followed was her harsh breathing.

And him speaking so softly no one but her could have ever heard it.

"I suppose it shouldn't surprise me to find that you think your salvation can be unearthed between the pages of a few dusty tomes. Yet oddly, I think I am. Like I thought better of you, somehow. Even though you've given me so little to go on," he said. Casually, like he was talking about the weather. Instead of being so scathing it felt like getting a paper cut clean through her skull.

She couldn't reply, for a second.

She had to take a calming breath first.

"Five more minutes, and maybe I'll have a lot more for you."

"Was that a threat, little bookworm? Well, aren't we getting bold."

"Not bold. Just honest about what I might soon be able to do."

He gave her a withering look—eyes rolling and then sliding sideways. "Yes, I saw you practicing. Your form is dreadful, by the way."

"It was enough to grab you in the maze."

"You got lucky."

"So maybe I will again."

"Let's see then, shall we," he said; then just as she was about to argue back, he added one last sudden spat word.

"Draw."

Like a gunslinger, she thought wildly.

Though she didn't expect him to *actually* go for his wand. That seemed ridiculous, impossible—until his hand whipped down, and then up, so fast she didn't even have a chance to move out of the way. All she could manage was grabbing the nearest book and holding it in front of her body. Like a shield against whatever spell was emerging from the end of the sharp little thing he had jabbed at her.

Something violent, she thought and braced.

But the book didn't just explode, or maybe end up with a hole through the middle. Instead, it seemed to collapse in her hands. It spilled between her fingers and poured over her palms, so quickly she didn't at first understand what was spilling and pouring. She just felt it; she just had the impression of something brown and in bits.

And then she realized *the brown* and *the bits* were soft.

They were small and furry.

Spiders.

He had turned the book into a great writhing heap of spiders, scurrying and sliding and scampering to get away. They flowed like a waterfall to the floor, where they raced around her feet. Or at least, *some* of them did. Others went up, instead of down, and oh god, they were in her hair. They were tangled there, too frantic to easily swipe way. She swiped and swiped and batted, and still they skittered over her scalp.

It was unbearable. It was infuriating.

"You fucking demon," she spat, as she flung the last one away. She watched it melt into the shadows between books. But he didn't seem furious that she had managed. Or that she had spoken to him that way. His expression was flat, featureless. She couldn't figure it out at all.

"Yes, I am," he said, cold as the heart of a glacier. "*Now* do you understand what you're facing here? It's nothing that books will help you against. And even if they could, you shouldn't be trying to learn at seven minutes to closing, in a library that turns into a nightmare the moment those doors are locked."

"It's not seven minutes to closing. I only just got here."

"Another thing you clearly don't understand," he said in a voice that almost sounded exasperated—like a teacher with a particularly difficult student. And he carried on in that way, too. "Time moves differently here, bookworm. You have to keep careful track of it. You need a watch on your wrist, an analog watch, preferably one that you wind. And you must keep it wound, and then pay attention to what it says, even if your mind tells you it's only been ten seconds."

She couldn't take his words at face value, however.

She had to brush them off. "The guidebook didn't say anything like that."

"The guidebook tells you whatever it feels like telling you."

"That's a completely deranged system. It doesn't even make sense."

"*Now* you're getting it. *Now* you're seeing that this isn't a fun wonderland, where all your dreams come true. It's *hell*," he said, that last word so overemphasized it sounded like it had two syllables. "And you're down to three minutes, by the way."

"That's not possible. It's been thirty seconds."

"Yes, and I told you what thirty seconds can be here."

"I don't believe it. You're just trying to stop me from unearthing your weakness."

"And what weakness is it that you think there is to find, little bookworm?"

He stepped toward her the moment the question was out. Just a little, but a little felt like a lot from someone so enormous. His shadow slid over her before he was even that close. And she could feel that cold. That burning cold. It made her want to beg him to step back. Or burst out with a *none of your business.*

But before she could do either, the lights went out.

All at once, directly to darkness.

And it was followed by a *thunk* that she knew was a lock sliding home.

"Well," she heard him say, through the dark and hovering silence that followed. "Time's up."

But she didn't wait for whatever he had planned next.

She simply shoved the table between them, hard enough that she felt it hit him. Then before he could recover, she ran. Right into the deep velvety darkness, as fast as she could go. Faster than that even. She thought of him cutting her off in the hall of headmasters, even as she went flat out. And she went harder. She flung herself, at full tilt.

But it made little difference.

She heard him loud and clear, a second later—despite the fact that he didn't seem to speak loudly. His voice was almost hushed, yet still it found her. As if he was barely an inch away. "Don't be a fool, bookworm," he said, as she pressed her back against a bookshelf. "The deeper you go into this place, the deadlier it gets."

And even though it seemed like a bad idea to give away her position, she couldn't help it. She let words burst out of her, thick with venom. "The only deadly thing in here is you, you horrible fuck."

"You're wrong. I'm the last shot you have now of getting out of here alive."

"Oh? And what exactly do I have to do to receive this sudden generosity?"

"Leave Harrowhall the moment we escape. Leave and never return."

She laughed mirthlessly into the darkness. "So the low, low price of giving up everything I've ever longed for."

"Somehow, I don't think you longed for being ripped apart by wraiths."

Liar, she thought the second he said it. Mainly because the books hadn't said a thing about creatures like that, haunting the library after closing. He was just trying to strong-arm her, to scare her until she took his deal. It was obvious, absolutely obvious. A fool wouldn't have fallen for that.

Yet somehow, she held her breath anyway.

She listened, just to see if she could hear anything moving around in the darkness. Wraiths were the tattered remnants of souls that had made terrible mistakes with magic, she knew, and they were meant to make a sound like sobbing. Like grief, if it was turned into a noise.

But she couldn't hear anything like it.

Just the flutter of a wing. A rustle of one of those birds she had heard earlier, a little louder than before, but still normal sounding. It definitely wasn't the movement of a spectral cloak around the graying bones of a lost body. There was no way, she told herself. No way they just waited up there, until darkness descended.

Then floated down to brush against your cheek.

That was just a cobweb, she thought frantically.

But she crouched down anyway. She skittered along the floor to a safer feeling spot, hand constantly brushing at her face where something had definitely touched her. And was that a sound she could hear now? It was low and more like the moan of the wind than anything else.

Yet it was there.

It was the reason he laughed, she thought.

"Oh yes, you can hear them now, can't you?" he said, voice as hollow and horrible as he actually was inside. Masks off now. "So what's it going to be, bookworm? Leave or let them ravage you?"

Stay quiet, she told herself.

But she was too full of rage to listen. "I'd sooner be reduced to bloody ribbons than go back to that *hell* I was living," she spat, surprised and horrified to hear a broken sound in her voice. And maybe he was surprised too, because he didn't say a thing for what felt like eons.

Continents shifted and oceans shrunk in the time it took him to reply.

"It can't have been that bad. It can't be as bad as this."

"This is only bad because you are making it be. Because you are trying to take it from me. All my life I've waited for wonders, and all you want to do is rip them up in front of my face. I can't even have the books, not even them," she said, intending at every step to be furious, but knowing her voice was starting to collapse even harder than it already had. She got to the word *books*, and suddenly there was a real break there. A fracture that sounded so thin and high and desperate.

And now her face felt wet. She swiped at it angrily with her sleeve. Knew that he had to know she was crying. He had to, and yet for some reason he didn't say anything. The silence spun out again.

Although it wasn't exactly silence anymore.

That moaning was getting louder and more unsettling. And in between she could hear a strange rattling sound. Like bones, like skeleton bodies brushing against one another, as they flew around above her head. *Wraiths use their half-corporeal bodies to slice their victims into pieces*, she remembered reading.

But it wasn't this that made her panic.

It was the creak of the floor somewhere close to her. Like a heavy foot, trying to creep up to her while she was crouched here, crying and vulnerable. *Him*, she thought, and just couldn't help it. She broke for the door, thinking completely impossible things, like *Maybe I can force it; maybe I can escape.*

Though in fairness, she could actually see it the second she got out from between the shelves. Moonlight streaked down from somewhere, some high-up window, and it illuminated that blue wood, the brass plate where you pushed. It was barely the length of a football pitch away, and there were no obstacles to make it difficult.

All she had to do was run.

Go, go, go, she ordered herself, and she did.

She just didn't get farther than a single footstep. Something hit her from the side the moment she started moving. Something skeletal, she half hoped. Something that would end this fast, shred her to pieces, and leave her to speedily bleed out. But of course she knew it wasn't immediately.

This thing had heft. It had weight.

It was like being shoved by a great blundering beast. She practically careened through the air on contact, and when she hit the ground, she didn't just land in a great heap. She had enough momentum to actually slide. She skimmed along that tiled floor—like a hockey puck over ice.

It stunned her.

For a second, she couldn't breathe or get her bearings. She lashed out at what she thought must be him over her. But she didn't do it well. Her arm struck something too hard to be his body—a shelf, she thought. And sure enough, books rained down on her. She smelled leather, felt their fluttering pages. Gasped and tried to fling them away from her.

Then there was nothing.

She couldn't feel him, couldn't see him; he didn't try to grab her or shove her again. And she could no longer hear the wraiths. It certainly seemed like silence and stillness, and something close to safety. She even sagged against the bookcase behind her. Body still trembling, breathing still shaky, arm hurting like a motherfucker.

But she was okay.

She didn't even think much of it, when she heard the sound.

It just seemed like her own breathing—or maybe some far-off stirrings of one of the wraiths, settling down now their food had gone still. There was a rattling quality to it that reminded her of them.

Only after a second, she realized:

The rattling wasn't random.

It was rhythmic.

It followed a pattern.

Up, down. Up, down.

And there was another note to it, too. A thick, clotted sort of note underneath that rattle. Wet, it sounded like, to her. Wet, and oddly familiar, in a way she couldn't piece together at first. But then it struck her, in a rush. The thing it reminded her of:

The deer, on the side of the road. The one her father had glanced with the car. The one trying to breathe, while drowning in its own blood.

They got him, she thought, in a flash of bright shock and panic.

Sure of it, yet at the same time barely able to believe. It could have been a trick, after all. It could just be him trying to lure her in. Yet somehow, she crept toward the sound anyway. On her hands and knees over the dusty tiled floor, as low and quiet as she could be. Half of her scared of finding a lie.

The other half scared of finding the truth.

Silly, she thought.

Until she got to him and had to bite back a scream.

It didn't just look as if something had stabbed him. There was no sign of some simple neck break that a spell might fix. A wraith had very clearly run right through him, and shredded almost everything as it went. His clothes were in tatters; his body was now a row of deep bloody grooves.

And his face . . .

God, his face . . .

She had never seen anything like it. It laid in utter ruins, completely unrecognizable. In fact, she could only tell it was truly him because his one remaining eye rolled to her the moment she got close. And even surrounded by gore, it was completely familiar to her.

That deep brown, edging toward black.

The strange light in it, like amusement, only not.

It can't be amusement now, she thought.

So maybe it had always been something else. Maybe it had always been fear and panic.

Though she didn't suppose it mattered now. When he tried to speak, blood bubbled up instead. It spilled over what was left of his lips, a brilliant red when it caught the light from one of the high windows, a deep and glittering black when it slid down over his cheek and throat and into the darkness.

So she did the only thing she could.

She told him not to. "Don't say anything. You're making it worse," she said and was startled to find there were tears in her voice. As if she was saddened at the thought of her mortal enemy dying. As if it hurt to see it happening, somehow. *I don't, it doesn't, it can't possibly be the case*, she tried to tell herself.

But she yanked off her jacket anyway.

She pressed it to the biggest wound she could see, on his side.

And let out a sob when the material disappeared into a hole too deep for him to survive. This was it—he was dead, he was done. There was no coming back from this. She shouldn't have *wanted* him to come back from this. She should have been gloating over his wrecked body.

But somehow, she wasn't.

Instead, she felt herself gripped by the strangest feeling. A kind of deep loss—as if she had known him for far longer than this. As if she had liked him for all that imaginary time. She even found herself saying words that felt so familiar but so strange to say about him. "No, no, no, don't leave me," she let out.

And for a moment the world seemed to turn upside down.

She was on the ground; he was above her. Everything fading.

One of those strange memory-like flashes, she thought. Though it made no sense to her at all. It didn't seem like the kind of thing that would make her feel more for him. It seemed like the kind of thing that should make her feel less. Like he was the one who had wounded her somehow—but then it flickered out.

She was left with him trying to say something.

Trying to lift his hand. *No*, she thought he was telling her.

Then his breathing hitched once, twice, and he was still.

That one eye went dull and fixed. Still resting on her, but with nothing more behind it. She could fully see there was nothing behind it, and yet for a moment she couldn't quite believe it. It seemed staggering that someone who loomed that large could be gone.

And to the point where she simply had to double-check.

She leaned down, just to see if she could hear one hint of him.

Some faint breathing, another word, anything, anything at all.

And she *did* actually get something.

His hand coming up, whip quick, to get her by the back of her neck. Hard, so hard she couldn't get away, even though she immediately and violently jerked back. She put a hand out to shove him and instead buried it in what felt like a mess of blood and guts.

But somehow it didn't seem to matter. He was still terribly strong—and apparently seemed to feel no pain at all. She squeezed whatever she had just sunk into, and he barely reacted. He just gripped her harder and yanked her down, and when he did, she knew.

She knew what was going to happen.

It felt like she had always known somehow.

Like that black gaze had given it away. Like that coldness had told her what she was too afraid to believe. She could barely believe it now, even as she felt his mouth on her throat. The sting of razor-sharp teeth, hotter and brighter than she would ever have thought, from seeing guesses at it in films and reading about it in books.

But she let herself embrace the word, as she sank down into oblivion.

She saw it behind her eyes, printed, like on the page she had read only a little while ago. The thing he was, his secret, his weakness, the thing he most likely suspected she had known, the way she knew it now.

Harker St. James wasn't human.

He was a vampire.

Chapter Eight

She woke like someone who had slumbered at the bottom of the ocean for a thousand years. Slowly, heavily, and with little memory or understanding of what the surface was like. Her world was the still, strange darkness down there now. There was no easy way back to even the wild sort of normality that existed at Harrowhall.

How could there be?

Her mortal enemy was a vampire.

He had bitten her, hard and brutally enough that she wasn't even sure how she was still alive. It was supposed to have killed her, something like that. And even if he had somehow stopped short, resisted, spared her—there were other things that definitely should have finished her off.

Because when she finally managed to focus on her surroundings, she could see she was still in the library. That was a line of burgundy book spines directly in her line of sight. She looked down, and there was the polished parquet floor. And she recognized the brown leather beneath her body.

It was one of the couches that lined the borders of the main space. She was sprawled on it—as if she'd maybe gotten away, and staggered to it, and collapsed into its plump, pillowy embrace. And then for some inexplicable reason, the wraiths had left her alone. They had not touched her. They had let her sleep off being drained by Dracula, out of the goodness of their hearts.

Could be he marked you as his kill, her mind threw up.

And that made enough ramshackle sense for her to try to get it together. She had to, really. She could hear the staff starting their day, from the direction of the main desk. A student was asking a question in a high fluting voice that grated against the insides of her head. As if she was just hungover.

It felt like she was, truthfully.

She sat up and the world spun, then settled into a slow sway. Her stomach lurched, and most likely the only thing that spared her was the lack of anything in it. Her last meal had been the inch of an egg she had managed with Anaya. The meal before that some packets of crackers.

And now she was missing god only knew how much of her blood.

She even wondered if she was still losing it. She put her hand to her throat gingerly, expecting something horrible. A gory mess, blood fountaining over fingers like it had over his lips. Then jerked her hand away when she encountered nothing of the sort. The skin there felt slightly uneven, true. It felt sore.

But it was dry and smooth.

Which was good, in one way. It meant she wasn't going to drop dead, or need a visit to the infirmary that she wouldn't be able to fully explain. However, in another, it seemed bad. It suggested things she very much did not like. She stood on legs that didn't want to hold her up and staggered to the table she had used the night before. Flicked frantically through pages until she found chapters on vampires.

The one that said how they were made.

A person, even one imbued with magic and with a strong connection to the Underneath, cannot be infected by a vampiric bite; a vampire can only be born to the Underneath or made by their magics, she read and sagged against the bookcase after she had. She breathed freely for the first time in what felt like an age. She wasn't going to become a bloodsucking creature of the night.

She was safe.

Or at least as safe as anyone could be when their mortal enemy was a vampire. *Once he's licked his many wounds, he's going to be coming for you even harder*, she thought, as she let herself sink into one of the chairs around the table.

And that only meant one thing:

She had to come for him before he could.

SHE DIDN'T KNOW where or how he would make his move. And when she first saw him again across the quad, laughing with friends as if he was just the same as them—a glowing golden boy, fat with family money and as smug as you like—it honestly seemed like no move was even being planned. He seemed oblivious to her. Like he was just going to bluster through the whole business.

It never happened, his boisterous laugh seemed to say.

And then his friends turned to watch two people firing warning shots at each other from their wands, and Harker St. James did not turn with them at all. He saw them looking at something other than him, and he seized the opportunity. He let his gaze slide to the left, to where she sat, on the bench beneath the willow tree.

As if he didn't even need to search for her.

He simply knew exactly where she was, at all times.

Once they have a taste for certain blood, it will call out to them, she had read in one of the books she had checked out. But what it hadn't said was exactly how that would feel. What it would be like to experience someone's eyes always on you, drawn to you, to sense their presence like a second shadow, so close to smothering you at all times . . .

She had thought she was prepared after a few days of research and gathering supplies and making plans. But even so, bearing it proved difficult. She had to walk to class perfectly calmly, like she wasn't constantly aware of the predicament she was in. Like there was no predicament at all.

Even when she could have sworn she felt his hand reaching for her. Sometimes the air would stir behind her, and her hair would seem to lift in a way that couldn't quite be explained by a breeze or by the rush of the crowd in the foyer, and then there would be a kind of coolness on the nape of her neck.

Almost a caress but not quite, not quite.

It chilled her more than any truly tender touch would have done. Sometimes she almost froze to feel it. Others, she felt like she needed to frantically bat it away. And the more times it happened, the worse it got. On the sixth day of him not making his move, that cold touch almost made her scream, as she walked into the lecture on the Underneath that Professor Hargreaves was giving.

But she bit it back.

She kept walking, eyes forward. She had to, for a number of very good reasons: like the fact that Anaya was already obviously and frighteningly suspicious. And the there was how important it seemed to appear helpless and oblivious, if she truly wanted to get the better of Harker. And finally, and most simply—it was just the most normal feeling tack to take. It meant she got to be an ordinary student, learning things she desperately wanted to know, instead of someone who'd been elbow deep in someone's guts, and gotten bitten, and was now being hunted by a psychotic vampire.

This way, she figured, she could hear what Hargreaves was going to say.

And god, she really wanted that. The woman was fierce about the rules and realities of that shadowy place and how they impacted the world above. *We cannot afford to play fast and loose with the divide between the two*, she had written, in a paper Mina had found in one of her full-daylight but still frantic forays back to the library. And now she had questions.

So she took her seat in the lecture hall with her back to the wall, and waited for the Professor to arrive.

Though god, it seemed like an age until she did, with Harker sitting three seats in front of her.

By the time the woman swept in, Mina felt as if she was on the verge of bursting. Like before, when she'd sat next to Harker—but worse, so much worse. Now it wasn't just mutual loathing or some beef he had with people who didn't fit in. It was blood and secrets and shadowy things.

She had to dig her fingernails into her palms just to stay in her seat.

The pain was excruciating by the time the professor started her lecture.

But it felt worth it. *The history, purpose, and characteristics of the Underneath*, she had put on the chalkboard. Only she hadn't written the word *Underneath*. She'd called it by the name the beings that lived there did. The one Mina had seen herself in the books she'd taken from the library.

Calabaraia, it had said.

"Now," Professor Hargreaves began. "Can anyone tell me when Calabaraia was first discovered by humans?"

And because of Harker, she knew the answer.

She put up her hand. "There are rumors that it was found and formed a relationship with as early as the seventh century, in some parts of the globe. Though, of course, many such places ensured this knowledge remained protected."

"And do you know why that it is?"

"Because we were not trusted."

"Indeed. And do you know when—"

"In England, it was discovered in 1812, by the wealthy landowner Lord Henry Amberson. He accidentally opened or found a doorway in his garden and began his first explorations due to losing his eldest son through it," she said and knew when she did that Harker turned to look at her.

She kept her eyes on the professor, but felt his just a few inches below her sightline.

She paid no attention, however. The professor was looking at her too curiously for that. "Very good—Miss Morrow, is it? Well. Nice to see a student with such a keen interest in history. Perhaps you might even enlighten the rest of the class a little further on the subject of his son," she said—and when she did, there seemed to be a sharp light in her eyes.

Like this was a test of a different kind.

Less deadly than before.

And one she had an idea of how to pass.

"He was found and brought back to the manor."

"I see. Well, we cannot all be aware of every—"

"Only he wasn't the boy anymore at all. He just looked like it."

Hargreaves had already turned her attention to her stack of neat lecture notes.

Now her attention turned back. She had very pale eyes, and they zeroed back in on Mina with an intensity she wasn't quite prepared for. Mina knew why, however. The official accounts didn't mention that part. They behaved as if Amberson's meddling in the things he hadn't understood were heroic, with no consequences.

Only Hargreaves's paper had acknowledged otherwise.

"And do you know what that is called Miss Morrow?"

"Arbrigor. It means . . . replacing or doubling."

"Indeed it does. Though, of course, the practice is very rare and only liable to occur when humans perform corrupt and unpleasant acts. Remember, all of you, that the accords of 1843 were put in place for a reason. We may only trespass on their lands with great care, and they may not trespass on ours save for a few very regulated and rule-based set of circumstances. The library, for instance. Demonstrations and the like. Mingling among our kinds is unseemly in ways that are never to be encouraged."

She eyed her class on the last word. As if she expected each one of them to start drawing doors and jumping through them or using summoning spells for purposes they shouldn't. *Like fraternization with otherworldly things*, Mina thought. *Or maybe so they could sit three seats down from you, plotting your demise.*

"But I was wondering, Professor. Do they always obey the accords?" she asked. Not pointedly, not aimed at him, just out of curiosity really. But once the words were out, she knew he shifted in his seat.

And the weight of his eyes on her grew greater.

"Well, of course. It is binding upon them."

"Because we learned how to use the magic they gave us against them."

"I wouldn't put it quite like that. We learned to recognize what we could wield, and opened doors to better let it through. Then simply put safeguards in place to make sure that certain perilous practices could no longer occur."

"You mean like monsters emerging from the depths, to stalk us."

She could have heard a butterfly bat its wings in the silence that followed that. And she knew why, too. Every single person in there was most likely thinking of the quiz, and the werewolf, and what it meant if something could simply break through without any sort of way to avoid them at all. No questions you could answer correctly, and stay safe. No Professor to create any kind of boundaries.

Just chaos.

Every creature Hargreaves had forced them to acknowledge were real, suddenly roaming around.

And then of course there were the others that she hadn't mentioned at all.

The ones that still teetered in their minds, between the myths they'd been taught, and the potentially terrible reality. Vampires, for example, didn't sleep in coffins, or wear cloaks, or fear sunlight. They weren't even actually called vampires, in the Underneath, in the magic world. That was their fumbled, cobbled-together title, made by a man who had most likely half glimpsed them once. Their real name, she knew, was Areifen—*arei*, meaning "wrong," *fen* meaning "fey" or "fairy." Or at least the fairy- or fey-like beings that existed down there. Some looked winged and pretty, like people thought.

But she knew now that some didn't.

That some had teeth instead of eyes.

"Yes, precisely so. That sort of thing no longer happens. And it shall not as long as there is constant care and vigilance," Professor Hargreaves said. But when she did, Mina thought of the people of Stanley Bridge. The ones who had been told it was just a collapsed stanchion. Instead of what she suspected it had actually been:

Tentacles as big as buildings from a being that closely resembled Cthulhu.

She'd seen pictures, in an unverified account in a book the librarian hadn't wanted to give her. And Cthulhu was not alone. "If it did, though, if you thought it had, if you believed a being from the Underneath had breached or maybe slipped through one of the doorways without permission, what would you tell that person to do, Professor?" she asked. And now everybody was looking at her. It felt like she was drowning in a sea of eyes—not least of which were the professor's.

There was a flinty look to them now.

Like Mina was disrupting something, instead of what she was actually doing:

Trying to goad that fucker. Trying to warn him. It was time for her plan now.

And the professor fit her answer into that perfectly.

"I would tell them to speak to me directly. Most fears are unfounded—we call it the first-year frights, as exposure to these many wonders and horrors can be quite unsettling. But in the event that they are not, I should like to know. My forte is dealing accordingly with anything untoward, Miss Morrow. So do feel free to come to me, any time you feel the need," she said.

And then she turned away, as did the rest of the class.

Except, of course, for the one she had been really speaking to.

Chapter Nine

She was tempted, very tempted, to take the professor up on her offer. It was even easy to picture: a most likely austere little office, with mean chairs and a view out of the window of a wall. Hargreaves stood ramrod straight, face getting sourer and sourer as Mina spilled the beans. *He is attempting to sully you, and I shall not have it,* she imagined the professor saying, before she took her wand from between the folds of her black skirts.

Mina had seen her do just that in fact, the other day.

In the halls, over a student using his flying tool—a bespelled hockey stick, it had looked like—to fly up to the second floor. She'd made him drop like a stone with a flick of her wrist, then left him crying in a heap. *I think my leg is broken*, he had sobbed. And Hargreaves had replied, *Well, you should have thought of that before you did something you know you shouldn't.*

Plus there was the quiz. The rap of that book being shut.

It was clear she brooked no nonsense.

And had the power to back up that stern disapproval.

Yet somehow, when she came to the turn that would take her to Hargreaves's office, she kept on going. She stepped out into the dying daylight. And she hadn't the faintest idea why. Because he was Harker St. James, boy wonder? Because it wasn't supposed to be something that happened?

Maybe, maybe.

But there was something else there, too. Something about the way Professor Hargreaves had spoken—like she might blame more than the creature that had attached itself to some hapless human. That she might think someone like her had encouraged such attentions. And even if she didn't, there was every chance the magic authorities might feel differently.

She had read the other day about them banishing people from the community for doing things they weren't supposed to. *Being shunted*, it was called. And it didn't just involve going back to where you came from.

It meant memory erasure.

So yes, true, it was risky to deal with this alone.

Sure, there was every chance she was very wrong about certain things.

But she had to take it. Truthfully, some part of her *wanted* to take it. As if she was starting to shed some fundamental part of herself, some small, sad part, that always tried to say she couldn't. And in its place was a girl who got to her room, and sat on the edge of her bed, and waited for the boy who thought she didn't belong.

She stared at the door, willing him to cross that last line.

To cut that tension and end whatever this was.

Still—it jolted her, when the doorknob stirred. Just a little, almost like someone had brushed against it by accident. But as she watched, it moved a tiny bit more. It started to turn, slowly. Excruciatingly slowly. She knew she wouldn't have seen it if she hadn't been paying attention. If she'd just been brushing her hair and getting ready for bed, oblivious, she might have had her back to the door when it began to open.

It was possible he even thought she might be asleep. She knew her breathing was slow and calm enough. That she was still enough.

She made herself be, just to get that satisfaction.

And it *was* satisfying, too, to see him revealed. He simply stood there, in the open doorway, once he'd finished his careful attempt to enter unnoticed. Face a picture of surprise, and something else. Something like exasperation, it seemed.

Though it was his clothes that really struck her. How casual they were for someone about to commit murder. He had on a V-necked sweater, in deep burgundy. A pair of jeans, some sloppy sneakers. He looked like he was going to play Frisbee somewhere on the grounds. He looked like an advertisement for summer, if a season needed something like a marketing campaign.

No one would ever know that twilight turned beneath his skin.

That he had taken some real boy's place, or maybe just learned to hide his true face—or something else, something she didn't really understand. But she did have some idea how to fight it. Their eyes met for a moment. And then his gaze flicked to the crucifix in her hand. The one she'd made herself out of pencils and string.

"So you do remember, then," he said simply.

Mask dropped. Almost amused about it really.

"It's sort of hard to forget when someone tries to kill you," she replied, and the ghost of a smile on his lips faltered. Those black as pitch eyes darkened even further. Like they had in the hall of headmasters, she remembered and wondered again how long he'd thought of biting her.

"I didn't try to kill you, bookworm."

"In the same way you've not come to kill me now, you mean."

"That isn't what I'm here to do. I'm just here to talk. To explain."

"Is that why you opened the door like a thief, hoping to steal in before I saw?"

He didn't answer immediately. He simply stared at her, in a way that made her think of that shadowy place he came from. Those endless gray hallways, that upside-down sky, the glittering emptiness. And that sound some explorer had described. *It is as if there is a constant desolate wind blowing, somewhere just beyond whatever walls surround you*, he had said.

He'd never been the same after hearing it.

She was sure she would never be the same after seeing it in his eyes.

"I knew you wouldn't let me in if I knocked," he said finally. But he had dropped some of the pretense now. His voice was flat and dark, as if he was no longer interested in convincing her.

He was just waiting for an opening.

"You make it sound so unreasonable that I might not want to."

"I didn't know what I was doing. I was dying."

"No you weren't. Areifen can't be killed like that."

Hollister's Complete History of Vampirism had told her that one. And all the other texts had agreed. A creature like that could be dismembered and drained of all blood, and after a while they would be back to their old self again. It was the reason her own wound had healed—vampiric saliva was apparently wonderful at knitting a wound back together.

It just took time.

Though not a lot of it, if he was anything to go by.

God, she thought. You would never know his face was a ruin a week ago.

"So you've learned a few terms and a few facts, and you think you're safe," he said. Not quite jeering at her. But certainly there was something withering in there.

As if he had any real right to be.

"Safer than I was, at least. Safe enough that you're staying where you are."

"Yes, but you really have to consider *why* I'm staying here."

"The thing I have in my hand, obviously."

"Yes, well, about that," he said in so pointed a way she knew what he was going to do, before he finished the rest. She even braced, as he spoke the words: "It was never a deity we don't believe in that repels us."

Then sure enough—he went for her. He practically lunged, and so violently she almost jerked back. She had a split second of fear, thinking she had gotten it as badly wrong as he assumed. But just as she went to, it happened. The thing she'd planned for, the trick she'd set up.

It worked.

He got to the point of actually getting past the doorframe, and his whole body seemed to just slap to a stop. More than that, really, worse than that—it was as if he'd rammed into something. *Like a bird against glass*, her mind gasped, as she watched his thighs seem to flatten, and his arm bang off absolutely nothing at all, and his head snap all the way back, so violently it was as if he'd been punched.

When he righted it again, his nose was bleeding.

It was bleeding, and it was *crooked*.

The impact had *broken* it.

Holy fuck, she almost whispered. "I know," she said, as he touched his nose and then looked at the blood on his hand, stunned. "It was never articles of faith that stopped a vampire. It was the *material they made the articles of faith out of.*"

And on the last word, she tossed away the pencils and string. Her cobbled-together little thing that she had only pretended to believe in. Because now it was clear that she had gambled on something else entirely—and she had won.

But even better:

He knew it.

He looked at where that barrier was wonderingly.

Then he looked at her, with something that wasn't withering disdain anymore. "You rubbed fucking iron filings into your doorframe," he said, and for the first time since she'd met him, she let herself grin.

"Oh, you *bet* I did, motherfucker."

"But *Hollister's Guide* doesn't even mention it."

"The most popular text is notoriously not often the best."

"So you dug up what? Some obscure witch's account of warding off vampires?"

She spread her hands, as smug about it as he had been from second one. "She seemed to know what she was talking about. Though even if she hadn't, I would have erred on the side of caution. Better to collate evidence from several sources than rely on just one," she said, as if that was just so obvious.

And it maddened him as much as she had hoped it would.

"So I have a broken nose because you're a conscientious bookworm."

"You have a broken nose because you just tried to kill me, Harker."

"I told you. I'm not trying to kill you. That was just me proving a point."

"By lunging at me, fangs bared?"

"Don't be dramatic, my fangs weren't bared," he said and rolled his eyes. Then he paused, before adding almost casually: "*This* is baring." And god, she couldn't help the sound of shock that came out of her when he followed through. He snarled, hard enough that it seemed to change his whole face. Creases appeared where they shouldn't be; things shifted in ways that looked unnatural.

And those *teeth.*

It wasn't just two neat little incisors.

His mouth bristled with razor blades. It was like seeing into the maw of a shark—only so much more unsettling than that. Because once he was done showing off, he drew back. And somehow the teeth did, too. They seemed to melt down into something more ordinary, all at once. As if that flash of fang had just been a kind of optical illusion.

Though, of course, she knew it hadn't been.

Her trembling attested to that.

As did his satisfaction on seeing it.

"So now you can see. If I actually *wanted* to murder you, Mina, I would have done it by now," he said. Then just as she was trying to find a way out of that, he continued. Almost casually. "Do you know how many times and in how many ways I could have killed you before today? You took a wrong turn the first time you set foot in this place—and down the deadliest hallway in the building, no less. Anyone who felt like murder was a great idea would barely have had to lift a finger. Then there was the maze and all the mistakes you made in there. Telling the competition things you could keep to yourself, letting yourself get caught out by a maze shift, not staying hidden when you should. And then just in case any of that wasn't bad enough: You *went* and *slept* outside your *bed*. You *knew* not to, you had the guide that *told* you not to, and you did it anyway. Anything at all can get to you when you do something as foolish as that."

He shook his head over that last idea.

As if her ability to throw away her every chance truly amazed him.

But she couldn't fight back. She couldn't defend her decisions. She was too busy thinking of what all this meant. What him knowing about the sleep thing suggested. *Oh god, it wasn't a dream at all*, she thought in a great rush. Hardly able to believe it, but forced to admit it all the same. "That was *you*," she gasped.

And he didn't even try to deny it.

"Of *course* it was me."

"But that's unhinged."

"I don't see why."

"Because you just left me. Why did you just leave me? Why didn't you end it? Why *haven't* you ended it? If you want to get rid of me, just get it over with. Stop dancing around it, or settling for trying to drive me away with threats and schemes. Drink me dry and then dump me somewhere," she managed to say. And was amazed at herself for doing it, with her mind still reeling from the memory of that thing stepping up onto her bed. Of it reaching down, with clawed hands.

But he just *shrugged*.

"Do you have any idea what a mess a human body makes?" he asked, as if he was talking about a minor inconvenience. And one he felt she should just automatically understand. He didn't even elaborate further—he just attended to another problem, as he waited for her agreement:

His broken nose.

It had stopped bleeding, but it was out of shape. So as she was still trying to digest the first thing, he reached up and just snapped it back into place. One-handed, not even a flinch about it—despite how *disgusting* it sounded. It crunched, like someone stepping on bird bones.

But she couldn't deny it looked better once he had.

You'd barely have known it had been broken, if it were not for the hint of blood he left behind, when he swiped at it with his sleeve. Then he licked over that space between his upper lip and his nose, and even that was gone.

She had to try not to sound stunned in reply. To be as blasé as him about something that made her sick and shaky. "Ah. Then it's not just that you don't want to. It's that garbage disposal is hard."

"I wouldn't say hard. Just likely to expose me to attention I cannot endure."

"Yeah. What is the price for trespassing here again?"

"They behead and then burn you."

He said the words so matter-of-factly, she knew they had to be true. But for some reason, she had the strongest urge to say he was wrong. That this could not be the case. The books had made the price sound like barely anything at all—just a slap on the wrist.

And instead, it was something that made her want to clutch at herself.

She had to really fight her own horror over the way things were, to use it against him. "Well, you better be careful, then. And not just when it comes to hiding corpses. I mean who knows what someone might say, if they were given enough reason to," she said.

And tried to take some satisfaction from the way his face dropped.

"Are you actually trying to *threaten* me?"

"It's not as if you've left me with any choice, if I want to live here in peace."

"There will never be any peace here for you. Three third years are plotting to strand you in the forest, as we speak. They think it'll be funny to watch someone so helpless trying to fight off those trees. You know—the ones that exposure to the Underneath has turned into things that need to feed."

"If they do, they will be disappointed. I read how to avoid getting eaten by them, in Barrett's paper on thinned spots and their effects on flora and fauna. You have to draw a circle around yourself," she said, one hand reaching into the pocket of her nightgown as she did. For the stick of chalk she always carried now, just in case.

His eyes dropped to it, and for a second she thought she saw a hint of begrudging admiration there. But it passed pretty fast. "That won't work on me, though, bookworm. And even if you somehow manage to keep my conscious parts at bay with threats of tattling, there are other parts that no longer listen quite as intently to anything like reason," he said; then just in case the meaning wasn't clear, he let his gaze drop to her throat.

And that gaze turned black fast.

She actually got to see it go from a deep brown to something darker. Something that swallowed his pupils and spread to the whites. After a moment, there was nothing but inky black there. Though still, she couldn't quite believe it.

"You cannot possibly be saying what I think you are."

"And what is it that you think that I am saying, Mina?"

"That you don't *want* to kill me. But oh no, oh dear me, addiction to that one taste of my blood might make you . . . So I better leave here before you snap and sink your teeth in again," she said in a singsong sort of voice.

It had no effect on him, however.

"If what I'm saying wasn't true, I could have just stuck with finding you annoying and wanting you to leave. I don't need to invent other reasons that I want rid of you."

"Yeah, but this way you don't look too weak to act, stalling all this time and fearful of repercussions you had to at least imagine I knew about. You look like you're just valiantly trying to resist the siren song of my blood, and any second you might actually snap, against all sense and reason. So I better still be afraid."

There, she thought. *That wraps up everything in a neat bow.* Though he didn't seem to think so. "This is not a ruse, you little fool, designed just to get rid of you the easy way. And telling yourself it is will only put you in more danger."

"If you really cared about the danger I was in, *you* would go."

"I think you know we cannot usually leave the boundaries of places like this."

"So then return to Calabaraia. Go out through a door there to some other country, where they don't have all the rules and treaties and regulations we do."

"Believe me, I would if I could."

He slapped that invisible barrier as he spat out those words. Genuinely frustrated, it looked like to her. And she knew what that meant, even if she wasn't sure she could fully believe it. "If you're trying to say you stayed in the real world too long—" she started to say, but he cut in before she got to the end of her eye roll.

"I *did* stay too long. And now I cannot go back. I am stuck here, in the grounds of this horrid place, and I will always be. But *you* aren't. You can escape any time you like, and I highly recommend you do. You are simply not equipped to survive me, or any of the things here that are already out to get you. Hell, you're barely equipped for practical lessons. You almost died trying to save some fool. You can't gather. What are you going to do when it gets to the next term? They're not going to wait for you to read a book. They'll push you out of a window and expect you to fly."

"And did it ever occur to you that I don't care?"

"It's madness to not. Complete and utter madness."

"Not if magic is worth more to me than my life."

She said the words before she could think them. Too fiercely too, too full of feeling. Like in the library, over the books. Only this time, she had to face his scornful expression in the aftermath. She had to look at him, as he mocked her.

Though it was a strange sort of mocking, she had to say.

His eyes flared wide. He went to speak, then stopped. And when he did, she got one of those flashes. Strong, this time, so strong it made her feel sick. She tried to bat the image away immediately, just to keep the nausea down.

But it lingered. She could still see it behind her eyes, as he replied: the man with the same dimple as him, grabbing her by the back of her dress over some sort of precipice. The edge of a building maybe. She heard him say something—*laugh*, it sounded like. *Laugh, you have to laugh.* And then it was gone.

And he suddenly looked as smug as ever. "Well, then. You had better start really thinking about how you're going to survive," he said. Arms folded over his chest. Expression almost bored, and certainly infuriating.

It made it very easy to argue back.

"I'll use everything I'm doing now. It seems to be working just fine."

"Tricks like that won't hold me forever, Mina. You have to know that."

"So I'll find magic that will."

"Not fast enough to fight me off."

"I don't know—I'm a quick study. And the library is right there."

"Books won't be enough. You need someone to show you. Someone to teach you everything you need to know. A tutor who can guide you through all the practical elements, all the ways in which to draw magic to you," he said, like a patient schoolteacher, just trying to help a particularly foolish child.

Even though she knew what he was really doing.

"Give me a break. This is just you, trying to convince me my plan is impossible—I mean, nobody is going to want to do that, and you know it. There isn't a powerful person here who has any incentive to help someone like me, with not a thing in the world to recommend them. No connections, no power they can use, personality plain as paper, and face as forgettable as a pane of glass."

"That's true enough. They have no reason to do it."

"They really don't."

"Right. But *I* do."

He said the words so lightly she thought she had misinterpreted, at first. She even went to say something else, some comeback that had nothing to do with his actual meaning. Then she took in the strange, steady way he was staring at her, and the tilt of his head, and the way the air between them suddenly felt—like it was full and fat with a sort of tense expectation.

And she knew.

It burst through her, hard enough that she got to her feet. She took a step toward him, so she could hit him with her answer harder. "You cannot be seriously suggesting that *you* teach me," she said, half laughter and half scorn.

But he didn't even have the decency to act like he had been joking.

He lifted one shoulder in a kind of shrug—as if two was too much effort. "I mean going on everything you've just told me, I'm the only logical choice," he said, as breezy about it as she was incensed. Or at least, breezy on the surface.

She could see something else there, just below.

A kind of waiting. A tension—like he knew he had to do this carefully, if he wanted to reel her in. Even though he had to also know she could never be fooled like that. "There is nothing logical about my potential murderer somehow volunteering to help me stop him murdering. Unless, of course, he wants to lure me in, and then find a way to make me hurl *myself* into oblivion."

"That would be awfully risky to try, when she's smart enough to know that."

"You don't really think it's risky or that I'm smart. You think I'm a fool."

"A fool who loves to look all the important facts up," he said, and just as she was about to respond, he carried on, in the same faux conversational manner. "Like, for example, the *way* they go about beheading any creature who breaks the accords. Did you know they do it with a blunt instrument? I don't even think it has any particular benefit, process-wise. It doesn't curse your soul to never return or anything like that. They just like to."

Then he leaned back against the hallway wall, hands in his

pockets. The perfect image of casualness. An obvious ploy to sell his gambit harder—and yet she had to admit, it hit her hard anyway. She took the words *blunt* and *like to* like a blow to the stomach. And her mind immediately went to every undercurrent of that human viciousness toward the uncanny that she had ever picked up on.

Yates calling them lower beings, Derrickson talking about tumors. *We are the tumors,* she had thought, when she read that one. *We are the ones feasting on their magic, like parasites. Take, take, take while giving absolutely nothing in return, not even admiration or love. Just like always, whenever those on top think they can exploit anyone else.*

But of course he knew she felt like that.

Somehow, he knew.

Maybe he'd seen her wincing over Professor Hargreaves's similar-seeming sentiments in class. Perhaps he'd overheard her and Anaya talking about the old white men who had shaped half the world, in the image of their ideas about how things should be. Everything powerful should be suppressed. Everything beautiful should be seized. Everything they don't understand must be ruled over.

It was possible. They weren't subtle.

And she knew now that he was always around.

So it was important to not let him use that against her. "That's a good try, but I'm not going to believe you're actually scared of me, or scared of killing me, and then drop my guard enough to say yes to this deranged scheme," she said finally. Voice firm, with a healthy dose of withering disdain running through it.

He didn't seem fazed, however. "Good. Because guard dropping would definitely be a mistake around something like me.

And especially when you're going to be spending a lot more time in my company," he said, with so much conviction she had to laugh. A little hysterically, truth be told. A little rattled sounding.

But she got it out.

"You *actually* think I will agree to this."

"I don't think, little bookworm. I know."

"Oh, really? And where did you get this great knowledge?"

"From you. From that hunger that flashed in your eyes the moment I suggested it. From the way you stalked forward, without even being aware you were doing it. A predator knows a predator when it sees one. You might not seek a bared throat, but you are ravenous nonetheless. Desperate for words, for understanding, for all the things I can give you," he said, every sentence so silky, so perfectly poised in that molten metal voice. Then on the end, he reached into his pocket. He took out a little silver case and slid out a cigarette. Set his teeth around it, delicately, and lit it using a blue flame sparked from his fingertips.

The smoke smelled as strange and sweet as it had that night, in her room.

That night when he could have killed her very easily. But somehow hadn't.

I don't know what game you're after, she thought.

But she knew the end of that sentence was: *yet somehow, I want to play it.*

It was there, even before he added the final note, to this warped symphony.

"All you have to do is let me," he said around a coil of smoke.

And what else could she do, in the face of that?

The only possible answer was this:

"Then I suppose I will."

Chapter Ten

She didn't truly believe that he would keep his word. It felt much more like he intended to make her drop her guard, then do something he wouldn't have any trouble disposing of. Like trap her somewhere for all eternity or thrall someone else into doing it for him. Really, it made no sense to go to the place he proposed they meet, in a letter she found in her drawer the next day. She cracked the actual wax seal and read it there, in script that now seemed disturbingly old-fashioned: *six in the morning, in the abandoned east wing theater.*

Like some sort of university version of *Phantom of the Opera*.

He was probably going to drop a chandelier on her head.

But she knew why she went anyway. It was exactly like he'd said.

She was ravenous. And for all the things she could see behind her eyes, the moment she thought of him teaching her anything. That magic he had done, in the maze. The beauty and brilliance of it, in his hands. How it had bent to his will, with almost no effort expended at all. He was undisputedly an expert, a virtuoso, a genius. And not even a human one, either. He was made out of the place magic came from. It was in his body and his soul. His lessons, even reluctantly given and probably half-heartedly conceived, would be invaluable.

And not just to her.

To Anaya.

She could *share* whatever he offered with her.

She simply couldn't pass even a chance at that up.

Though she took precautions. She used the iron filings she'd mixed with Vaseline on her own throat, her wrists—anywhere she could think that might seem tempting to him. The iron fork she'd pinched from the dining room went in one pocket of her pinafore dress, the iron nail she'd found in the other.

Then finally, she did the riskiest thing.

She set up the letter. The one that would drop into the drawer that sent things, if she wasn't back in time to stop it. Addressed to Professor Cobble, because Cobble seemed kind. He seemed understanding. The lecture before last, he had tapped his lectern, and told that horrible Henry Godwin to cease trying to bespell her notebook.

It was at least possible that he might listen to what she'd written, if she suddenly disappeared. That he might make sure Harker didn't hurt anyone else—and in a way that didn't unsettle her. *He won't have him beheaded*, she found herself thinking, as she wrote the thing. Because try as she might, she couldn't shake how horrible that idea seemed. It haunted her, somehow.

Though of course she didn't let it show in her words to Harker. She didn't tell him that she'd taken great care in her letter to Cobble. That she'd erred on the side of Harker *doesn't know what he's doing.* Instead she detailed her plan in great and gleeful detail. *To my not quite mortal enemy*, she began. Then ended it on: *just in case you were planning on something other than what you claim this will be.*

And was surprised when he wrote back almost immediately.

Oh, what a disappointment it would have been, little bookworm, if you had given me anything less. I do hope you intend to continue living up to my high expectations of your seething hatred and distrust of my every move.

Yours faithfully,

Yes, Immortal Is the Right Word to Use Now

Though her surprise was even greater when she got to the end, and a bubble of laughter rose up. She had to crush it down, hard. Smother it in its sleep. Now was not the time to find him amusing. It was the time to crumple that letter up into a tiny ball, and toss it, and then go to the east wing theater, with a face like stone.

Impenetrable, ready for anything, hand already on that nail in her pocket, as she eased the creaky, half-collapsing door open, and just let herself peer through the crack she had made. No body parts going past the threshold, no making a racket. One look, and nothing else.

But one look did nothing for her. All she could make out was a long stretch of wooden floor, slightly warped with age and disuse and probable damp. And a stripe of a velvety-looking crimson curtain, tattered at the hem but still somehow sumptuous. It made her think of baroque performances, where everyone wore makeup so thick it gleamed and moved in unsettling ways.

In fact, for a second she could almost see it.

She could hear the slightly discordant music.

She shut her eyes, and she was there on a seat amid rows of them, in the dusty darkness, as performers parted over-lipsticked mouths, to show their disturbingly large teeth. They cavorted and capered, in a play she could almost see the title of. A word from the Underneath, something someone whispered to her, and when he did, he put his hand over hers, and she knew. She knew then that they were going to end the night tangled together in—

"I wasn't sure you would really dare come."

Her eyes snapped open the second she heard him speak. Heart already racing, half of her sure she'd dropped the ball already. But he just stood there, hands in his pockets, in the sliver of space she'd revealed when she opened the door a crack. Like he'd done no more than step to the left, so she could see him. And even after she had, he didn't make a move.

He waited for her to make one first.

To step inside—and she did. She slipped through and shut the door behind herself. Carefully, and with her eyes never on anything but him. Then she stood like he was, hands in her pockets, her battered little Mary Janes positioned primly together, face as expressionless as she could make it.

And only after she was satisfied that she had made the right, slightly defiant, and ready-for-anything impression did she speak. "Well, I do have my little safety net now. So it didn't seem like such a dangerous thing to do."

"This will always be a dangerous thing to do, bookworm. And especially when hunger exponentially increases, the more time a vampire spends in the company of the thing they hunger for."

"If that's the case, how do you even expect to do these lessons?"

"By making them fast enough and brutal enough to beat the clock, of course."

"That's ridiculo—" she started to say. But before she could even get to the end of the word, he cut in with one she already recognized all too well. "*Draw,*" he said, like a whipcrack. And this time, she had no time to grab a thing. No chance to put a book in front of her. There wasn't even a book to be *had*.

All she could do was lurch to the left, hard enough that she went down on one knee. The bone there brayed at her; some muscle in her side definitely got twisted in a way it didn't like. But the mess that came out of his wand missed her by what felt like a millimeter. She honestly thought she felt heat kiss her flailing arm.

Before the bust of some old dead man burst into flames, behind her.

For a second all she could do was stare at it, agog. But the only thing he had to say about it was this: "Well, at least you can sense a spell when it's coming for you, and dodge in the correct direction. Even if you can't instinctively shield."

"You just almost fucking incinerated me to prove *that*?"

"Don't be dramatic. I didn't almost incinerate you. I aimed for your hair."

"My hair is on my *head*, Harker. If one burns, the other does, too."

"Not when I can put it out this quick."

He flicked the wand still in his hand at the bust. And sure enough, the fire winked out, like it had never been there at all. Still amazing to witness, after a month of seeing similar feats in the halls and her dorm and all over the grounds. But even so, she couldn't respond with anything but fury. "Or you could have remembered I can't even gather, and told me how to first."

"You don't need to gather to feel magic coming for you. Ordinary people sidestep it all the time, without even knowing they're doing it. And you aren't ordinary, so your sense is keener. Now, let's see if we can juice you into doing something more than dodge. Ready?"

No, she went to say.

But he didn't even wait for her to answer. He just snapped that wand at her again. And this time, she knew it wasn't fire he was throwing. Somehow, she knew it was worse. It was something *much* worse, and it was aimed right at her heart, and she just wasn't fast enough. She could feel it—exactly as he'd said—but she was too slow. She wasn't going to make it; all she could do was throw herself onto the ground and squeeze her eyes tight shut and hope.

And god, this time she felt it do more than kiss.

She got pressure, sizzling over her left shoulder. The sense of something sharp, the *snick* sound of something being sliced. When she looked, she honestly expected to see blood. And instead she watched as the strap of her dress suddenly drooped, and slid, and finally settled into two separate pieces, on either side of her body.

Shouldn't have worn a bra that shows through this blouse, she thought mindlessly. "My fucking dress, you absolute arsehole," she spat.

Much to his amusement.

"It really shouldn't be something you're mourning."

"Of course I'm mourning it. Unlike what you're probably used to, this isn't one of many."

"You know I'm a vampire, and you still think I'm a wealthy prick?"

There is no concept of money in Calabaraia, she thought automatically.

Though she couldn't bring herself to concede.

"If you don't want me to, maybe you shouldn't act like one."

He spread his hands. "But when you do, you fit in. And it's not as if I can afford to not."

"So that's the reason for the captaincy, and all the holding court."

"Well, you can't deny it makes for good cover. And I *do* need a hell of a lot of it. Doubly so, when delicious meals are suddenly on the floor in front of me, hearts beating like jackhammers, skin showing through their flimsy little blouses."

She grabbed that split strap when he said it. Tried to pull it back over herself, so he couldn't see. Though it wasn't as if she'd ever actually seen him look. And he didn't look now, either. He held her gaze, as he let his tongue curl up, over his teeth. His suddenly very sharp, very numerous teeth.

She wasn't about to be intimidated, however.

"How do you even talk with those razor blades in your mouth?" she scoffed.

And it seemed to work. His expression went back to something less predatory.

"*That's* the question you want to ask me? The breadth of my knowledge, my skills. The fact that I am a near-mythical creature to everything you were before this. And your curiosity is about where my teeth go when I'm speaking."

"Oh, I'm sorry I wasn't appropriately awed, your lordship," she said, as she doffed an imaginary cap. "Please do tell me about the time you sat on a throne of skulls in Calabaraia, as the King of the Fen handed you a giant crown made from the blood of your defeated foes."

"There is no King of the Fen."

"I was joking. I know hierarchies don't exist there."

He raised an eyebrow. "Really? And do you know why?"

"Of course I do. Because they are completely baffled by the

idea of anything ruling over anything else. They can't understand it, even when we explain. There, only a kind of chaos reigns," she said—and now both his eyebrows were up. In something like surprised admiration, she thought it was. Though it melted down into withering so quickly, she couldn't really claim it definitely had been.

"You should really stop reading and accepting all the unsanctioned accounts. You're going to get yourself in trouble, bookworm," he said, as he shook his head in this weary of her nonsense sort of way.

She had no idea why, however.

"How much trouble can that be, when those accounts are in the library?"

"The library does whatever it wants. Students do whatever they are told."

"So everyone else just reads whatever any professor says you should."

He spread his hands again. "Exactly so, yes."

"But what if they're lying? What if what they say is dusty and dry and doesn't help you at all? I could fall into the Underneath and get melted by fen, because I thought you should bow to royalty that isn't actually real," she said, and though he looked annoyed, he didn't do anything other than sigh. So she stuck it to him. "You don't actually have an answer for that, do you?"

"Well, apart from the obvious one: that this is precisely why it's a bad idea for someone like you to be in a place like here. I knew it as soon as I saw you. So sure of what's right and fair, you completely forget nobody else cares, and that every one of them resent how it makes them feel to hear you do."

"One look through a windshield couldn't have told you that."

"You only think that because you didn't see the expression on your own face."

"The expression is irrelevant when nothing I've done backs that assessment up. I just slink to lectures and lurk in the library and say nothing about how unjust this whole goddamn place is."

"You say it to that little friend of yours. You're saying it *now*, to your worst fucking *enemy*," he said, half laughing with incredulity as he did. And to be fair to him, it did sound ridiculous, when he put it like that. Or at least, ridiculous enough that she could somewhat accept it.

"So that's why you don't like me. Some idea of me as too bold."

"Stop searching for reasons. I am Areifen, fickle chaos. I need none."

"Then let's just go back to the lessons. I mean, it's not like I relish talking to you, anyway," she said, more sour sounding than she intended. As if she was actually enjoying the conversation or wanted to know about his deep-down feelings. Instead of seeming as normal and furious at him as she wanted to be.

Though if he noticed, he didn't let it show.

He just folded his arms across his chest. Leaned back against the rickety stage behind him. It groaned in protest at his enormous body, but it held. "Fine," he said. "You're gathering wrong."

"And you think I'm not aware of that fact."

"I think you're aware of it. I don't think you know why you're fucking up."

"Well, maybe somebody here should give lectures on that, before they give lectures on the entire life story of a man who didn't even discover the Underneath, was a terrible magic wielder, and eventually got eaten by a goblin that had replaced his son."

They were on part three of the same story so far. Cobble was a kind professor—he was sweeter and more approachable than Hargreaves, or Yates who supposedly taught Horticulture but spent lectures screaming at everyone for being useless, or even the elusive headmaster, who everyone just referred to as *the overseer.* But he was also a rambler.

She had gotten more from one book than she had from hours of his lessons.

Hell, she was getting more from Harker, even though he'd yet to really teach her a thing. "They don't have to for everyone else. Everyone else has already been told," he said, and all she could think was *at least he's willing to admit it.* Even if she kept her response sharp.

"Yes, I'm aware of what money and station and access to inner circles affords people. And what that means for someone like me. Or even for the things that magic is used for. That doesn't change the fact that they *should* do things differently. That they should start with how to make a fucking shield, before a deranged vampire burns your fucking face off."

"I told you. I didn't aim for your face."

"Maybe not. But other people could."

He went to say something after that. Something exasperated and contemptuous, she figured. Only for some reason, he stopped midway through making the words. The eyes he was almost rolling went to her instead. And for just a second, she thought she saw something flash across them.

Before he glanced away, in a manner that said it hadn't.

He looked almost bored suddenly. And he sounded it, too.

"Was it that third year? Sebastian something or other?" he asked, as offhandedly as he'd mentioned the forest thing. The trick he had said some student she didn't even know had wanted to play. They hadn't, so she had wondered ever since if he had been lying. If he had just tried to scare her.

But something about this said otherwise.

It made her think of the sandy-haired boy she had seen in the dining hall the other day, glaring at her over his soup. And hadn't he shoved by her in the hall once? *Maybe*, she thought. "I don't know," she said. "Nobody ever offers their names, when they're busy being rude over my charity shop clothes, or the hair I can't even spell dry. Never mind style into anything they'd approve of."

"So it's just insults. No one is physically hurting you."

"Not as of yet, no. I just mean that they could."

"And you're telling the truth there. You're not lying to me."

"Why would I lie about something like that? It's hardly a risk for me to tell you that you have a rival for your murderous intentions. Worst-case scenario is you let him do what he was going to do anyway. Best-case scenario, you kill him to secure first dibs on my beating heart. Or have I got which is worse and which is best the wrong way around?" She gave him a little faux-musing. "I suppose it depends on which way he wants to go about ending my life. Dismembering sounds more horrible than being drained of blood, after all."

"Don't say dismem—" he started to tell her. But then he seemed to cut himself off, before he could get the whole word out. He pinched his lips together; she saw the muscles in his jaw clench. Like he knew he was getting too frustrated, over something he shouldn't have been frustrated over at all.

What did it matter if someone decided to remove her arms? It was a strange thing for him to seethe about.

But he did it all the same, for a second.

And then he seemed to wrestle himself back under control.

I bet that countdown clock to extreme thirst is spinning like a top thanks to all your taunting, she thought, and that seemed to fit. He turned his back, and when he looked at her again, there was something steely in his expression. Resolved.

Ready to get this over with.

"You think gathering is about getting hand placement exactly right; it's not. Like all the basic forms, it's just a way to help you get into the right frame of mind. Then the others focus on whatever you manage to call to you. Like a pen—once you pick it up, you know what's going to happen, and you can then decide what you want to flow out of the tip and onto the page. But first, before you do, you have to do whatever it is that fills it with ink," he said, all in a big burst. He even did hand gestures of the kind you might expect to see from a swimming instructor trying to explain how to breaststroke, while someone drowns right in front of them. Spread, hitting the air over and over, full of impatience.

But she couldn't deny it: Damn, he explained it well.

It hit better than anything she'd read. Suddenly, it seemed clear.

She couldn't praise him for it, however. "All right, then. What *does* fill it?"

"Emotions. And the stronger you feel them, the better."

"That can't be true," she insisted. "Every book says it's clarity of mind."

"Yeah, honestly, I think most of them just wish that was the case."

She shot him a skeptical look. "Why would they wish a thing like that?"

"Because they were written by old, stuffy, rich white men."

"Careful, Harker. Now who's the one questioning things?"

He sighed for that. And he didn't just gesture, when he started speaking again. He paced. "That wasn't questioning, it's just the truth. *Barrett's Guide, The Complete History, A Secret Etymology*—they were all written by the sort of humans who would vastly prefer everything run on reason, and rationality, and clean, cool logic. But it just doesn't. You already know it doesn't. You've met chaos in the flesh. You've accepted that chaos runs the Underneath. You've felt the chaos here, seething under the surface of the brick and mortar and wood they've tried to contain it within. What else could it be but purest feeling?" he asked, by the end so almost passionate about it that she had to believe him. This was something he meant. Something he felt deeply, in a way that most likely had nothing to do with her.

This place made him angry, too, quite clearly.

He just played the game of it, for his own ends.

Though he tried to cover that up a little, once the words were out and ringing in the air. He took out that silver case again and drew out one of those cigarettes. Lit it, in that same casual, "I don't care" way he had the other day. But of course, even that said something now.

It helps him stay cool, she thought.

And filed that information away for later. "So I just need to . . . be joyful," she said, as if she'd never clocked any of this at all.

"You need to strongly feel whatever best connects you to magic."

"But how do I know what does? How can I possibly discover that?"

"The same way you would anything else. Learn. Try. Test it out."

He waved the hand holding the cigarette, and she got a wave of that scent.

Familiar somehow. Though she shook it off.

"I can't just test out different emotions," she said.

Much to his scorn. His eyes practically rolled out of his head. "Of course you can. Think of whatever sparked it when I had you on that stone table. Loathing, most likely. Think of something that you loathe."

"You. Looking at me with that smug face. While probably tricking me."

"I *am* tricking you. And then I'm going to laugh when you fall flat on your face. In fact, all of us will; we'll stand around you in a circle, jeering and crowing. And nothing will stop us, not even when you cry. That might even make us wor—" he said, all of it so suddenly awful it caught her off guard. The words just built and built, each one better designed than the last to strike at her heart, until she broke.

She cut him off, before he could say another word.

"Stop it, you horrible beast," she spat.

But of course, as soon as she had, she knew.

It was there, in the way his expression immediately dropped from vicious to completely neutral. He hadn't been serious at all. He had just been trying to goad her into fury—and it had worked. She could still feel her heart pounding in her throat. Her face was burning.

And it burned hotter when he spoke.

"And? Anything happen for that?" he asked, casual as you like.

"You could have just let me come to it on my own."

"Why, when I can fill you with disgust just by blinking wrong?"

"That was hardly a blink. That was fucking horrible."

"Well. Horrible is what I am. I don't know what else you expected," he said in a way that made all the sense in the world. But strangely, for a second, she found herself wondering. Why had she just said that to him; why had she just accused him of being horrid?

It almost sounded like there was some other way he could be.

Even though he always was. There was no other way to see him.

"I expected some skill. That did nothing," she said.

And he nodded. He went back to the point.

"Then it isn't loathing. What else did you feel when I was over you?"

"Terror. I was terrified," she said. Though she didn't think back to it, when she did. She couldn't think back to it. She *never* thought back to it. And if he was going to . . . "But don't you dare try to make me feel that. I *will* stab you if you do."

"What if I do it from over here?"

"I don't see how you're going to manage that."

"It's probably wisest not to challenge me, bookworm."

He kissed the cigarette to his lips. Let smoke coil out from between them. It hung like a veil over his face, almost obscuring his expression. But not quite, not quite. She could still make out that hint of feral threat.

She took a step back because of it.

Yet all he said was, "Perhaps I should tell you a scary story." Then before she could tell him that was a ridiculous idea, that she had grown up on tall terrifying tales and none had ever stirred her, he drew out his wand. He flicked it in a particular way, and a chair slid across the room from the side, to slot behind her.

She sat, without knowing if he had made her or not.

And he began. "Once, there was a girl, a student here, called Lilibet. And she was very bright, and very courageous, and very . . ." He paused, almost like he had gotten a little lost in the story already.

But then he seemed to shake it off and continued. "She was very lovely. So lovely, in fact, that she attracted the notice of something no sensible person should ever want the notice of. A shadow built from the bones of a broken thing. But unfortunately for Lilibet, she barely noticed the breaks—and she welcomed it in."

"Because she was kind. Because she had a kind heart."

"Kindness is just foolery, wrapped up in a pretty bow."

So edgy, she wanted to sneer. She probably would have done so, too, if it hadn't been for his tone. It sounded so dull and off it made all the sensitive points on her body prickle and bristle. Suddenly, she found herself leaning forward, muscles tensed.

"It didn't seem like such a terrible mistake on her part, at first. Shadows can seem very like other more ordinary and decent men, that you already know. They can call up familiar traits, familiar feelings, to inveigle their way into your life. And they are so charming, so sincere seeming. When the shadow gave her a gift of green velvet ribbon, she took it without even thinking twice about it. She wore it gladly, around her pretty throat."

"Like in the story."

"Exactly so."

"The one where she takes it off and—"

"Everyone knows the rest. She knew, too. But she thought she was safe—because of course she didn't have a secret like that. She wasn't the one keeping anything from him. If she ever took it off, she thought, there would just be what had always been there underneath," he said, his voice getting softer and softer. And was it her imagination or was the room getting darker and darker?

No, it couldn't be.

But she could hardly see him now.

It was like she was dropping into an abyss.

"I don't think I want to hear the end of this version," she said, her own voice even fainter than his. Far away almost, and so plaintive he had to listen.

Instead, he carried on.

"Until one day, she decided she wanted to see. He warned her not to, but it seemed so silly to worry. So she pulled the end of it and watched it unravel, and there underneath was not her own hidden ruin. It was the ruin he had wrought on her all along. The wound he had made deeper under cover of that velvet darkness, over every single day she had let him draw close to her, in seeming sunshine. All her life held in, until she pulled that thread. She pulled it and wore a waterfall of blood, for the rest of her life," he said. Then after a long, dark moment, he seemed to lean in close. "Are you terrified yet?"

To which she went to say, *No, of course not.*

Only somehow her eyes were closed. Her hand was on her throat, as if to keep that waterfall in. As if to hold her head on her neck, while the feeling of losing that fight got stronger and stronger. *She's drowning*, she found herself saying, *she's drifting away to that shadowy place.*

And when she did, her voice was full of tears.

She didn't know why. She didn't understand any of this.

It seemed as if he was making her feel it maybe—but then she heard his voice. The snap of his fingers. *Mina*, he was saying. Not *bookworm*, not some other snide insult. But her name, her actual name. *Mina, Mina, Mina, come back, come back. Come back to me.* She even thought for a second that she felt his hand on the back of her neck, on her arm.

Like someone trying to lift a body out of a lake.

Like he could drag her out of this.

But it wasn't him that managed.

It was the sudden ring of the breakfast bell, loud even down here in the bowels of the school. It clanged out, just as she thought she might sink into that oblivion forever. And when it did she snapped back to reality, like she'd never been anywhere else. She took a breath, and looked up to the place she was sure he was.

But he hadn't moved.

He was still over there by the stage.

Staring at her, with that flat expression all over his face.

"I guess terror didn't work," he said, as he eased himself out of the half-sitting position he'd been in. "Oh, well. I suppose we shall just have to try and make you feel the right thing tomorrow."

Then he simply strolled out.

Leaving her stranded, spent.

And not sure she could ever do anything like this again.

Chapter Eleven

She didn't sleep well. Half her dreams were of girls wearing dresses made of blood, of Lilibet whispering in her ear that she was falling into the same trap. And the other half were of him doing the trapping. Just luring her in with things that seemed like good advice, but more than likely were not.

Connecting to magic via emotion might actually make it burst out of you and burn your own face off, she told herself, in the middle of getting dressed the next day. And she told herself it again, as she sat across from Anaya before the breakfast rush, wolfing down thick slices of buttery toast and huge mugs of tea.

"I just feel like everybody has mastered basic stuff, even before we get to the practical classes. So of course, they're all going to survive being attacked by some possessed skeleton or a serpent scooped from the Underneath or whatever else gets thrown at us. But we won't. And with barely two months to go to the end of term," her friend was saying. So naturally, she wanted to tell her what Harker had told her. To share possibly valuable information, like she had before the maze.

But in the end, she just couldn't.

Not yet, anyway.

She had to figure out, first, if he was being honest.

After all, it was bad enough that he and his secrets were a danger to her. She couldn't endanger her friend, too. She couldn't endanger anyone. She didn't even want to be endangered herself, and yet somehow, she got to the theater at the exact time he had asked. *Seven*, he had said in his letter, this time. As if he wanted to give her a little extra time to fill her head with nightmares.

Though he didn't look like someone who would ever do such a thing, when she stepped into the room. He was sprawled across the stage, one hand propping up his head, the other holding a book. And the book was, inexplicably, *The Velveteen Rabbit*. As she watched, he licked his thumb and turned the page.

Even though she knew he could bespell those pages to move on their own. Hell, she'd read about one particular piece of magic that made the words in a book simply leap into your head, all at once. And she felt sure he could have done it, if he wanted to.

It made her wonder: Was it the novelty of not?

Or did he find using magic for things you didn't need wasteful?

She knew some did. Professor Hargreaves had talked about it the afternoon before, in her lecture "Conservation and Practicalities." *Magic is not a disposable tissue, there to be used frivolously and lazily and then discarded*, she had said. *In fact, I would invite you all to question if it is even natural for us to use it at all.*

And the memory made her come close to asking him.

As did the way he currently looked. He seemed almost soft now. Almost ordinary—lazing with a book, sleeves of that baby-blue sweater too long and almost covering his hands, hair hanging over his forehead, battered sneakers on his feet.

But then she remembered that yesterday, he had told her a story so terrifying she was still sweating about it now. Yesterday, he had almost set her hair on fire and split the strap of her dress. In fact, he'd split the material of the blouse below it, too. She found a cut so fine in the shoulder of the material that it looked like it had been done with a razor.

So better to keep seeing him as the monster he was, she felt.

And she was glad she had, when his gaze suddenly flicked up to hers.

For some reason, it thumped her hard in the gut. "I didn't think you'd return for a second round," he said, while she was still recovering from whatever those eyes had just done. *Tried to get me in a headlock*, she thought and looked away before she answered, in as unbothered a manner as she could muster.

"Well, you hardly managed to rattle me yesterday, so it seemed a little less foolish to. Though don't take that as me dropping my guard. I upped the iron dust, just in case you decided to really put your back into being evil," she said, in a tone that came so close to withering. In fact, she tensed for a second, wondering if she'd gone too far. Goaded him, instead of just making clear that she wasn't a pushover.

But when she let her gaze go back to him, he looked almost amused.

And just a little irritated. "I know. I feel like my lungs are on fire," he said, breezily enough that some of the tension went out of her. She didn't flinch, either, when he got off the stage in one sinuous roll and stepped a little closer.

She just sank into the first thought she had.

"So you do actually breathe, then. Like a human."

"Is this you trying to ask if I stole someone's skin to wear?"

"Well, there's at least a fifty-fifty chance you did."

"They overstate how common that is, to make anything that comes here in human form seem disgusting and like a thief. Instead of something that could have possibly gone there, and then returned."

"You were taken as a child, then."

He hesitated. Touched his pocket, where that silver case sat.

Then finally, he answered. Just one tight word: "Yes."

It didn't sound convincing, however.

"That seems like a lie, somehow."

"Even though I have no reason to."

"Maybe you want me to feel sorry for you."

"I doubt there is a single unendurable agony I could suffer that would garner your sympathy," he said, voice light and almost amused. Like it was a joke, like it was meaningless. Even though that choice of words stood out, a neon sign in the dark. *So it has been beyond endurance and absolutely agonizing, then*, she thought.

And didn't like how hard it made her stomach drop.

"You're right. Nothing ever could," she said.

Much to his satisfaction.

"Then you understand I'm telling you the truth."

"I don't know. There could be other reasons to lie."

"Name one."

"You want to hide something worse."

"All right. Let's test how human I once was then, shall we?"

No, she thought automatically. Even though she had no idea what he intended to do. She only saw the wand suddenly in his hand, and his free one open as if to take hold of something, and knew she didn't want to see this. And sure enough, he drew a line of glittering blue through the air.

And now he had a knife.

Near transparent, gleaming.

But keen as a shard of glass.

"Don't," she said, but too late, too late. He drew that sharp edge down the inside of his forearm, in one stroke. Like someone trying to end their life the fastest way they could, it seemed. And even more so when that red line split open. She could see parted muscle. She could see *bone.*

"Oh my god, oh my god, what have you done?" she cried, too horrified to even pretend she could cope with this. Blood had already covered his hand. It was pattering onto the floor. This was too much, it just was.

No matter how casual he was being about it.

"Shown you how human I am underneath my skin."

"And you needed to make a ten-inch gash to do that? Holy shit, you are bleeding everywhere; you are bleeding *so much.* I have to go get someone. I have to get you to the infirmary."

"Mina, you know how fast I heal."

"Right, but—"

"But what? You thought a hole through my body went away in a week, but this flesh wound was going to stick around long enough to need some kind of magical medical intervention?"

"I would hardly call a knife hitting bone a flesh wound."

"To me it is." He held up his arm. The one that had been all but split in two a moment ago—but now had no split in it all. There was just smooth skin beneath the coating of blood. "See. All gone. Good as new. And plus now you've seen the sort of thing you need to conjure in order to actually kill me."

"So that's the only way to cut off your head, then."

"Yes. A knife forged in magic, with a particular sort of edge." He turned the blade so she could see. It almost seemed to disappear;

it was that fine. "Though of course you need to do it yourself. A spell cast cannot be turned against—"

"The caster, I know."

"You can hold it, though."

"What would I want to do that for?" she asked. But she took the knife when he spun it in his hand, and held the hilt out to her. She marveled over the lightness of it, like she wasn't really holding anything at all. And how it shimmered, in the low light.

But of course that meant she wasn't paying attention, when he stepped back, slowly, into the shadows. When the shadows started to gather and deepen, until everything dimmed. "For practice," he said, suddenly so low and deep, into that abrupt veil of darkness. "Now come for me, before I come for you."

Then she looked up, just in time to see one of those velvet curtains lift and reach for her. Like a ghostly arm, like there was something underneath it—even though she knew nothing was. It was just material bespelled. He was trying to frighten her with cheap tricks.

Yet somehow it was no less terrifying for it.

She stepped back so fast she stumbled and almost went to one knee. In fact, she only managed to stay upright because her hand flailed out, and fell on the back of the chair she'd sat on the other day. It helped her, and helped her again when that red velvet hand stretched farther. It almost stroked her cheek, and she lifted that rickety wooden thing and tried to throw it.

Only the thing wasn't wooden anymore.

It was melting in her hand, turning pliable and soft and, god, disgusting. God, it felt disgusting. And it wouldn't let her let it go. It stuck to her hand when she shook it; it seemed to squirm and slither until it became clear. He'd turned the chair into a sort of creature. A snake thing, that looked at her with one gimlet eye.

Use the knife, she thought, as it twisted its way up her arm.

But just as she went to try to stab the thing—unsure if it would work against creatures he had magicked, but willing to try—the velvet hand snatched at her. It got her by the wrist, while she was too busy paying attention to anything else. And after it had, she didn't need to worry about the snake anymore.

It smothered her so fast she knew she had no more than seconds. She went to scream, and it seemed to fill her mouth. The only breath she could take stuffed her throat with material, heavy and thick and tasting of tattered ruins. Though even if that hadn't been the case, she suspected the result would be the same.

The velvet had her around the throat and chest.

And it was tightening, tightening, tightening. It made her think of medieval torture devices, of being trapped while someone turned a handle—and of course, she knew who was doing the turning. It was him; he was doing this. She had let her guard drop enough, and now he was seizing his chance to torture her to death.

And it was her fury at that injustice that made her act.

She couldn't move her hand, but she could move the knife within it. She could tilt it up, until it touched velvet. Then it was just a matter of forcing, of pushing, and making that fucking material rip.

It shocked her when it did, though.

She felt it give and almost sobbed with relief. Because the moment she managed that, the rest of it seemed to retreat. It melted away from her, as fast as it had come, while she continued to tear and stab and wrench her way back out. She burst free, like something being born.

And there he stood, laughing at her. *Laughing.*

She'd almost suffocated, and he thought it was hilarious.

"You didn't even get anywhere *close* enough to kill me," he said, with so much contempt and so much amusement that she wasn't sure what happened. She just felt something boil up inside her, something that felt like her and yet not, something that knew how to hurt someone without needing to be near at all.

Toss it up and catch it by the blade, this voice said.

Because by the blade makes it easier to—

"Throw," she said, and then somehow she just *did.* Like someone had taken over her arm briefly, and made her something other than clumsy and slow. It took only a split second to turn the knife, to get it by the tip. And even less time than that to hurl it. One straight shot directly at his heart.

Perfect in a way she knew she wasn't.

But once you were, the voice said.

As the knife thudded into his chest, easy as pie.

Chapter Twelve

The first thing she thought was: *No, no, no, this isn't right.* It couldn't be right, because she'd read the thing he'd said herself. You couldn't kill someone with their own magic. It just wasn't possible.

And yet the results spoke for themselves.

He staggered back the moment the blade went in. Eyes wide, mouth a circle of shock, one hand going up to clutch at the hilt. Like he wanted to try pulling it out, it looked like. But he didn't even have the strength to hold it for long. He let go after no more than a few seconds, and suddenly that arm went limp.

All of him seemed to go limp, in fact.

He sagged back against the now curtainless side of the stage, as if he needed something to hold him up. And just as she was thinking, *No, this can't be; vampires cannot even be killed by a dagger through the heart,* he met her gaze. He looked at her with eyes full of wounded shock.

How could you? they said.

"But I didn't mean to," she blurted out in protest. Though, of course, she knew protesting wouldn't do any good. You couldn't unkill someone with good intentions, or an insistence on some misunderstanding. All you could do was try to fix things—and she had a good idea how to.

He'll heal if you take it out, she told herself, and didn't even think twice about it. She scrambled to her feet, heart somehow thumping harder than it had in that suffocating velvet darkness. And she stumbled forward to take hold of that knife. "Hold on," she gasped, as she clutched the hilt. Eyes on his face, so she could see exactly how much damage she was doing.

But that just meant she saw his expression change the moment it did.

Like a switch being flicked. One second it was hurt and shock. The next it was the smug fuck she had come to know all too well. "I just cannot *believe* you fell for that," he said, so firm and clear and kind of exasperated, it was as if he had never bled at all. Though it still shocked her anew, when the red on his lips evaporated. When the blade dissolved. When it became obvious that all this had just been an illusion designed to draw her in, and nothing more. And now he got to grab hold of her wrists, as he carried on saying the most annoying things in the world. "You were doing so well. I really thought that was going to be it. I really thought fury was the key, but not only was it not, you gave in to sympathy the second you felt it. Even though you knew, even though you read it with your own eyes that vampires cannot be killed like that, that my own blade could never even be turned against me, you still caved to *kindness*."

"Kindness isn't a weak thing, you fucking cheat."

"It is when you think cheating is something your enemy should be above."

"I don't think that. I just thought that you—I didn't think that you—"

Do not finish that sentence, she ordered herself. Because she knew the end was *would do that to me*, and god, that made almost no sense at all. He'd just tried to suffocate her to death. He'd made her scream around a mouthful of old velvet. He was rotten, he was rotten, he was rotten.

He was worse than that.

"It doesn't matter what you think of me. It matters that you do not ever hesitate. Because I will *never*. I will see my opening and seize it," he said, and as he did, the whole room revolved, so violently she thought she might be sick. Bile rose in her throat; she got that buzzing in her teeth that usually meant her dinner was coming back up. And then she felt something against her back, and all motion stopped.

But absolutely nothing got better.

Because somehow, she was in the maze again, laid out on that stone plinth, like some ancient sacrifice to a god she didn't believe in. While he crouched above her, just like before, caging her body in. Only worse, god, it was so much worse. He still had hold of her wrist, and now he had it pinned above her head. His body seemed closer, his face even more familiar.

"This time, I *am* going to drop you into the Underneath," he said, low and heavy. It wasn't the sound of his voice that disturbed her, however. It was the words. The words. Like he had known exactly what had been in her mind, when he had done that to her.

"So you *are* in my head, somehow," she said, as she strained against his grip.

It wasn't a comfort, however, when he shook his head.

"No, Mina. I don't need to be, to know your worst fear."

"But that place isn't it. Not even a little bit. Not at all. It's—" she tried to say, thinking only of him. Just him and all the ways he made her feel. Everything he did, everything he said. *You are my every nightmare and all my torment*, she thought, but somehow, she couldn't get it out.

She looked up into his face, and saw only the long grass.

Felt that shadow behind it all. The slow sink into losing herself in it.

And it must have shown all over her, because his seemed to change.

"What connects you to magic," he finished for her. "Whatever it is you have to feel, you are afraid of feeling it; you hide from it. You hide it from yourself. One hand acting, to distract from what the other does in secret."

Then before she could say no, he reached up. Like he was about to strangle her, she thought, and tried to escape it. She struggled, her free hand going to protect her throat. Body bucking against his, suddenly half mad with the need to escape. But all it did was make the long, heavy length of him roll against her. All it meant was feeling her own pulse, thrumming between her fingers.

He would kill you if he could, she thought desperately.

Just as he used that hand to find the curve of her cheek.

And then he stroked over it, so slow and barely touching that it almost seemed like a dream. Like something she would wake up from, and tell herself she didn't really feel.

Even as it sent a wave of warmth through her, so intense she didn't know how to speak because of it. She went to say stop, and all that came out was a great bloom of light, between their bodies. It filled the hand she had on his chest, so strong and sure she couldn't believe it. Couldn't even use it. Didn't know what to do with it now that she had it. Or at least, she didn't know what to do with it, at first.

But then he said two last words.

“It’s desire,” he whispered.

And when he did, she just couldn’t help it. She used that magic to send him into the sky, in one violent rush. All the way up to the barrier above, so far she could hardly see him.

Then she simply didn’t hesitate.

She scrambled down from the stone table and fled.

She ran, with the sound of him falling, falling, falling far behind her.

Chapter Thirteen

She didn't want it to be desire. Or at least, not the kind of desire he had definitely been talking about. The kind that went with words like *sensuous* and *seductive* and made her feel so unsettled she couldn't even talk to Anaya about it. Even though it was kind of something she *could* mention, if she wanted to. She didn't have to hide that from her friend. She could just say she unearthed it in a book, or overheard other students whispering. It's *not clear thoughts, or intense focusing on what you want to appear, or the exact right hand gesture or wand movement—it's emotion*, she imagined herself saying, on more than one occasion.

And especially when Anaya seemed to be hitting a wall now.

During Professor Yates's class on preliminary applications, she managed to light a candle. But she couldn't turn the candle into a key, even though wax and iron were supposedly the easiest of materials to alter into each other. "Look, it says here that they are resonant, yet I can't even do that," Anaya said, as they lounged together on Mina's bed on some freezing cold Thursday free period, books piled between them, her friend's thumb holding open *Simple Transmogrification Pairings for Foolish Beginners* at the right series of diagrams.

Then once Mina had squinted at the tiny drawings of wax shapes, she flicked to the harder stuff. Stone into organic matter, that sort of thing. "Never mind *this* one," she said and pointed to a pebble pictured next to a doughnut.

"Nobody can do that one. Yates said that the less pure an item is, the harder it is to turn it into something else and vice versa. A doughnut is twelve different things; you'll end up with some sort of flour and butter rock monster," Mina pointed out. Then for good measure she mimed what this poor unfortunate creature would look like. A hand coming out of its head. Body half melted. "Killlll meeeeee."

"Stop it. Just because Damien Farweather turned his foot into a depressed chair doesn't mean it's not possible to do it right. Or that we shouldn't be aiming for it. I know for a fact that *you* are aiming for it, even if you're keeping how a secret."

That jolted her. Hard enough that she couldn't say anything, for a moment.

Anaya had to break the silence, once she seemed to register that silence needed to be broken. "I wasn't saying that resentfully, Min. I know you would never hoard information," she said, then seemed to hesitate. She bit her lip. Before just bursting out with it. "But I'd be a fool if I didn't know you were getting that information in some kind of weird and probably dangerous way."

"It's not dangerous."

"If it wasn't, you would just tell me what the source is."

"Maybe I just don't think both of us should be in trouble."

"So it's illegal, then. It's going to get you expelled. Or dragged in front of a magical tribunal for crimes against the natural order." Her friend's voice dropped low for that last part. And even lower when she added one last thing, while leaning forward, eyes wide. "You know they execute people in really weird ways, right? I heard that they use a rusty spoon. And they don't cut your head off. They cut your *elbows* off. Do you have any idea how long it'll take to die of having sawn-off elbows? Years, probably."

"Well, good job, you're being ridiculous on purpose, then."

"Maybe I am, but the head and rusty spoon part still made you flinch."

No, she wanted to say. But the thought of Harker got in the way. Harker saying what they would do to him. *Who are you really protecting?* she found herself thinking. Anaya*? Or him?* And it didn't make her feel any better about things when her mind answered, Anaya. After all, Anaya was the only person who should even be in an equation like that. Who cared if he got brutally executed?

Not her. No, sir. Not a bit of it.

"Look, you don't have to worry, okay. I'm being very careful. I've got things in place to protect myself." She swallowed too thickly around those last words. And had to rush on, before Anaya could point at said swallowing as evidence of her lies and her nerves. "And once I make sure that whatever I'm learning is accurate and safe and not going to blow you up somehow, I will share it. I just need to see if I can . . . replicate it. By using certain methods."

"Do the methods involve emotion?"

Anaya said the words casually.

But she met Mina's gaze as she did so, and held it.

"So you've guessed that, then," Mina said. "It feels that way to you."

"Kind of. Sometimes. I did wonder about whether it was something to do with feeling relief? The first time I gathered, it was once I was safe on top of the hedge. My whole body sagged with it, and then somehow I could feel it coming to me. It kind of bloomed. And when I think back on that feeling, I can make it happen. Like some sort of . . . emotional muscle memory."

Anaya held up a hand, light suddenly blooming in it.

Then she seemed to look at Mina pointedly. And Mina realized her friend was waiting for her to do it back. To show that she had mastered this muscle memory, too. Or at least started to give it a go.

But of course, it wasn't that easy.

"Well, see the thing is, though . . . my emotion is sort of embarrassing."

"You mean you have to, like, pick your nose to feel it?"

"What? No. *No*. Gross. And probably not a thing. *Hopefully* not a thing."

"I dunno, Min. I saw Humphrey Smythe the other day in the spooky hallway behind the quad, muttering to himself while rooting around with both fingers. And I don't think he was searching for clear thoughts."

Mina flicked back through her memories of their various classes, searching for a Humphrey. And when she got him, it didn't make this information any easier to digest. "Oh god, is he the guy with the monocle?"

"It popped off while he was attempting it."

"This is the worst thing I've ever heard. I don't want to talk about this anymore. In fact, let's just go back to the life cycle of a unicorn. First, there is the horse orgy. And then . . . and then they . . . and then—" Mina started to say. But she couldn't finish the thought. And judging by Anaya's pointed expression, Anaya understood why. Most likely Anaya could see the blush spreading over her cheeks, and was now connecting the dots.

"It's a sex thing, isn't it?" her friend said finally.

While she scrambled for a way out of it.

"I have no idea what would give you that impression."

"Your face is bright red just because you had to talk about horse shagging."

She threw up her hands at that. Before putting her head in them. "I'm just not used to thinking about these things, okay? Or talking about them. Or feeling them. The closest I ever got to experiencing a sexy sensation before now was that time in school when Jenny Haverman tripped and accidentally brushed my boob with her boob. And now here I am at nineteen years old saying the word *boob* to my probably reasonably experienced and very cool friend."

"Min, I am not experienced at *all*. I had braces so big and thick all through high school that one boy started crying when I suggested we kiss behind the bike sheds. He said the idea traumatized him. He had to go to the nurse. And even if boys had made it through, my Baba used to squirt any who came too near me, with the thing he used to mist the tomato plants in his sort of greenhouse," Anaya said. Exaggerating quite plainly, but oh, it was amusing enough to make Mina drop her hands, and sag back against the frame of her bed.

"I get what you're doing, you know. Telling silly stories to try and make me feel more comfortable about this. But the simple truth is that I've never been. And I don't know how to be. Or even if I can be," she said, but even as she did, she could feel something long asleep inside her, stirring. Deep down, beneath layers of sad disappointments and dull encounters. And all it needed was something more to unearth it, something like darkness and danger and the sense of everything being turned upside down. Something like him, stroking her face in the middle of a maelstrom of emotions.

And so softly, too.

Like she was something fragile and forbidden.

A gothic story with a hero red in tooth and claw always did make your heart race, some voice in the back of her head said. But god, it was unbearable to hear it. She shoved it away before it could take root. It simply couldn't be that, and even if it somehow was, it definitely had nothing to do with him.

He was just a stand-in.

Anyone could have prompted the same feelings, in someone so unused to them. She just needed to practice on her own. And apparently, Anaya thought the same thing. "Maybe I should leave you alone to explore this a little more intensively," she said, half laughing.

But not unkindly.

And she gave her a half squeeze as she made her way out the door. Then it was just her, alone with her thoughts. *Close your eyes*, she told herself. *Lay back*, she told herself. Think of the fantasy version, not the real version. A woman running through a maze wrapped in red veils, something chasing her, thunder rolling above, everything lush and deep and dark.

And for a moment, something seemed to shift. The books she'd laid back on melted away; her breathing slowed, slowed. She could almost feel the chill air on her overheated skin, could almost hear the ragged breaths of whatever was after her. *The hunt*, she thought, *the hunt*, and then somehow her hand was nearly between her legs.

And that silvery feeling—it was there. It was within reach.

Just a little more, she thought, as she turned her face up toward that lovely magic. Hands coming together, ready to gather. Every part of her sure this was entirely divorced from him. Then she heard it, clear as a bell, in her head. His voice, just as it broke through.

And she shut down so fast, it felt like a slap.

SHE DECIDED THE best thing to do was just not push it. Let it come naturally, away from him. If she could just get a moment's peace, she could sort all this out herself, she was sure of it.

But unfortunately for her, there wasn't a moment's peace to be had.

She had barely gotten herself settled in for an evening of fervent study and serious thought, when she heard the familiar sound of a letter in her dresser drawer. And she knew as soon as she saw it that it was from him. She recognized his handwriting now. That old-fashioned script.

He's probably a thousand years old, she thought bitterly.

But she picked it up anyway. She broke the seal and spilled the contents all over her bed. First a letter, with just one line written in it. *You cannot stay away from everything you fear forever*, it said. Then beneath it, a sumptuous piece of card, embossed with gold lettering.

Familiar, because she had seen it in the hands of other students.

It was an invitation to the All Hallow's Ball. The one being held that very night, but that she hadn't considered for a second. It was not for the likes of her, whether she was fearful of it or otherwise. She was the sort of person who stayed in, while other people danced and drank and did fun things. *I don't even have anything suitable to wear*, she thought.

But then she heard a rustle from her wardrobe. And when she opened the door, there it was. A deep red, among the worn browns and grays. Vivid, even through the gauzy wrapper, and underneath, silk, taffeta, layers all furled and furrowed, like the frosting on a cake. Beautiful enough that her eyes and fingertips marveled, even as her heart hardened against it. *I'm not a doll to be dressed just so, in the hopes I'll be accepted. And even if I was, it won't fit,* she told herself, as she tossed it aside. She kicked it into the corner of the wardrobe, alongside the shoes that had also appeared.

Crystal slippers, obviously.

Faceted to catch the light, and so fragile looking she wasn't even sure she would dare step into them. And she'd definitely never be able to walk in heels like that. She picked one up and almost cut her hand on the high sharp point. Impossible looking, and certain to shatter the second she tried to walk.

Maybe that was even the joke. She'd dare and slice her feet to shreds.

You can forget it, she wrote, on a sheet of paper torn from a notebook, under notes on Professor Jameson's lecture on maintaining a code of silence. Then she stood, and went to the drawer, and held it above, waiting to drop it in.

She probably would have even done it, if it hadn't been for the knock on the door. Too soft to be him, she knew. But it still jolted her. Her heart still did the same thing it always did, whenever he was around. She had to force herself over there and make herself open it. And it wasn't even a relief to see Anaya on the other side.

Because Anaya was also wearing a dress.

A gorgeous emerald-green creation, with a halter neck that revealed only the amount of skin that Mina knew her friend was comfortable with. No sign of her bust, but her toned arms and smooth as silk shoulders were bared. They glowed, in the low light of the hall.

Perfect for her.

And even lovelier with her hair done up like that. Tendrils floated around her elegantly made-up face—done with magic, Mina knew, because Anaya had sent her a note about it the other day. *If you want me to show you how I did it*, it had said. And for just a moment Mina had thought how nice that would be. To be able to rely on her friend instead of her enemy.

But of course you couldn't kill a vampire with eye shadow.

And even if you could, Mina was pretty sure Anaya wouldn't be able to teach her. It wasn't the mechanics of spellcasting that she had a problem with. It was feeling things she barely wanted or understood, apparently.

But she pushed all of that aside to focus on her friend. "I didn't even know we were all invited. Let alone given dresses like this," Anaya said, as she bustled excitedly into the room. She snatched up the red silk on Mina's bed, already cooing over it, while Mina's heart sunk over something she didn't even know how to explain.

I think you've been invited to make sure I come, just so he can do something horrible to me, she thought sadly, at her friend's back. But of course, she couldn't say that. She couldn't ruin it for Anaya. And doubly so when there was a good chance it wasn't true. Maybe someone thought Anaya was as lovely and magical as Harker thought she was awful and ordinary, and they desperately wanted her to be there.

It was possible.

She was clever and beautiful.

"It's the least you deserve," she said.

Then slipped out of her sweater and skirt, ready to try on a dress.

Chapter Fourteen

She knew from various books and talk about the school that balls were always held in a place called the arboretum. Though it wasn't really an arboretum at all. It was just a building, a little way past the lake, with a huge domed glass ceiling that you could see before you made out a single other thing. It gleamed in the dying light, like a diamond.

Anaya squeezed her arm on glimpsing it.

"I'll never understand how a place can be so rotten and so glorious, all at the same time," she said, as they made their way up the winding, cobbled path to the building. Though Mina thought her friend did understand, only too well. Money and power made things pretty. It surrounded them on all sides—in the hovering lights that bloomed as darkness sank over them, in the sound of flight above their heads, in the ripples on the lake as iridescent things stirred beneath the depths.

But it couldn't mask the looks they got from the students around them.

The ones who were dressed in ethereal gauzy wisps, or black-tie dinner jackets types of things, and saw Mina and Anaya for what they were. Imposters, dressed in clothes that didn't go with some theme they hadn't even known. That they could never have known, because he hadn't said. He had given her a dress that fit like a glove and shoes that felt like walking on air. All of it beautiful enough to convince her that this would be okay.

But of course, it was the wrong kind of beauty.

It was lush and gothic, instead of fine and elegant.

"Maybe we should go back," she said, just before they got to the great glass doors that led in. Close enough that she could hear music—that thin, high, haunting melody she sometimes heard around the dorms—and smell food even more mouthwatering than anything the dining hall came up with. Clouds of sugar, fruits that weren't from this earth, meat from creatures she couldn't imagine.

But still so removed from it all that it felt impossible.

"Oh, let them stare. The only reason they're doing it is because you look incredible. They're used to seeing you in brown sacks, and now you're swanning in like a vampire's bride," Anaya said. Well meant, of course. But it just made Mina's stomach sink even further than it already had.

She thought of his hand on her cheek.

The gleam of his razor-sharp teeth.

"Don't say that," she said.

Much to Anaya's puzzlement.

"But it's true. Francis Ford Coppola could have directed you."

"Anaya, I think I should tell you something. Something really important."

"You don't have to. I know you and the king of this place have something going on. I know that you're scared of it. I know it doesn't feel real. But I'm pretty sure it is. In fact, I'm pretty sure he's obsessed with you," her friend said, so full of surety that it cracked Mina's heart to hear it. She turned her head and looked into Anaya's soft eyes, so sweetly accepting. Maybe even happy for her.

And didn't know how to say the way things really were.

"What makes you think that?" she asked instead.

But Anaya just looked past her, into the ballroom.

She nodded her head, in the direction of it.

"Because he's coming toward you right now," she said, and as soon as she did, the world seemed to slow down. It took forever for Mina to turn her head and take in the sight of him, walking up the steps toward her. And even longer than that to let everything about him sink in.

Because he wasn't wearing a black suit, like the rest.

He wore a kind of long coat, as soft and gauzy as a cloud, yet somehow sharp at the same time. The collar of it went high on one side, and came to a point along the line of his jaw, fine enough that she could imagine it slitting his throat if he turned too clumsily.

Though, of course, she knew he never would.

On any ordinary day, he moved like water.

Here he practically floated.

He looked like something out of a fairy tale. All the ones she'd read as a child—the ones that were secondhand and cobbled together, but more true than anyone beyond walls like this knew. Creatures like him *did* wear moonlight and dance in shadows. And if they ever held out a hand to you, you were supposed to refuse.

All the good girls in those stories made sure to.

She really didn't know why she took his, the moment he offered. She only knew that it happened. Her fingers slipped between his, and his closed around hers, and that was that. He led her into a room like the insides of a snowflake, glittering and glowing. And then he spun her over a floor made entirely of glass.

Incredible looking.

But even more so when she caught a glimpse of what was beyond it, as the room whirled. Not the foundations of the place, or something pretty, or even another floor. No, god, no—*it was the Underneath.* It was a whole other world, right beneath their feet. Somehow, they had made an enormous window to it, and *god*, the things she could see through to. A second sky, like a skein of gray velvet, sewn through with stars like droplets of dew. Beings you barely see, beneath it, upside down on the other side of the glass.

She could see the soles of their feet.

Or at least, what passed for that on them.

Sometimes they didn't seem to have bodies, in any way she understood. She could only make out a shape because of the clothes they wore—moonlight fine, like his. Glittery, like his. *Magpies*, some of the books called them. And it seemed there was some truth to that.

But it was a mean sort of truth.

They were so much more than any human words could make them. It was the reason she blurted out, "Oh god, so lovely," in a far too gushing sort of voice to use, in company like his. But to her surprise, he agreed. "There isn't a thing in existence that is lovelier," he said, and she looked up to see his eyes on her face.

Sad, but completely sincere.

Because of course, of course.

"You miss it," she said, and he hesitated. He held her gaze.

But in the end, he went ahead.

"Honestly, I can barely stand how much I do. It makes a fool of me."

"There's nothing foolish about longing for home. If that *was* your home."

"Nothing has ever been more so. I belonged where that loveliness was."

He looked away then. But not before she saw the sudden sheen over his eyes. Tears, quite obviously. Though she tried not to let that knowledge sink in too deep. The last time she'd let herself feel sorry for him, he'd mocked her for it and pinned her to a stone table.

This dance was enough.

The dress was enough, too.

He had been right: Sympathy was a step too far.

"Perhaps if you stopped tormenting people for five seconds, you'd have time to find a way back. I read in something by some witch the other day—the boundaries and rule breaks are never as set as they seem," she said, far more kindly than he deserved. Because somehow, the words just made him harden.

"Don't talk like that."

"Well, why not?"

"I told you. Because it will get you into trouble."

"And you care about that, in between all the suffocating."

"I didn't suffocate you. It was just a trick, not a serious threat," he said, and as he did, he leaned down. His hand shifted on her back, until it felt like more of an arm around her than a thing to guide her into the right moves. And just as she went to push him away, she saw all the other girls with their dance partners. Lifted up and twirled like ballerinas in a music box, as the music hit a certain note.

Then felt the air beneath her own feet.

Saw the room spin, all around her.

Before he set her back down, and retook her hand and her waist, and went into whatever the next move was. Because these *were* moves, in some kind of set pattern. Everybody was doing the same thing. But what struck her about this was not the fact that he had done this with her.

It was that she had been doing it, without thinking.

She hadn't stumbled once. She hadn't been clumsy.

She swayed when he swayed and spun when he spun, and somehow it all just seemed to fall into place. And of course, some of that was him guiding her, she could see that. His hand was firm on her back. He led her smoothly into certain gaps between other couples.

But she couldn't deny that this didn't cover all of it.

"Are you making me understand this dance?" she asked.

Then looked up at him, in time to see his irritated expression.

"If you're asking whether I've thralled you, the answer is no."

"You say that like it's weird for me to wonder, when it would explain so much. Why I came to you for lessons. Why I keep coming even though you're cruel. Why I came tonight, after all the ways you tortured me. And then the other thing, the other stuff that happened, the—" she fumbled out, every part of her trying to say without saying. Acknowledge what she had felt, without acknowledging it.

But he just slipped in first, before she could manage.

"So that's how you're explaining desire to yourself."

"It makes more sense than actually feeling it for you."

"Maybe you just felt it for the situation. For the sudden touch."

"That hardly seems like enough to cover what it did to—"

She cut herself off before the last words. Mostly because she realized how those last words sounded. Like she been overwhelmed with pleasure, or something similarly ridiculous. But it was too late. His expression was all smug amusement.

"Glad to hear it was good for you. I had no idea I was so talented."

"Talented at fucking with my mind maybe."

"If I had really fucked with your mind, you would know."

"And how do you figure that, when the whole point is to make it impossible?"

"Because it feels like *this*," he said, the last word so low and dark she knew what was going to happen. She even braced for him to say something that would turn her brain to soup. But what she didn't expect was everything else, around the words he spoke. *Hear me; hear me and do not fear what I am*, she thought she heard him say, soft as syrup, and now even lower and deeper and darker than before.

Then all around them, everything just seemed to stop.

People froze mid-twirl, mid-kiss, mid-cry of delight.

Someone had thrown confetti in the air; it hovered there, in a spray of color. She could see a girl's teeth, caught just as she opened her mouth to laugh. The wild eyes of people in the middle of a revelry, now unable to come back down to earth. It was like moving through a painting called *The Bacchanal.*

Because they *were* moving.

He was moving her.

He had her by the waist, and he used it to pull her through the maze of mannequins everyone had become. Fast, so fast she couldn't catch her breath. She couldn't think how to even start to get out of this. And of course, all the while his words sank her in deeper.

"Come with me, come with me, my love, let me take you, let

me hold you the way I long to," he said, voice now almost a burr of something soft, against her cheek, her throat, the insides of her head. *Stop*, she wanted to say, but it was like drifting into a dream. Like before, when he had told her the story of Lilibet.

Only stronger. So much stronger.

Oh, this was undoubtedly something more.

Whatever that had been, it wasn't thralling. Because *this* was thralling—this sense of walking without moving her own feet, of being drowned even as she did her best to swim. She was never going to break the surface of this, never. It was impossible to, even when he pulled her into some dusky darkness, behind a curtain that concealed a room beyond.

To savage her, she assumed.

But she was a fool to, and she knew it. Being savaged was a thing he could just do, if he wanted to. But persuading her to do something soft—well. That was something else. That was the real prize, the true proof of his power. If he could make that happen, he had her in his thrall, unquestionably.

Yet somehow, it still shocked her when he said it.

"Kiss me," he murmured, the moment they were alone. Syrup soft, like all the rest of the words he'd used to put her under his spell—but with a strange current of something else. Hunger and desperation, all tangled together. Impossible, and yet it was there in his eyes, too. It was in his face.

He looked down at her through a kind of fog, as lost in this thrall as she seemed. Eyes heavy, one hand coming up to almost touch her face again. And when it did, she came so close to doing it she actually felt his breath fan against her face. She saw the flecks of black in his brown eyes. Felt her own hand on the nape of his neck, pulling him down to her, in a way she knew he couldn't possibly want.

This was just about tormenting her.

He wanted to claw through her soul, to turn her upside down and inside out. And yet it still didn't look like it. She saw it clear through the fog of whatever this was—his face changing, when her lips were within an inch of his. Those eyes filled with a strange sort of despairing softness, like someone resigned to losing their life. Then they seemed to drop to her parted lips, as he leaned in.

And it *was* him who leaned, in that moment.

She didn't pull him. She didn't move at all.

Somehow, she had stopped—as if his influence had suddenly dissolved.

Even though she knew it hadn't. She could still feel it, as strong as ever. But it seemed easier to resist, for some reason. She pushed, and it drew back. And when his lips almost grazed hers, it pulled back so far, she couldn't even say it was controlling her at all. She was just nearly kissing him, and he was nearly kissing her, as if they were suddenly two different people entirely.

And she knew why.

The girl in the long grass, she thought.

The one with the ribbon around her throat.

Once, that girl *had* kissed someone like him. She even got a flash of it, then—sitting in a deck chair, as dusk settled in. The smell of mown grass in the air, the sense of someone sitting next to her. He had long legs, like Harker. Dark hair, like Harker. That interesting dimple in his chin.

But the hand he had in his lap was nervy, always fidgeting.

He constantly cracked the knuckle of his forefinger over his thumb.

And he didn't turn to the girl sitting beside him in a confident way. He snuck a glance, eyes as big as moons. *Lili,* she thought she heard him murmur. *Lili, about the other day. I wasn't feeling like myself. I don't know what came over me. Sometimes it feels like something gets hold of my body and makes me do awful things.*

Like a shadow has a hand on your shoulder, Mina thought.

But she couldn't follow that idea. Because a moment after she had it, Lili replied to the boy in the deepening dusk. *I don't think something can be awful if I* welcome *it,* she murmured back. And then she leaned forward, slower than sinking into syrup. And she pressed her lips against his parted ones. She kissed him—and oh. Oh. Oh.

It was simply too sweet to resist.

No clashing teeth, no rough fist in her hair.

Just exquisite tenderness, and a sense of overwhelming heat. As if this moment was so much more than just a kiss. It had meaning behind it, of a kind she didn't understand, she couldn't know.

All she *did* know was that *then* and *now* mingled so deeply, for a moment, that she almost went ahead and kissed Harker. She came so close it almost seemed like she tasted that sharp mint scent on his breath. That the sensation pouring through her was because of him, and not that sultry and strange memory.

And it was only magic that stopped her.

That heavy desire made it bloom within her. And when it did, she couldn't help looking down. She stopped and stared at her hands in wonderment. At that bright glow gathered there, without even the need to cup or call or anything. It simply was—and it brought her back to her senses immediately.

This wasn't the boy in the deck chair, making her feel so delicious.

This was the thing, lurking in the shadows.

This was Harker, and she was Mina.

And the moment she registered that again, she just let that magic burst out of her. She let it surge toward him, hard enough to hurt. Hard enough to burn him, before he could drag her any deeper into this nastiness.

He staggered back, wincing, shaking the hand she'd just singed.

Though she didn't get the satisfaction of hurt or anger.

No—he laughed as he went. Curled his tongue up to his teeth, almost ruefully, before sinking his hands into his pockets. "There. Now you know what thralling feels like. And also exactly why I have never bothered to try it on you. Even when it's something easy to persuade someone into, you apparently just flick it away, like a speck of dirt from your sleeve," he said—all matter-of-fact about it. Like it was some sort of obvious given.

Even though it hadn't felt that way to her.

Her whole body seemed like something ripening past the point it could stand, in the sun. Any second and she thought her skin might split. And he found it amusing. He found it so *nothing.* "I caught myself by the skin of my teeth, you absolute fucking nightmare," she hissed.

And all he did in response was roll his eyes.

"Don't be so dramatic. I wouldn't have actually let you do it, even if I had somehow been wrong about your will being strong enough to deflect it. Which I wasn't, by the way."

"It was the magic that stopped me."

"You wouldn't have even been able to use the magic, if you didn't have the strength of mind. But you did, and so now you can understand. Whatever you do with me, you do of your own free will," he said—as if her free will was important to him.

When of course she knew it wasn't.

This was all just nonsense.

"And you couldn't have just *told* me this?"

"Would you have believed me if I had? Would you have trusted it?"

"So that's what this was? What it always is with you. Tricks and traps until I learn my lesson. Tests, everything tests, toward some end I don't even understand anymore. I mean this dress, the dancing, the ball—did you really give me all this just so I wouldn't be fearful of taking my place? Or was it something else?"

He didn't speak for a second.

Almost like he couldn't, like he was struggling.

Though that impression faded so quickly, she wasn't sure she had really seen it. And his voice was cool and collected when he finally spoke. "I thought it might be an opportunity to plunge you up to your neck in something seductive, something that makes you look like you do right now—breathless, flushed, full of all the things you don't know how to feel. On the edge of your own magic, ready to seize it. Then once you were, well. We could just see if you have the ability to use it, to compete for a prize," he said, almost as soft and low as he had sounded for the thralling.

Only this time, she knew it wasn't.

Even though she had to shake it off, all the same.

"Ah, so now comes the big reveal. Lure me here, and then suddenly plunge me into a fight to the death in some god-awful setting. Get me dispatched by every single person who just seethed with jealousy, to see me on your arm."

"They were hardly seething. Most of them don't even like me, for reasons they probably barely understand. And this isn't a Gauntlet, bookworm. It's not a Brawl. We just try to ring the bell, every All Hallows, at midnight."

"Somehow, I don't think a bell ringing is all it's going to be," she said.

Yet somehow, she didn't try to pull away, when he lifted the curtain, and gestured for her to follow him through to the now empty ballroom. She just went, like curiosity and a thirst for understanding overwhelmed every sense she had. *Even without thralling, he knows just how to get you*, her mind warned her.

But she went anyway.

She followed him out of some doors on the side of the building and stopped when he stopped at the top of some stone steps, overlooking a great bowl of grass. Then she stood there and watched the scene before them, as he did. A great mass of students, running and shrieking and firing magic all over the place, loud enough that she could make out what they were doing before he even told her.

The bell wasn't a bell at all.

It was a burning bright wink of light, small as a firefly, darting through the darkness. And this time it wasn't some book she had read that told her what it was. She felt it, deep in her bones. The magic still buzzing through her grew louder; it sung to see that familiar thing. A star from the sky of the Underneath, fallen from its own sky and now lost in theirs. And if you caught it—

"It grants you favor through the halls of Calabaraia," he said, almost as if he'd heard her thoughts and wanted to finish them off for her. Though why he wanted to—why he would want *any* of this—she had no idea. Favor was a prize beyond measure, she knew. It was endless amounts of time there to drink in all that magic, without ever being driven mad, without being murdered, without losing any sense of self and getting stuck. Anyone who managed it would eventually be powerful enough to do almost anything—never mind fight off one vampire, or survive petty student squabbles, or pass every brutally cruel practical lesson.

She couldn't imagine what use it would be to him, to see her win it.

And she *could* win it.

She knew she could.

She watched them all down there, fighting with one another for a chance at snatching or shooting it down, and just knew. Like she'd done all this before and could now just do it again. *You don't compete to wound it over someone else; you give something of yourself to guide it back,* a voice whispered to her. And she knew who that voice belonged to. *Lilibet,* she thought. *It was Lilibet who did it. Before she ended up in her bloody dress, she chose her weapon and made her shot.*

And before she could even fully consider this, her hands simply took hold of something. A shape in the air but more solid than anything she'd actually ever touched. A bow, like the bow Penrith had strung to shoot the monstrous stag of the upside-down sky. A bow like something that belonged to her, like something she instinctively knew how to draw back, even though she'd never even done so with a toy.

And when she did, the arrow emerged in a wave of light. It hung suspended, like there really was a string, like there really was a bow. All she had to do was aim as true as that girl who wore a velvet ribbon around her throat, and with as much magic at her command. All she had to be was bright and brilliant and enough.

And just as she was thinking she couldn't be, she felt Harker lean down, until his lips were almost kissing her throat, her ear. His breath burned over her skin, in a way that made that bloom through her body almost burst out of her. Then he whispered soft as silk, *You don't have to be more magical than you think; you only have to know that you already are.*

Then everything in the world was silver.

And through it, she held on tight. And she let fly.

Chapter Fifteen

She only knew the wound she had made in the world had let the star fly through, when the sound of a bell rung out, and everyone turned. Every one of them at once, even though some still sat astride brooms. Some were still in the middle of dueling. One student had turned themself into a centaur, and he stopped and looked, just the same.

She wanted to say, *It wasn't me*, under their sudden scrutiny.

And not just because she'd never liked crowds. There was something undeniably unsettling about it. Something too silent, too still. Like she'd committed some terrible faux pas. "So this was the secret plan? To make me think this was something worth winning, when they're all now going to kill me for it?" she asked into that ringing silence. But she knew as she did it that she wasn't entirely serious.

It was hard to be, when he had said those words.

Most likely not meant at all, yet even so. They lingered in her mind.

And lingered even harder when he answered, "They could try, I suppose. But once you walk those halls, they will never be stronger than you, and they know it." He shook his head, eyes bright with a kind of rueful amusement. "I mean, did you really think I was popular because I'm so charming and handsome? Everybody here is charming and handsome. No, bookworm. I'm popular because I am powerful. And power is the only thing any of these people ever understand."

"Yes, but here's the thing, Harker: I haven't gone through a door yet."

"Maybe not. But you did just perform an impossible feat, in front of them."

"And you think that's enough to keep them at bay?"

"Even if it's not, they will never get past me," he said, and she knew what he meant. She knew why he wanted to protect her. He thought that letter would drop if she was too dead to stop it. But the way he worded it—the way he sounded, so suddenly heated—made her look at him anyway.

She searched his face for something more.

And found precisely nothing. His expression was as bland as always—not to mention unfocused on her. He had fixed it on the other students, as they climbed the steps toward them. Like a retinue, greeting their king and queen. Some of them saying "well-done," others smiling, a few as resentful as she had imagined.

But nothing serious.

She even turned back toward the ballroom. Safe suddenly, among the crowd, in a way she had never felt before. And now she could see Anaya, in the glowing light beyond. She had stood on a chair, so Mina could see her above all the heads of everyone trooping in, and she waved her arms in excitement.

Like she had seen and wanted to celebrate with her.

I wonder if I can take Anaya *there with me*, she thought, as she waved back frantically. Though she suspected Anaya had other plans, for the foreseeable future. As Mina watched, one of the boys she had seen holding serving platters swept her down, off the chair, and into a kiss. And he was as handsome as she had imagined, when she had thought of her friend having someone. Eyes like stars, a jawline to die for, skin a soft brown under the glittery lights.

It made her heart sing to see it.

She had been right about her friend having something sweet for herself. A little secret love affair that she couldn't wait to tease her about. In fact, she was only thinking of that, when she felt the sting over the back of her hand. The one that was still lifted to wave, and entirely exposed.

"Just to make sure," she heard someone say and saw the sandy-haired boy, Sebastian, with his wand raised. Then she looked, and there was blood. He'd nicked her, just a little—to see if she was actually human under there, she assumed. *No big deal*, she thought, *not exactly an attack*.

But Harker moved anyway.

He put himself between her and Sebastian, and she saw his arm sort of jerk, just a little. Like he was hardly doing anything at all. And yet people immediately backed away, all the same. They started disappearing indoors, fast. And now Sebastian was looking at Harker aghast; he was clutching his hand.

Or at least, he was clutching the place where his hand *used* to be.

There didn't seem to be anything at the end of his sleeve anymore.

It looked like he'd just tucked it inside, as a joke.

Except that nobody was laughing. In fact, she suspected Sebastian was so unamused that he wanted to do something more here. Retaliate maybe. Strike back somehow. But whatever expression was on Harker's face seemed to persuade him not to. He took one look, then backed away with the rest.

Turned tail and ran into the crowd.

Leaving only her and Harker on the stone steps. Everything suddenly quiet, quiet, quiet. Everything suddenly dark. Someone drew a set of curtains over the closed glass doors, and it got darker. She turned to him through so little light she could only make out the shape of him.

Like that shadow, over Lilibet's shoulders.

"You didn't need to do that; it's just a scratch," she said, so caught up in the idea of Harker actually doing what he'd said he would—covering anyone else who tried to hurt her—that she didn't really process how he now looked. He had gone very still and very quiet.

And when she put a hand on his arm, he didn't seem to want to turn.

Instead, he said: "I can only give you a countdown from thirty."

Then he covered his eyes. Both hands, she could see.

Like a little kid playing hide-and-seek.

At which point, it clicked—and so hard she felt her stomach drop right down into her feet. She got a flash of a passage from a book on being hunted in the Underneath, of how the childhood games played here were the things done for real there. If a human was caught and had no favor in the halls, this was what you got.

A head start before they sought you out.

Though, of course, none of that explained why.

She didn't get it; she didn't understand at all, until she remembered what had started this. She looked down at the back of her hand and saw the blood. Barely there, but barely there didn't matter.

Because it was also on him.

She could see it between his cupped hands.

It had made a stripe, over his lips.

"Thirty," he said. "Twenty-nine," he said.

And then she ran.

SHE DIDN'T WAIT for her heels to hold her back. She kicked them off and went barefoot across the grass, huge dress hoisted into her arms, hair a black streamer behind her. Every part of her knowing she would never be able to outrun him to a place of safety. But all of her willing to try just the same.

And especially when she realized in a hot rush:

She didn't have to make it to her room at all.

The only thing she needed was a door. A door through to Calabaraia—where she would now be safe, but he couldn't even cross the threshold to. He'd bounce off it as surely as he would bounce off the iron barrier she had made for her bedroom. So really the only question was: Could she make one?

She knew it was forbidden without permission, of course.

But it was also relatively easy. Just draw an outline on anything at all.

Though, of course, in order to do that, she had to stop. And when she glanced back over her shoulder, she was sure she could already see him. A dark shape in the glow from the moon. Going slow, almost sauntering, but still too close.

It wouldn't take him hardly anything at all to cross the distance, once he saw what she was attempting. But when the rotunda attached to the east wing came into view, she knew she was going to try anyway. She practically flung herself around the curve of it, until she was out of his sight line. Leaned against that cool gray stone, as she brought her cupped hands together. Once, twice.

Nothing.

What's the good of being the queen of this place if you still can't cast? she thought wildly, as she glanced back around that curve, for some sign of him. Then when there was nothing, she took a long, slow breath. She tried to focus on something that sparked it—those words in her ear.

And there it was. A bright bloom of light, that melted down into a familiar cylinder the moment she positioned her thumb and finger just so. She clutched it like a pen, before it appeared. Now all she had to do was draw the shape on the stone beside her. Easy-peasy, really.

Or at least it *would* have been.

If it had not been for the state she was in. For some reason her eyes were blurry with tears. She couldn't seem to control her breathing—it grated in and out of her chest, fast enough that it was starting to make her dizzy. And her hands shook when she touched the pen to the stone.

She had to steady one hand with the other—and even so the line she drew came out shaky. It came out with gaps that were probably going to make it fail. She found herself going over them frantically, almost scribbling, tears now cooling on her cheeks, heart trying to beat out of her body.

And still the thing came out crooked.

The top was practically on a diagonal.

The whole door was too small, too low—she was going to have to stoop to get through it. And that was *if* it even worked. It seemed doubtful, considering the door handle she was trying to grind into the stone. A sloppy mess full of jagged lines, half of them going outside the circle she was trying to make.

It looked pathetic.

She stepped back and almost laughed.

In fact she most likely would have done so if it hadn't been for that sudden prickling feeling. That coldness all along one side, like she'd felt that first day in the lecture hall. And then she turned and saw him.

Barely ten feet away, eyes blank and staring, mouth full of teeth.

She didn't know why she reached for that door handle. It didn't even seem like she'd be fast enough—never mind believing that it would be good enough to work. But it did, oh god it did. Her hand seemed to sink in and clasp around something at the same time. Light bloomed around it, and around the edge of the crude door she'd drawn.

Go, go, go, she urged herself, and tried to push right away.

First with her hand, then when nothing happened, her shoulder. She slammed against it, hard enough that she felt some bone or muscle protest. Pain shot through her, and still she tried again. She had to try again.

That was the sound of him growling, at the thought of losing his quarry.

And it was close, so close, god, she could almost feel the breath he'd used to push that grating rattle out. It brushed against the nape of her neck, and she nearly lost her mind. She didn't just shove at the door; she begged it with her body. She flung herself against it, half screaming, sure it was done.

And that was when it gave.

It swung inward, so fast she couldn't stop herself tumbling through. She practically fell to her hands and knees, wrists barking and dress suddenly around her face—though she could hardly care, of course she couldn't. Because all she felt of him was the rake of his claws over that silk, that velvet, that taffeta.

Then she was through.

She was on the other side.

She was in the Underneath.

Chapter Sixteen

She didn't move from the door for a long time.

She couldn't—the creature on the other side held all her attention.

Because it *was* a creature. There was no sign of Harker there anymore. His deep brown eyes were blank and black, almost sightless seeming. Like all he needed was instinct, and instinct said his prey was close by. Just on the other side of a thin membrane, barely visible. The only thing he had to do was find a place to slip into.

But god, the way he went about it.

He didn't search. He scrabbled, feverishly. He went over and over the edges of her door with clawed, hungry fingers, looking for holes. Looking for some crack that might let him in. Horrible to see—but something else that she didn't expect, too.

Sad. It was desperately sad. Even though she hated him, even though he was awful, her heart swelled to see someone so robbed of all their senses. She pressed the heels of her palms into her eyes, just to make the idea go away.

Yet still, remnants of it remained.

They followed her as she finally stood, and closed the door on him. They made her do it slow, too slow, as if hoping he might switch back at any moment. And even after he was sealed on the other side, she couldn't quite tear herself away. She stood with her forehead pressed to what was now stone surrounded by nothingness, for a long time. *You are starting to think he means his help*, her mind whispered. *To see it as something a begrudgingly made friend might do, instead of a forced enemy.*

Even though that was ridiculous.

In fact, *all* her focus right now was. Calabaraia lay spread out behind her, and all she could do was think about him. Like nothing had changed from her first moments at Harrowhall, to where she was now. Truth be told, she had gotten *worse*. Then, she had gladly pushed him from her mind.

Now it took time.

It felt like pulling a tooth out, from the root.

She was sure she bled, as she finally put her back to the door. And this time, somehow, what she saw couldn't quite wash that feeling away. It lingered, as she let her gaze wander over a landscape that the historian Hornbeck had once called *featureless and dull*, and the explorer Alvin Broadbeam had declared *singularly barren without a bit of civilization about it.*

But it was, in truth, a wonder beyond all imagining.

Because it wasn't really the gray desert they had described at all. It was a shimmering series of dunes, dotted with silver. Each one of those rises so soft seeming, so subtle, it was like seeing something that wasn't all there. It appeared nebulous almost, like you could sink into the ground with one step.

And that thought finally made her understand: It was not the ground at all

It was the *sky*. It was the upside-down sky. She was standing amid stars, amid the velvet darkness of the night, amid the furrows made by something like clouds. And somehow, it all took her weight.

She could walk on these things, with her human feet.

She did right then and there.

She took a step, heart in her throat, and it all held her as softly as sand.

And they hadn't appreciated a single thing about it. They had looked at it and found it lacking, simply because it wasn't covered in roads and buildings and things that didn't even matter here. Nobody lived in a house. They didn't even need to choose between the ground and the sky.

There was none of that to them.

It was all just everything, all at once.

She looked up, and there were staircases suspended in nothingness. Twisting things like trees, weaving sideways through the spaces in between. Somewhere in the distance she could hear music, sweet music—like nothing on earth and yet so familiar at the same time. It made her think of that Sunday school song:

I danced with the devil when the sky turned black.

It's hard to dance with the devil on your back.

She even found herself humming it, as she stepped toward the sound. And she felt absolutely no fear when she did. Because of the favor she had been granted, she thought. Because of the safe passage that was now hers.

But the farther she walked, the more she wondered if that was the truth.

Or if ringing the bell was more about something else. Not about claiming safety, but about showing that *you* were safe. That you would not hurt anything here. That you didn't have terrible intentions and would not do anything deeply unfair. Like their way of granting permission to come, she thought, in places where humans had decided for them what permission they gave.

We say that we grant it to them, and they grant it to us, Hargreaves had said the other day. *But that is not entirely the case. The beings of the Underneath do not, in truth, seem to understand such a concept. They only know what we enforce and impress upon them. They only know to abide by our wishes.*

And that had seemed like a strange thing for her to say, at the time.

This very feeling she was getting seemed strange, truth be told.

But it looked less so after she saw what she did, in the distance. A rope of deep blue gauze, it looked like, flickering in and out. But as she got closer, she realized what it really was, with a sharp intake of breath. It was a *being*. It was something that lived here. Fen possibly, if the soft loveliness of that shape and color was anything to go by.

But it could have been something else.

A shrey, a wilderun. *Like violent dogs they are*, Hornbeck had said of the latter. But what did he know? He was *dead*. And he'd never understood anyway, if this was anything to go by. It seemed to approach, then darted away again. Seemed to become more solid, then not once more. Sometimes she thought she could see its face and sometimes not. In fact, it was only when she stood completely still and calm that she saw it had anything like a face at all.

It looked formed out of water and moonlight.

Mostly eyes, of some description, all a deep blue, with no center to them. But full of recognizable feelings. They confirmed what she had first thought, when she had seen its hesitation in coming to her.

It was *timid*.

Almost afraid of her.

And it only stopped when she smiled in welcome.

Then suddenly she could see something resembling a body, some sort of clothes. Like the long coat Harker had worn, only not quite. *We don't have words for what they do and wear and how they present themselves,* she thought and ached to write that down. To scribble over everything she had read in a million silly books with just how marvelous that idea was.

And that was *before* it spoke.

"Lilibet, it is you. Have you come to dance with us once more?" it said, so clearly and with such obvious joy in its voice that she couldn't deny the words or what it meant. Despite the fact that this joy and this voice didn't sound like anything she could ever have imagined. It was one long hum, that resonated at a frequency she could just somehow understand. Impossibly pleasant and completely magical, even with the mildly terrifying implications.

And it was the terrified part it seemed to sense.

It drew back. That strange face creased down the middle.

"Ah, no, no," it said. "You are not her. I have mistaken your inside face."

Then it retreated even farther. It shrank down, seemed to flicker in and out again. Ashamed of the assumption and disappointed that it wasn't the case, she realized, and wanted to reach out a hand immediately, to reassure. But somehow, she knew just feeling the emotion would be heard.

And sure enough, the being seemed to brighten.

"You are kind, like she was. Perhaps this is what I touched? So few of the large ones of your sect are, only the small sort. I cannot find their word for it to you. Might you tell me of it? Lilibet does not come, and I forget," it said, and now the meaning behind everything came thick and fast.

She thought of what it searched for immediately.

"The small ones are called children."

"Yes, yes. There, children. That is so. The ones who come to us only when lost. The ones she gave thanks to us for, for our kindnesses to them. She thought it very well, indeed, very well, even as we tried to do the explaining. It is only as things must be, we showed her. Yet we could not have shown her rightly, for it only made the sadness from her eyes greater. There is a river that came of it, not far from here. I could take you, if you will it," the being said. Then it waited patiently for her answer.

She didn't know how to say that she couldn't. That he had almost made her sad from her eyes, too. That his words made her think of Lilibet, breaking into pieces over all the ideas of what this place was. And to what extent it was the opposite. "I should probably stay here," she tried. "But thank you."

Then watched the being bow. "It is not so strange that you do not wish to. She did not do a visiting to its banks often. And when her Bram came alone, he did not seem to like it so well."

Hers, she thought. *Bram*, she thought.

And automatically after it:

The boy in the long grass. The boy on the edge of the building. The boy in the deck chair, with the nervous hands. "So she had someone, then. Someone who would come here with her. Someone good and loving."

"He was her one above others. As gentle as she."

"Do you know what happened to him? Did he die, too?" she

asked, too desperate to actually uncover something about that ghostly girl, to even think about her tone or what her question meant.

Though she regretted it immediately.

The being recoiled.

"Oh, she has done the terrible ending."

"I'm sorry. I think so. I don't know for sure."

"Yes, you do not all feel each other. I recall."

"But you can feel this good man. This one above others."

"Not anymore. So perhaps you are right. Perhaps he has gone on without us, too. Perhaps a dreadful thing befell them both—oh, oh, it cannot be held in me. I must fade; you must let me," the being said, its form starting to dissolve before it even finished asking. She had to race to ask one final thing, before he was gone for good.

"What dreadful thing could have befallen them? Could someone have hurt them? A rival maybe, someone bitter about them, something untethered that stalked them, searching for people to latch on to," she said, barely sure of what she was even thinking but needing to know. It would explain it, after all.

Why she saw them, like a warning. The sense that something was haunting them, in every flash to that past. Then the fact that Harker looked just a little like him, that Bram had said he felt like something took him over . . .

No, she thought. *No, no, no, no. That is mad; that is impossible. Harker is not some weird thing walking around in someone else's body. He showed his flesh and blood to you, underneath. There's no way it could ever be the case.*

But just as she did, the being spoke a final time. "They had a shadow on them, always on them. We tried to tell them that it could not be shaken, but they did not listen. Be careful, one who is not Lilibet," it said.

Then it was gone, and she was alone, in the Underneath.

Exhausted, suddenly. Desperately sad. And completely unsure what to do.

Sleep, her brain said. *Things will make more sense in the morning.*

Then before she could wonder how she might go about a thing like that, something seemed to spring up around her. Branches, bursting with flowers and moss, coiling and curling to make a kind of bower. A bed for her, it seemed—as if this place had heard what she most needed.

Because she did need it.

She drifted off before another second went by.

Chapter Seventeen

When she woke, the being was still gone. It was just her, in that cup of strange branches and flowers. They shifted about her and set her down on her bare feet, the moment she sat up. And to her surprise she found those bare feet weren't the least bit sore. None of her muscles were. Somehow her body seemed completely replenished.

The only real problem was her mind.

It's too many things to take in at once, she thought, as every one of them rattled around inside her head. The ball, the dancing, the whisper in her ear. The bell she'd rung, the run across the grass with her dress in her arms. And then everything that being had said. About a shadow being on Lilibet and her beloved. About Lilibet seeming like she was in danger, in a way that explained the warnings, the flashes of the past, the feeling of someone trying to guide her.

Though what Lilibet was trying to guide her to do was still unclear.

And it got even more so, when she made it to the door. She hesitated, thinking of that rabid thing beyond. But instead of warning her away, that voice whispered something else. Something more like *safe*. As if somehow she'd gotten things wrong or mixed up. Imagined he played a role in all of this, when he didn't.

Maybe he just knows what happened and fears whatever it was or fears doing the same thing, she thought. *He doesn't have to have been something deranged, like the evil half of a set of vampire brothers or some monstrous double waiting to slip into someone else's skin. And if he was somehow, why make sure you gain more power than he can hope to equal? How would that make any sense?*

She just didn't know. But it felt a little like the reveal of what was on the other side leaned weight to the latter theory. He didn't immediately try to burst through the barrier, or scrabble at it when he found he couldn't.

He wasn't even standing there.

He was sitting on the grass, arms around his knees. Hugging them, almost—like he was cold, somehow. He was even shaking like he was. She thought she could hear his teeth chattering, behind his tightly pressed together lips. And his skin had an ever so slightly bluish tinge, of a kind that confused her.

But then it clicked, in her head.

It had been in that book she'd read on vampire weaknesses. *When one of these creatures goes without a hungered-for food source for an extended period of time, he will begin to starve. Eventually, a kind of catatonic state will be entered, colloquially referred to as the long sleep*, she remembered.

And of course if that happened . . .

"We need to get you inside," she said, fast enough that her good sense simply couldn't keep up. Though said good sense stared at her incredulously, once the words were out. *At least wait until you've dug in to whoever Bram and Lilibet were before you start putting your head in the lion's mouth again*, it tried to tell her.

But the problem was: He seemed to think the same damn thing.

"No we," he ground out from between gritted teeth. "You go."

As if he didn't like her being in immediate danger any more than she did.

Which definitely put another point in the *not some past serial killer* column.

"And what's going to happen if someone finds you here?" she asked.

"It doesn't matter. It doesn't matter."

"Yes, it does. They'll behead you."

"Your care for me is touching."

She rolled her eyes. "Still smug even while you're dying of vampirism," she said, then sighed just for good measure. "This isn't me being kind. This is me thinking of our deal. You can't teach me anything else while decapitated."

"You don't need anything else."

"Because I rang a bell with the help of a ghost? And spent the night sleeping in a Calabaraian tree? It sounds like starvation is making you dense, as well as ten seconds away from foaming at the mouth and going all rigid and all the other things I now wish I hadn't read about vampires," she said.

Though she knew even as she did that it wasn't the physical details of it that had gotten her. It was the reason the details had been listed. *Once in this state, the creature becomes a kind of living corpse, perfect for anatomical study,* she remembered, and shuddered. But it strengthened her resolve, at least. "Now, I'm going to try to get you on your feet. And you're going to let me. And then we're going to act like you're still drunk, and I'm taking you back to yours."

"They'll think we're fucking."

"I've got bad news for you, pal. After you swooped me around the fancy ball and whispered sweet nothings in my ear and defended my honor against whoever swiped me, they already do. So come on, give me your hand."

He groaned and turned his head away. "I'll bite you."

"I'd like to see you try, in this state."

"You just told me you still need lessons to do a single magical thing."

"Right. But I don't need them to knock you over with a light tap of my foot."

She lifted her skirts, on the last word, and nudged him a little on the shoulder with her toes. And sure enough, he went over like a house of cards in a stiff breeze. For a second, he couldn't even seem to get back up again. He just laid there, sprawled on the grass, more exhausted looking than anyone she'd ever seen in her life.

He barely even turned his head for the hand she held out again.

But this time, he took it. He let her haul him to his feet.

And once he had managed, he didn't let go. He clung to it, like a lifeline.

So now they just stood on the grass, holding hands. *Like we really did fuck*, she thought—and after that it was her turn to wobble over the whole thing. She came close to pulling away, and even closer when she realized where his arm was going to have to go in order to get him somewhere safe.

He needed help staying upright.

And that meant laying that big thing *right over her shoulders*.

Even though the hand alone was bad enough. It felt as if it was swallowing hers whole. She could make out the tension in it, like he was trying to touch her without touching her at all. Or avoid crushing her with his impossible strength, before he could think about it.

Another tick in the *not a serial killer* column, she thought.

But it didn't help. Now he was being all nice seeming and trustworthy, just as she gingerly attempted to lever him closer. And it made it difficult in all kinds of other ways. She tried to stay on guard but had to do so while he trembled at the feel of her hip, her side, her arm around him. She put a hand on his back, and he let out a sound of fear and desperation.

It was a miracle she managed to stop herself doing anything more.

She had never had a stronger urge to reassure someone in her life.

So she forced herself forward, instead. Staggering and stumbling, but she managed to keep him on his feet. And when it seemed like he was faltering, she did what she had to in order to keep him conscious. "This would be a *lot* easier if you were shorter," she said in between panting breaths.

Then got the kind of sass she'd come to know and hate.

"It's not my fault you're only two apples tall."

"Please. Five foot three is hardly two apples. You're just gargantuan."

"I wish I was. Then my face would be too far away from your body to catch your scent. God, do you have any idea how glorious that scent is? I dream of it. I live for it—every day I feel an inch away from losing myself right into it. And if I did, if I do, oh, Jesus, just drop me here, just let me die," he gasped.

While she did her absolute damnedest not to listen.

It was just the ravings of a starved vampire.

Once she got him sorted, she would never have to hear him talking ever again. Or at least, not in a way that made her feel all weird and shaky and like she was about to burst with magic. She just had to focus. "Don't be so dramatic. Just tell me where your dorm is," she managed to get out. But god, he was no help on that score at all.

"I don't live in a dorm."

"Of course you don't. Okay, your majesty, point me to your palace."

"It's down in the basement. North wing, seventh staircase from the left."

What the heck? she thought.

She couldn't linger on this fact, however.

She had to just keep up the veneer of sardonic calm she had slapped on.

"Christ. Well, at least you've come to your senses enough to let me take you."

"It's not my senses talking to me now. It's the part of me that knows you'll be trapped down there," he said, in a way that made her want to update her serial killer tally again. But when she tried, she found she couldn't.

Because even an overt threat afforded her a strange sort of safety.

"Good of you to be honest and warn me, I guess."

"There's enough of me still left to, darling."

"Don't call me darling. In fact, don't say anything else at all," she ground out, from between teeth that were now gritted. Though she was surprised when he fell mercifully quiet. They made their way through a warren of increasingly dim hallways in silence—or near enough to silence anyway. There was still the rattle of her increasingly harsh breathing, echoing in the emptiness. And the click of his expensive shoes on the polished floor.

She didn't even know how he was still wearing them.

He'd lost his fancy coat somewhere in the middle of the night. His shirt was missing a sleeve and most of its buttons. Like he'd tried to tear it off and only half succeeded. Though he went for the rest, the second they were at his door. "This one," he said, once they'd passed several of the same, all featureless wood.

Like storerooms, she thought.

But didn't have time to think more.

He was half naked now. Through the door but on his hands and knees. "Oh god, I'm burning up," he moaned, as he crawled into the room. "I feel like I could tear off my own skin." And she simply couldn't let him do that. She followed him and shut the door behind her, fully expecting him to spring up and get her.

You fool, she imagined him saying.

But he didn't say anything at all. He didn't do anything. He just made his way across the threadbare rug-covered floor, until he got to the bed. Old looking and a little rickety, with what looked like a metal frame. *An iron frame*, she realized with a start. And that wasn't the only thing that got her in the guts.

There was also the window above it.

The one that looked a little off, to her eye. She glimpsed a deep twilight-colored sky, a hint of velvety grass, maybe a tree in one corner, and went back for a longer look immediately.

And sure enough, it wasn't a look through to the outside at all.

It was a painting. Someone had *painted* a window view onto the wall. And this seemed so odd, for a second she forgot everything else. She just stared at this thing—and then at other strange things in the room, too. Old statues and busts stacked about the place, rugs rolled into corners, what seemed to be a large brass tub in some small, dank room beyond. And the bookcases—oh, there were so many bookcases.

It was practically a cave of them.

Gorgeous to her, of course.

But absolutely wild for someone like him. He mocked her love of them constantly. The most interest she'd ever seen him pay them was that one he'd had in his hand, at the start of one of their lessons. Yet here they all were, jammed into shelves and spilling onto the floor and surrounding her on all sides. It made her want to take a closer look, to see what exactly it was that he liked.

She only resisted because of the sound he made.

It was so desperate now it cleaved her heart in two. Her feet actually tried to step toward him; she only held them back by the skin of her teeth. Though it wasn't any easier just watching him. He seemed to be searching for something, desperately. He had an old suitcase out, from under the bed, and was trying to unfasten the straps.

And failing, obviously. His fingers fumbled awkwardly.

Like they were already frozen.

"Let me help you," she said.

But he batted her away.

"No. No, you've helped enough."

"But you're going to just turn into a husk down here, on your own."

"I have someone. They will do what's needed. You don't have to worry," he said over his shoulder, offhandedly, quite obviously not thinking about what he was saying. But she thought about it the moment he had. She actually jolted to hear it, for the second time, and immediately went over all possible candidates for such a thing.

A friend of his? The lithe, long-limbed girl?

No, no. It sounded like he'd known them a while.

He would have had to, if he had leaned on them as long as he'd been here. And she felt pretty sure he'd been here more than the three years it would take someone like him to graduate. So what did that leave? A professor, she thought. Someone like Cobble, who you could trust.

But she couldn't bank on that. She had to ask.

"Well, tell me who they are, and I'll go get them."

"Who they are isn't your business."

"Then let me at least open that suitcase for you."

"You wouldn't want to if you knew what's in there."

Lilibet, she thought.

But even the parts of her that hated him recoiled from the idea.

No, it had to be something less horrible. Something simpler.

"I'm guessing it's blood. Or maybe body parts," she said.

Though even that made him balk. He looked at her, incredulous.

"You think I have *body parts* stored under my bed?"

"Well, I was thinking of animals, not people."

"So just a dead dog, then."

"No. No. More like a rat. Or a bird."

He stopped fighting with the suitcase at that. Laid his head on the bed, turned away from her, as if he was too exhausted to continue. It even seemed like he might have gone to sleep—until he made a sound. A wretched thing that seemed to go through his whole body. "Just please leave me now," he moaned.

But she definitely couldn't after hearing that.

"I will when you manage to make yourself better."

"Nothing can make me better. I'm too sick for you to ever be."

"So what you're saying is that nothing but my blood will do."

"I'm not going to answer that."

"Well, why not?"

Another sigh then.

But this one was gentler. Almost wistful. And so was his voice when he finally spoke. "Because you are too kindhearted, little bookworm. Even toward me, a man you have every reason to loathe—I see the way you're starting to soften. To talk yourself into thinking maybe I'm not so bad, and that even if I am, is it really all right to watch me suffer and starve? And so when I say, yes, you will think that perhaps, just perhaps, it might be okay to offer me a taste. Just one little taste, you'll say, because one little taste isn't really so bad, is it? And I'll want to tell you, yes, it's very bad indeed—it's the worst anything could possibly be. But instead, I will say, no, no, it will be all right. And it won't be. It won't be, because I won't be able to stop," he said, each mad word building one on top of the other, until she was practically bursting to tell him he was wrong. About her kind heart, about her softening, about what she would want to offer him.

But somehow, none of that was what came out.

She thought instead of how strange it would be for a monstrous double to confess something like that. To persuade you not to put yourself in danger, even if it was only fear of being caught that made him. And she answered, before she could stop herself "So then we take away your choice to," she said.

As if this was all just some puzzle to be solved by a scrap of logic.

Instead of something so strange and terrifying even he looked aghast. "You mean you want to tie me down," he whispered, voice hushed and hoarse. Gaze full of a kind of fraught light. Waiting, she thought, for her to step back from the precipice.

Even though he was the one who'd accidentally led her there.

"I didn't mean anything at all. But yes, I imagine that would work."

"It won't. There isn't anything in this room that could hold me."

"Then make something. Make something out of magic."

He gave her a withering look. "You know full well I'm too weak."

"I also know that you're just saying that in an effort to put me off."

"I don't even understand *why* I have to. You should be put off anyway."

Maybe I would be if you stopped saying things like that, she thought.

But that didn't cover it, and she knew it. She had to scramble for other excuses.

"Yeah, and I've already told you the reason I'm not: I still need you to help me do this. Quite clearly, because if I didn't, I would be making some goddamn manacles myself right now. But I'm not, because I just know when I try that it won't be there. I can feel that it isn't there," she said, unsure as she did who she was really trying to convince. But surprised when it worked.

The words built to a crescendo of actual stress.

Actual fear of all the things she couldn't do.

And she could see that idea sinking into him, too.

He stared after they were out, long and assessing. As if he was weighing something up. Then finally, he seemed to decide. She almost saw him nod, as in, *well, that's settled, then.* Before he took a slow breath and spoke in the most suddenly casual and kindly way she could imagine, coming from him.

"You're just exhausted."

"Yes, I know I am."

"Not to mention stressed out and frustrated."

"Well, of course. Wouldn't anyone be, in my place?"

He nodded sagely. "You're right. Things like this happen to a lot of people."

"Right," she said. "Exactly. Exactly. This is absolutely understandable."

"You probably just need to give it a minute. We can always try again later."

She went to say something in response. But then she saw his expression, with just that hint of amusement to it. And suddenly everything he'd said turned on its head. It took on another meaning entirely, of the sort you might offer to a man having performance issues. *In the bloody bedroom.*

"You fucking arsehole," she burst out.

But he just shrugged.

"Relaxed you, didn't it?"

"Honestly it made me even more tense than before."

"You can't get away with that with me, bookworm. I can hear your heart rate. I can see every minute change to your body, from the softening of the muscles in your shoulders, to the slight tension around your lips that tells me you wanted to smile. You wanted to laugh even. But you held it back, to stop me having the satisfaction," he said, his expression a picture of *got you.*

Even though he hadn't.

"So you'd be satisfied by my amusement, then."

“You say that if it seems so strange that anyone would be.”

“Not anyone. Just you.”

He tilted his head on one side. “Liar,” he said.

So confident about it that she couldn’t try a denial.

“Can you hear that in my heartbeat too, can you?”

“Sometimes, yes. When you’re most scared of the truth.”

“So tell me what exactly you think the truth is, in this situation.”

“That you can never imagine you make someone happy. That they might want to see you laugh and be pleased if they manage. That your delight is their delight, your pleasure is their pleasure, their dreams are whatever makes your dreams come true. The very idea is alien to you, impossible. Even if it was right in front of your face, you would struggle to see it,” he said, hands spreading as he did. One shoulder almost lifting in a shrug. Just as casual as everything else he’d told her.

But this one left her breathless.

She couldn’t even hide the shake in her voice when she replied.

“Maybe if someone actually told me these things, I wouldn’t,” she tried to shoot back. But it lacked the tone she wanted. It sounded like sadness over scorn. Vulnerability over a sense that she didn’t really care.

And of course he hooked his claws into the softest things.

“And exactly how do you think that hoped-for conversation would go?”

“The whole point is that I have no idea. You can *see* I have no idea.”

“Yes, but you can imagine, surely. You must have imagined someone saying your name, soft as fur against your skin. ‘Mina,’ they might whisper. Over and over—‘Mina, Mina, Mina,’ like something they were forbidden to speak, and so now they must say it a thousand times," he said, low enough that she could hardly hear him. She almost took a step forward just to get every word, every use of a name he had never spoken aloud, as he spun this strange little scenario.

And only stopped herself at the last second.

She stepped back from the edge, instead.

"That doesn't seem like much for someone trying to convince me."

"Well, it depends what you want to be convinced of. If it was just the idea of someone liking your delight, a name might be enough. But if you needed to know that they craved your pleasure, I can imagine it would be more. A simple *let me make you feel good*. A soft sigh of bliss, when they do. When they watch your eyes grow heavy, and your lips part, and—"

"Okay, *stop*."

She didn't mean to say it so frantically.

It just happened, the second she saw what was coming. Something terrible, something she couldn't stand. Words she could never let him speak—not while she was like this. Caught in between the possible danger, and all the ways he didn't seem dangerous at all. The whispered words in her ear holding one side of her good sense, the countdown to the chase, in the other.

There couldn't be anything like that to tip the scales.

Nothing seductive. Nothing that made this surge of something go through her.

Not even when she already knew what it had done. She felt it, even before she looked down at her hands. The silvery wash of magic filling her body. The bloom of it in her hands, without her even having to cup them. Like he had been right, about the forms and the wands and the beads just being a thing to focus and shape.

Unneeded if you could focus and shape with a feeling.

If you could call magic to you, just by letting it in.

It was just unfortunate that letting it in involved him.

"There," he said. Voice suddenly flat and normal.

That shaky, exhausted look back, quick as a flash.

It made her throw up her hands.

"You said all of that just to make me spark?"

"Well, I certainly wasn't trying to seduce you."

He rolled his eyes.

While she tried to be angry, instead of dying inside.

"I didn't . . . I wasn't imagining . . . It was just a lot to say to me, all right."

"It worked, though, didn't it? Now you can do whatever you want with it."

"I told you what I wanted to do. To make a set of manacles. For *you*."

"Even though you're incredibly close to doing more. A knife would be *so* easy now."

He touched his tongue to one sharp incisor.

Like a different type of temptation altogether.

See how dangerous I am, it seemed to say. Big teeth, seductive words.

Not that teeth and seduction helped him, in this sense. "And what would I do with one now? Stab a defenseless man? I want to be able to make weapons so I can fend you off at your full and rabid strength. Not get you when you can barely keep your own head up. Now, shut up and let me concentrate," she said—as if she really needed to.

When she didn't at all.

It took almost nothing.

She put her arms together, to signify something defensive. Then down, hands forming two circles, thumbs and forefingers touching. Before finally, she pulled them apart. Fast and without letting herself think about it too much.

And there they were.

A set of manacles, so ghostly looking she could hardly believe they had a thousand times the strength of any metal. But she knew beyond a shadow of a doubt they did. She could feel the power in them, built out of all those far too intense things he had said. They still sung in her, as she held them out to him.

Though the worse part was, he seemed to know.

"You can't, under any circumstances, make contact with me," he said. As if he thought things were so conflicted inside her that she might be tempted to touch him. That she might like to or enjoy it when she did.

"Don't say that as if I want something like that."

"I would never think you do. But the thing is: I might persuade you to."

"As we've already established, thralling really doesn't work on me."

"Yes, but I wasn't talking about thralling. I was talking about you, and the way you react when I do certain things, and talk a certain way, and look at you like I'm looking at you now. When I make it sweet and good, when I seduce you, so you can just slip into your own magic, easy, easy, easy."

"That only works because I let it."

"Are you sure?"

No, she thought. *Yes*, she answered.

"Of *course* I'm sure. You mean nothing to me. None of this means anything to me. I see it as nothing more than a means to an end. And this will be, too. It's just a medical matter. Practical. Businesslike. Part of our deal. I'll go about it with all the professionalism of a doctor, lancing a wound. And that will be the case, no matter what you do," she said, so sure sounding about it that he only hesitated a moment longer. Those dark eyes drank her in, as if looking for cracks in the facade.

Then he took the manacles she tossed to him, satisfied.

Though she imagined he wouldn't have been, if he had seen the inside of her head. Her thoughts raced wildly, as she watched him snap one of them around his wrist. And not just because of the way it looked, once he had—like a piece of brutal jewelry, against his suddenly tender-seeming skin.

No. There was also the sudden understanding of what he would have to do here. The second manacle wasn't just going to go around his other wrist. Of course it wasn't. He had to thread the chain around something first. A sturdy something—like say, the obviously iron frame, at the head of his bed.

Still, though, she didn't expect him to really do it.

She imagined a metal hoop somewhere, drilled into the wall.

Some sort of pipe that wouldn't buckle under his strength.

Then was forced to watch him, as he laid down on the bed. As he arranged the chain and spread his bare arms above his head. Not lewdly, she told herself. Not purposefully, like something suggestive.

But the problem was, the effect was suggestive all the same.

She could see the exact perfect curve to his biceps, when he held his arms like that. How oddly thick they looked, in a way she could never see in his shirts and sweaters. And that thickness was in him elsewhere, too. There was something almost heavy about his chest, his shoulders.

Like a man who didn't work out.

He just did things that made him strong.

Or more possibly: *had* done things. He had grown into this in Calabaraia, most likely. Shaped himself on mountains made of glass and hunts that had no horses. Everything just about how fast you could run. How high you could climb. What you could do with your bare hands. *A lot,* she thought, as he shifted on the bed.

And every muscle in his body moved.

They all rolled beneath his honey-pale skin, in a way that was almost hypnotic. Certainly she felt hypnotized, when she walked over to him on legs that felt half hollow. And then she was looking down at him, and the sight did nothing to strengthen her.

Because true, he still had those trousers on.

It was just that the trousers weren't particularly modest.

They hung very low on his hips—low enough that she could see the trail of dark hair leading down, below the waistband. And the material seemed very tight and very thin. It pulled taut over his thick thighs, when he spread them—which he did, immediately. For comfort, she imagined.

But in the moment, it didn't really feel like it.

It felt like he was doing it on purpose.

Like some part of him had taken that *hate* comment as a challenge. And when she forced herself to look at his face again, the expression on it only backed that assessment up. There was something . . . watchful about it. Something sly. Like the person she was starting to almost like—or at least understand—was no longer in control.

Instead, there was this demon.

Eyes dark, tongue curled up to touch one tooth.

Just waiting for her to make a mistake.

This whole thing is, she thought. But she touched the knife she'd found to her palm, anyway. She pressed, thinking it would be difficult to draw blood. That she would be timid, too queasy to hurt herself, that it wouldn't be like it was in the movies. Yet red welled up the moment she did it. It spilled down her hand and wrapped around her middle finger, like a ring.

Then dripped onto him.

Only a drop of it, but apparently a drop of it was enough.

He bucked, to feel it. A sound came out of him, so close to a moan of desire she couldn't have split the two with a razor. It made her heart jolt in her chest, and that hollow muscle feeling increase tenfold.

Though it wasn't either of these things that really got her.

It was the way he turned his head, and then pressed his open mouth to his own upper arm. Right over the swell of pale muscle, teeth breaking skin almost immediately. As if he could quell the hunger with the taste of his own body.

And when he realized he couldn't, his gaze slid to her. Heavy, lustrous, full of longing. He murmured words, so low she almost didn't hear them—or maybe didn't want to. Because now they were in her head, running over and over on a loop: *You are my every torment, you are my every torment, you are my every torment.*

It was the reason she wanted to stop.

It was the reason she couldn't.

She let the next drop spill over his lips. His closed lips that parted the moment the red kissed them. He let his tongue dart out to catch it—quick at first, as if to get it over with. But then once he'd tasted it, once he had that salt inside him, his eyes rolled closed. And he licked again, long and slow.

Sensuously, her mind suggested.

Because her mind was a traitor. It was already turning on her, before he'd even tried to talk her into something terrible. And then he did, and oh, it was so much worse than she'd imagined. He didn't tell her to cut more deeply or press the wound to his mouth. He didn't strain up, hoping to sink his teeth in.

He said, "Let me lick you."

He said, "Let me stroke all wet and soft all over you."

He said, "I won't use anything sharp. Only the sweetest and tenderest of things."

And it got hold of her like nothing she'd ever known. For a moment she thought he'd thralled her—it was that intense. It made her heart thunder; it made her breath hitch in her chest. She could almost feel what it would be like, before she'd even lowered her hand to him.

Then found that she had lowered it, without actually being aware.

Her palm was now barely an inch from his parted lips. He could have lifted his head and done just as he'd suggested. But she suspected the reason he didn't. It wasn't as satisfying to take it, when another second might see her freely give it. Just a little more of this heavy tension, just a few more thoughts of what that sensation would be like. *Just one more word*, she thought.

And he gave it, too.

"Please," he said.

She had to put her other hand around her wrist, to stop herself from immediately giving in. And even then, she could feel her resolve crumbling. Her grip shook; it was like holding up a thousand-pound weight. One that gained another ton for every second she held it. Soon, she was so close she could feel his breath on her skin.

She could feel that tongue of his, stirring the air around her hand.

Almost *licking* her. Her almost *liking* it.

And all while he lost himself completely. That red was now flowing over his lips, and it made him frantic. It made him moan and rock—like someone being fucked. Every bit of him entirely abandoned to the sensation, unaware of where he was or what he was doing.

She suspected that was how it happened.

He didn't mean to do it. He just wanted to get as deeply into that deliciousness as he could go—and when he did, something slick simply brushed against the thickest part of her thumb. Barely anything, no part of the place sensitive at all. Yet the effect was stunning. It made her gasp.

She gave in to that weight without a moment more of fight.

Just to get it again, just to get it one more time.

That sweet flicker of his tongue over her skin.

And somehow, he did just that. He immediately followed the path that blood had made over her fingers, until he had found that curve between two. That intimate space, far more sensitive than where she had felt him lick first. Though she had to say, it wasn't the physical sensation that made her act.

It was the sight of it.

The rudeness of it.

The slick curl of that tongue easing between the split of her fingers.

Suggestive, in a way she simply wasn't prepared for. Her mind immediately went to spread legs, and someone with their face between them. And as soon as it did, she was gone. Her hand was over his mouth, pressing. Every bit of her sizzling, when he pressed back.

But oh, the best part wasn't that.

It was when he suckled at that bloody line she'd drawn. Sought it out, again and again, with his greedy mouth. It was unbelievable. Beyond anything. She could almost feel it connecting, somehow, with that unbearable ache between her legs. "Oh yes," she found herself moaning.

And she couldn't even regret it.

Because he moaned back.

The sound reverberated through him and into her, heightening every single deranged sensation as it went. Suddenly she wasn't just enjoying it. She wasn't just letting herself be lewd over it. She was leaning in. She was leaning down. Like she actually wanted him to claim something other than her hand.

She wanted him at her throat.

It feels so good, oh, so good, her mind murmured. *Where would the harm be to just feel him there? Where would the harm be to let him put that mouth on that curve?* And in that moment, she truly had no idea. All she knew was that her body was thick with sensation, and so desperate to drown in it that drowning felt like good sense.

Because yes, she'd suffocate.

But oh, wouldn't it feel glorious to do it?

Didn't she want to feel glorious, for once?

Yes, she thought, and tilted her head. Turned, so he could. Honestly, she thought she even felt his sharp teeth, grazing her neck. And then she saw it, out of the corner of her eye. The bloom of her magic, just as it had come to her before. Like a warning shot, like a life preserver.

And she seized it.

She took hold, as she had in the ballroom. Only this time, it didn't singe him.

It seemed to snap against her. It almost blew her back, hard enough that she found herself on the floor. Dazed, hardly able to believe what had happened. But still in one piece. Still unbitten. She had seen real sense at the last second, and saved herself.

Then she met his low-lidded gaze, across the bedroom, and saw those parted lips, red with blood—and she knew. The ability to get out of this was never going to hold, for long. She was deep in it, all the way up to her neck.

And there was really no escaping now.

Chapter Eighteen

She knew how dazed she seemed the next day. She could see it in the mirror over the dresser—her eyes were suddenly too large for her face; her skin looked so pale it was almost translucent. But it still shocked her when Professor Cobble stopped her in the hall, as she made her way to Hargreaves's next no doubt horrifying lecture.

"My dear, is everything well?" he asked and in so kindly a way she almost spilled all her worries. *The only way I seem able to emotionally connect with magic is when a potentially murderous vampire fills me with lust*, she thought. *And now I'm pretty sure everybody here wants to kill me for snatching a prize they think they deserve.*

But instead of saying that, she stretched a smile over her face.

"Couldn't be better. Just been burning the midnight oil," she said.

Then in reply she got an arm squeeze, and that soft, absent-minded smile of his, and him bustling off down the hall. She followed him with her eyes, almost wistful for what she could have had there. An actual adult in charge, to confide in and look out for her.

Because god knows there wasn't another.

She got to Boundaries and Bureaucracy two minutes late, and Professor Hargreaves looked at her like she had crawled out of a hole in the ground. Her thin, graying face seemed to get thinner and grayer; her cool gray eyes were suddenly chips of ice. "Well," she said, as Mina took her seat. "I suppose the golden girl no longer believes she must be on time for her lectures."

And everyone in the room tittered.

Some turned back to stare in that same cold way.

She felt pretty sure the seat next to hers suddenly bursting into flames was not an accident. She had to take the trip she needed to the library with a singed sleeve. The smell of burning hung in the air, as she flicked through old yearbooks and records and any accounts she could find of the last girl to ring the bell.

But all she got for her trouble was a tiny picture in *The Harrowhall Gazette*'s records, in the aftermath of the event. Lilibet in the center, fairly clear, and enough like her that she could understand why someone might squint and think so. The same billowing curls and waves of dark hair, similar big brown eyes. Something in her expression that seemed familiar, from a thousand looks in the mirror. More beautiful, of course, much more beautiful. But yes, it was there.

However, the man with her—she could see what that being had meant.

Kindness shone out of his face. It radiated from his being. She could almost imagine the warmth Lilibet must have felt, from the look he was giving her. And it made any resemblance to Harker *very* hard to imagine. It softened out every edge, every line. Made him seem like so utterly a different man that she couldn't imagine anything as mad as a monstrous double, living just beneath his skin.

It just didn't make sense.

And she couldn't find anything else that made it add up to

something. No sign of a secret sibling he might have had, no connection to the man she knew. No hint of anyone like him lurking in the backgrounds of their lives, watching their every move. In fact, there wasn't even a hint of their untimely deaths—despite the fairly reasonable record keeping she uncovered, for the era she now knew they had lived in.

Late eighties, it seemed like.

But there was no listing for Lilibet. No listing for Bram.

You were supposed to save me from sinking even deeper into being seduced by him, she thought sourly, at the books piled around her.

The books said nothing back.

She left with less than she had started with, and so late for dinner with Anaya that she completely forget to go change her blouse. And of course Anaya noticed immediately. "Did someone try to *burn* you?" she whispered over bowls of asparagus soup. "Just because you won that thing that makes you amazing?"

While all around them people stared, and made faces, and basically answered the question for her friend. "Honestly, it wouldn't be so bad if it *had* done that," Mina replied, as she poked at her food. "But I still can't conjure much of anything."

"I'm sure you will once you've spent some time snogging fen."

"I don't think snogging is possible with beings that have no faces."

"So you've been there already? You've been there and seen?"

"Only for a little while. And I didn't get far."

"You went alone, then."

She had been chasing a swirl of sour cream around her bowl, with her spoon.

Now she looked up at her friend. And sure enough, there it was, all over her face.

The barely concealed glee at the thought of digging up some juicy details.

"Yes. But honestly if you ever want to—" she tried, just to dodge having to explain everything that happened, without really explaining it all. However, all she got was a hand wave. And a slightly pointed, *you-know-what-I'm-asking* look.

"I know you would take me. But I think you get that's not what I was asking."

"Harker didn't come with me. He stayed in his room, while I went through."

"And after you came back out? And you were alone with him, in said room?"

Anaya raised one eyebrow. Leaned forward, in the exact way Mina would have loved, if this was a real conversation about being with a guy. It was the kind of thing she'd dreamed of, in high school. The world of cool hookups, and being able to actually talk about them afterward.

Only this was a bizarre bloodthirsty hell, instead.

Mixed with something else she couldn't explain.

And it made her protest too tensely.

"We didn't do anything. I was just helping him."

"So he was trapped inside his clothes, and you lent him a hand escaping."

"Not out of all of them; he had his trousers on the whole time I was there."

Fuck, she thought, the second she saw Anaya's cheekily satisfied expression.

She had confessed too much, without intending to. Now, in her friend's mind, the guy she had danced all night with had ended up half naked in front of her. And it wasn't as if she could explain. She couldn't say: *well, he ripped out of his shirt due to lust for my blood.*

All she had were weak denials.

"Things are not like that between us. *Really* not like that."

"Oh, I'm sure they're not."

"He hates me."

"I bet he does. That's why he danced with you like that and couldn't keep his eyes off you and is also now sauntering over to talk to you, with what can only be described as a desperate hunger in his eyes," Anaya said, voice so thick with amusement that Mina thought nothing of taking it that way. She even went to snark back that he would never.

But then she followed Anaya's gaze, aimed just over her shoulder.

And there he was. The bane of her existence, doing exactly what Anaya had said. Strolling in a way that made his hips roll. Focus all on her, despite the many people who tried to get his attention. The only deviation from Anaya's description was in those eyes. *It's not that kind of hunger*, she wanted to say to her friend.

But of course she couldn't.

She just had to sit there and wait, silently, for whatever this was going to be.

An embarrassing horror she imagined, about a second before Harker spoke.

"Good morning, ladies," he said. And *warmly*, too.

He looked right at Anaya and actually smiled.

So of course Anaya smiled back.

"Well, good morning to you, too, Harker. Can we help you with something?"

"Actually, yes. Perhaps you can persuade Mina to eat something more than a bowl of soup. Because as delicious as it looks,

I don't think it's really going to make up for the exhausting night she had."

"Yeah. I thought she looked pretty spent, too."

Anaya winked at her. She tried not to wither and die.

And that was *before* Harker tilted his head in that a-killer-blow-is-coming way of his. "Well, you know. I *do* tend to wear out the company I keep," he said, and of course she knew he was doing it to keep the charade alive. She knew this was only cover. Yet somehow, it still knocked her sideways.

Her face flamed briefly red; she came close to making a sound of shock.

I thought you didn't want anyone to think that, she wanted to say.

While they just carried on. "Oh, I'll bet you do. She's probably going to need steak and chips, after you," Anaya said, as if the half-naked confession had unlocked some friendship setting Mina hadn't understood.

Now everything was innuendo.

And other harrowing things.

"I was thinking the same thing. How about extra bloody, for that kick of iron? You know. To really get some color back into your cheeks," Harker said, as he turned to her. But apparently, looking wasn't enough.

He reached and touched her there, too.

Just with one curled finger, barely making contact.

But *god*, the effect it had. Suddenly her whole head was a mass of those strange memory flashes—and every single one of them seemed incredibly rude. A hand running down from her face to somewhere between her legs. That kind version of him, making her go up on her toes.

And even when she managed to force those flashes back, there were other things determined to take her attention. The blood. The bed. That tongue of his, licking over his upper lip. It all washed over her, one thing after another, until she could *feel* the glow around her hands, beneath the table.

She had to force it down for the first time, before she started rattling the cutlery. And then somehow answer like a normal person. "My cheeks are fine," she managed to grind out. But even after that, he didn't let up.

"Well, that mysterious flush has certainly helped. But they still look a little pale, to me."

"I'm going to make you go pale, if you don't shut up."

"And I'll shut up when you eat," he said, as the food he'd obviously had in his head arrived. He set it down in front of her, instead of the soup. Then came very close to nudging her arm. "Go on, get stuck in. It looks delicious."

How would you know? she wanted to say.

And apparently, she would soon get the chance to.

Anaya had stood up. For the guy she had enjoyed at the ball, waving at her across the room. Frank, Mina knew he was called. Though that obviously wasn't the only reason she was exiting stage right. "I'll leave you two alone," she said, as she gave Mina a one-armed squeeze.

So now she was alone with the university version of Satan.

He sat across from her, very satisfied with himself.

"You know I had *just* managed to convince her that we did not have sex," she said. Much to his amusement. He gave her a little faux frown, as he leaned back in his seat. And when he spoke his voice was almost musical.

"I thought you didn't mind if people imagined we did. Or have, many times."

"Yeah, I don't mind people thinking that. But my friend is a different matter."

"Because it's only her opinion that could make you ashamed of it?"

"Don't say it like anything actually happened. I fed you. Nothing more."

"*Fed* and *nothing more* makes it sound like you did what I have just done—ordered you a plate of food you're still not eating. Instead of what actually happened: you came pretty close to sparing me a horrible death. And at great personal risk, I might add. I could have killed you." He shook his head, almost disapproving. Most likely ready to say more things designed to throw her. Only then he seemed to stop, and his eyes dropped to her arm. "Though it seems I might not be the only attempt on your life around, if the smell all over you is anything to go by. Did someone actually try to set you on fire?"

"Not exactly."

"That means yes."

She looked away. "I don't see how you figure that one."

"Because I know you by now. Always trying to hide how hurt you are."

"So then you *are* aware of the amount of damage you do to me."

"Of course I am. It sinks in deep, every single time I land a hit," he said, just as offhandedly as he'd been about everything else. He even did things as he spoke—took up her knife and fork and started cutting up the fat, sizzling steak on her plate. She was still sitting there, baffled and uncertain of how to respond, when he skewered a juicy piece of it, and after adding a glossy coating of sauce, offered the handle to her insistently.

Maybe he's just actually grateful for what you did, her mind suggested, as she fought to figure out if she should take it. But before that thought could settle, she answered her mind back, *Either that or one taste has him desperate to fatten me up.*

Though she took the fork, as she finally replied.

"You say that like it's you getting stabbed," she said. A happy medium, she felt, between snark, and the space for him to confess why he kept saying things like that. But he dodged it soundly, as he forced her to eat another forkful.

"Stop trying to change the subject. Someone set you on fucking fire."

"They set the chair next to me on fire. And Hargreaves eventually put it out."

"So she took her time, then. She let you suffer a little first."

"It wasn't like that. She meant no harm."

"Yes, but someone did. So let's start with who."

"I don't even know why it matters. He's no more mean than you."

Come on, she thought. *Explain yourself. Admit the ruse behind your concern and your almost sorries*. And of course, he gave her nothing. "It was Sebastian, then. Or his friend, Jude. The one without a chin."

"There's now a chinless guy out to get me?"

"Everybody is out to get you. It's honestly exhausting keeping up with them all. I almost knocked out that boyfriend of your little buddy this morning, when it seemed like he was getting in good with her to get to you."

"For god's sake, stop acting like you care."

She didn't mean to say it so loudly. Or slap the table when she did.

It just happened, and to the point where everything went suddenly quiet.

They all stared in a way she didn't think they'd dared to at first. Harker St. James did whatever he pleased, and you didn't act like you were paying a gossipy sort of attention to him, unless you wanted trouble.

Yet somehow, she had managed to overcome that.

And it made his face turn cold. Dead looking, it seemed.

"I think blood loss is making you read too much into things. Now eat your food. You're going to need your strength for our next lesson—how to avoid being set on fire. See you at six tomorrow, bookworm," he said, tone so smooth and icy she could have skated across it.

Then he stood and walked away.

After which, she cleared her plate.

Chapter Nineteen

She tried to practice, before she went to her next lesson. Mainly because of the air of threat to his words, over breakfast. But there were other things in there, too. Frustration that it still wasn't coming easy. The feeling that other threats were closing in on her. A sense of time racing on, and every challenge that would bring with it.

Practical lessons began after Christmas.

And practical lessons would not wait for her to catch up.

She would either fly when pushed, or fall. Defend herself while dueling, or get cut down. Contain a fireball, or be incinerated. There was no in between when it came to things like that. So instead of reading *How to Navigate the Underneath* for the seventh time, she stood up. She closed her eyes. And she tried to summon the right sort of feeling, without falling back on any recent situations.

Like him lifting her. The look of him on that bed. His mouth—

Think of something from before all this, she ordered herself. *Something that is not him and all the ways he is obviously poisoning you. Because he* is *poisoning you. Making you think he means any sweet thing he says and does, making you sleepwalk into sympathy, and then telling you your sympathy is dangerous just to fool you even further. He is smart, and you have to be smarter.*

But when she tried, nothing came up.

It never came up. There wasn't anything there.

The best she could do was things she'd read in books, about swooning maidens being haunted by fiends. Most of which had never really inspired a whole lot of anything. And the stuff that had was pretty much useless to her now. Every time she tried to fall back on some story that had produced the slightest spark in her, the story simply reminded her of him.

Like she'd been primed to fall for this.

There was just no way out.

Desire for him was deadly.

But only desire for him would do.

And that was a very bad thing, indeed, when she had to walk into that theater knowing he was most likely waiting with a fistful of snakes. She had to let herself think of a nightgown being slid over milky thighs, just to make some sort of shield before she went inside.

Though she knew it wasn't a very good one.

She brought it up the moment she set foot through the door, and it actually seemed to wink out for a second. She watched that silvery blue dissolve, just as she felt magic rushing toward her. A knife of some description, she thought it was and tried to duck. To lurch to the left.

But just as she did, the shield wavered back.

She heard it *thunk* into that imperfect square, hard enough that the impact juddered up her arms. It made her stumble back and let out a sound of shock. But she got it back together fast. She had to. She could see him across the theater, arms crossed over his chest, looking at her like he had just *known* she wasn't up to scratch.

And it deepened her frustration like nothing else.

"I stopped it, all right? I did what I needed to do," she spat, as she yanked that very heavy-feeling blade out of her shield, and threw it back. Though of course it dissolved before it got anywhere near him. And so did the flimsy thing she had managed to conjure. It flickered and then winked out, while he eyed the place it had been pointedly. Before flicking his gaze back up to her.

"Yes, you did," he said. "With a shield so weak it's already lost cohesion."

"It can't have been that weak. It stopped that thing cold."

"Because I barely gave it any power."

"So now you're pulling your punches."

He held her gaze for that. Assessing her, it seemed.

Like he suspected she was starting to test the limits of his supposed hatred.

In the end, though, he just shrugged. "All I do is pull them. If I don't, you die."

"Well, that's a very thoughtful gift to give me. Not making me a corpse."

"No need to thank me. Just think of it as an early Christmas present."

She let out a scoffing laugh. "Do you actually even celebrate Christmas?"

"If you call unwrapping the single gift I get celebrating, then sure," he said, a little bored sounding about it. A little bored looking while the words came out. It was only after they had that she saw him stiffen a little.

Like this time, he *had* said too much. "So you don't get dozens, from all your admirers. It's just one special person," she said, and now his full and very focused attention was back on her.

"I'm not going to tell you who they are. You might as well stop trying."

"Where would the fun be in that?"

"There isn't supposed to be any fun. This isn't a guessing game."

"Yeah, but if it was one, I think I would definitely go with Cobble."

"I have no idea how you figure that one," he said, with an actual laugh in his voice. A pretty convincing one, too. It was just a shame that his face was typically such a stoic mask, really. Because it definitely showed when he experienced an emotion he didn't mean to.

And that seemed to be the case right now. She could see the hint of tension around his smile. The slight drop that happened, just below his eyes. It even seemed like a flicker of light crossed the surface of his gaze.

It made her laugh back.

"He's kind, he's not awful about anything that lives in the Underneath, he has the clout here to get away with keeping a secret like that. And he's pretty ancient, so he could have looked after you for a long, long time," she said, as she ticked every bit of reasoning off on her fingers.

While the tension in his face tried to deepen.

A muscle in his cheek twitched, almost like a tic.

Before he managed to get himself back together.

"I'm not a thousand years old, for fuck's sake."

"So just hundreds. then."

"No. I was born in 1972."

Not old enough to be a student in the years Lilibet was here, she thought, in a great rush of both relief and disappointment. Relief that he probably wasn't. Disappointment that the mystery had just deepened.

Though, of course, there was every chance he was lying.

Even if it did ring so true she momentarily didn't know what to say about it.

He actually looked like someone who had been born in the seventies, in the strangest way. *Maybe because of the hair*, she thought—that thick shaggy mess, the slightly too long sideburns. Or the clothes—so close to something that wasn't quite this generation. Or the last even.

He favored striped jerseys.

Those too-long-for-his-legs jeans.

He could have starred in a movie about teens getting killed in a summer camp, set in America. In fact, for a second she almost asked him if he had been born there, instead of here. If the accent was an affectation, too.

But she was on a roll now of getting him to reveal things.

And she couldn't let that go right away. "You realize that's still incredibly old," she said as lightly as she could. Almost a scornful tease, because scornful teasing seemed to work the best.

Though it still surprised her when it got him.

He looked briefly offended. "Yes, but to be fair I slept for a good amount of that time. When things got—" he started to say, before he realized, and looked furious at himself, and cut his words short.

As if that was going to stop her. "When things got what? Bad? Traumatizing? You made a mistake you couldn't take back, and then had to be a living corpse in that windowless room until the heat died down? Come back with some new name, some new approach. Just be cool."

"We should go back to lessons."

"But I just did a bingo. Don't I get a prize?"

"You'll get a prize when you successfully deflect something."

He moved before he finished speaking. To shut the conversation down, she knew, and yet it didn't make the slash of his wand any less scary. The second she saw it, she automatically ducked and put her hands over her head. She didn't even wait to see what he was throwing.

But that was her mistake.

Because this thing?

It was *big*. It made a whistling sound as it cut through the air, loud enough that she looked out from underneath her own arm. She tried to catch a glimpse of what she was facing and got just a flash of teeth, of something circular. Like a saw, it seemed, and so large she knew she'd never be able to get low enough.

All she could do was close her eyes and brace.

Only to have it hit and then just *slide right through.*

It didn't even sting her. In fact, the sensation was almost pleasant. Just a strange tingle, and then a sense of something she couldn't quite understand. Like being held, somehow.

Though it quickly passed.

And now she was left with him, all being an ass about it.

"You realize that would have sliced you in two, if it had been a real attempt."

"Well, then. Good job it was just you trying to scare the shit out of me."

"You will be scared, if you don't stop getting in your own way."

God, she wanted to kill him. She wanted to kick something in his face.

But she settled for punching the air in front of her.

"I'm not getting in my own way, you ass. The emotion I use to connect to magic is just really difficult, okay? I mean, Anaya's is relief. I heard someone in the halls talking about theirs the other day, and it was the satisfying feeling you get from peeling Velcro. And I just know that you have something easy for you, too. Like contempt or some fucking thing. So don't get on my case about it," she snapped, everything forgotten, now, aside from how annoying and unfair all of this was.

Not to mention hard on her knees. She'd bruised one of them while trying to duck. It didn't want to quite straighten. And there was dust all over her best woolen tights. She swiped at it angrily, in the silence that followed. In fact, she was still seeing to it, when he answered.

"Mine is love," he said.

So simply she didn't even look up, at first.

But then it hit, and she just couldn't help it

She had to see his face. His expression. How sincere it was.

Only to find it hadn't changed at all.

"No," she said. "No I don't believe you."

"I have no reason to lie. In fact, lying here would benefit my image more."

"Yes, because that's all you're ever concerned about. How cool you look. So how am I supposed to believe that you can whip that amount of magic out at a moment's notice, based on soppy feelings you barely understand?"

He sighed. "Because it doesn't matter if a feeling is out of reach. You find a way to get to it anyway. You claw your way to it, if you have to. You open wounds to make it happen. You use every trick in the book and force it from yourself."

"It's not that easy, with this."

"Seemed easy the other morning, with me."

He shrugged one shoulder. As if it to say, *Hey, no big deal.*

But the smile tugging at the corner of his mouth gave the game away.

"The cause was not you, you arrogant fuck. It was just the things that happened. All that excitement and then the bed and the manacles and the blood and the sensations. Anyone would lose themselves in something like that. But unfortunately for me, losing myself in those things is not something I can just do, every time I need to make a spell."

Or do for any reason ever, she mentally added. *Just in case I start liking it any more than I already seem to.* Then just had to hope it didn't show on her face. Or in her body language. Even though both were pretty rigid already. Her features felt like a mask of irritation; her arms had wrapped themselves around her chest without her even knowing it. She was safe.

She just didn't *feel* safe.

"So imagine it, then," he said, too soft for her liking.

She swallowed thickly to hear it. Shook her head to cover it.

"I don't want to do that, either."

"Because it was very disturbing?"

"Because it involves having to think about you."

"Then you're going to have to consider other things that turn you on."

A jolt went through her, over those last three words. And not just because of the sudden lewdness of them. No—there was also the thing that swam into her head, the second he said it. That little curled finger almost brushing her cheek. Inexplicably, impossibly, and right in the middle of him saying more things.

"There must be something. Someone. A boy you liked," he said.

She had to fumble into answering him, with a head full of nonsense.

"The boys I knew were not very pleasant."

"Then a story. One of those ones that dance on that glass you all love."

"Oh my god, you mean a *television*," she shoved out. "You're talking about a television. How on earth do you pass for just a person when you barely know what a fucking television is? That just seems impossible."

"There are plenty of people here who live in closed magical communities."

"I know, but even so. You must see how weird that should look to some."

"The only thing I see is you trying to change the subject again."

She went to protest. Or deny it. The words touched her teeth.

Yet somehow, under that knowing gaze, something else just came out instead.

"Because you want to talk about sex. And I have no desire to do anything like that with my mortal enemy. I don't even want to do it with myself, quite honestly. I tried this morning and there was just almost nothing there, and even the things that were felt as uncomfortable to think about as thinking about you. All that gothic stuff about being haunted and hunted and devoured," she said, all in a rush of embarrassment.

So of course he just made it worse.

He laughed. He actually laughed.

"And now you're mocking me."

"Yes. But not because of that sort of fantasy."

"Then what exactly do you find so funny?"

"You thinking those are the things you like about those stories."

"Because I do. I clearly do. It happens the second you show your teeth."

Why keep confessing things to him? she moaned at herself. Though really, she knew why she did. She had stepped off the edge of the cliff again. And now everything was descending into madness, at some speed.

"No, it doesn't," he said, as he took a step forward. Just one step, but it was slow and deliberate enough that she knew what was coming. More words, more soft words—god, he knew how to say so many words she had no defenses against. "It happens when you expect me to, and instead I do something else. I end the story sweetly. I end it different to how it usually does in reality. In reality, you get torn apart; everything is a tragedy. But in the dream, someone strokes a hand over your face so tenderly, it leaves you breathless. They whisper sweet nothings in your ear, until you're boneless. And the moment you think you might give in to something bloody and brutal, they do all the sensuous things you most like, and magic blooms through your body, and saves the day. You like kindness, Mina. And especially when you most believe that none is coming."

Jesus Christ, she thought.

Only it wasn't just because of what she'd braced for. He didn't just make it sound good. He was *right*. And so much so she didn't even really know how to deny it. "That is not. That is just. You. You can't know that," she stuttered out, half knowing that this would just make things worse.

And it did.

Now she wasn't just plummeting off the cliff.

She'd hit the sea, at the bottom. And it was like syrup, soft and warm.

She could feel herself sinking into it, right up to her neck.

"Of course I can. I can hear your heart, remember. I know what it races for."

"Maybe it just happens too close to something else for you to really tell."

"There is always a difference between a pulse that quickens in terror and one that quickens over something someone finds arousing. And sometimes those two things do overlap, I will grant you. But not so much with you."

"Oh, come on. How on earth could anyone pinpoint that?" she said and tried to laugh as she did. But the laugh died when she realized what she'd just opened the door to. Now he was going to answer.

After taking another step closer.

And dropping his voice one octave lower.

"Because one only makes your heart beat loud in your chest. But the other makes it beat between your legs," he said. Then he held her gaze, just for good measure. He waited, until the flush already all over her cheeks deepened. Before he continued, slow, slow, slow. "Do you want me to be more precise than that? I could tell you exactly where, if you want. I could talk about the sound of the blood rushing to swell your cunt. The way it beats like a second heart, in that sweet little clit. Sometimes, I think I can even make out the exact ache that goes through you there, when you most feel it."

And *god*, once he had.

She couldn't help marveling over every explicit word he'd chosen. No more covertly seductive poetry. Now there was things like *cunt* in there, things like *clit*. Raw and real, and in a way she'd never really heard from anyone before. She'd barely seen things like that in books.

It was really no wonder she struggled to answer.

"No, you can't," she tried to insist, so faint it seemed almost breathless.

While he only got stronger, more sure.

"Even if I couldn't, those aren't the only clues."

"What other ones could there possibly be?"

"The way you flush—not just in your cheeks, but down your throat, over your chest. How your pupils dilate, how your lips part, how your breathing changes. And most importantly, there is your scent. Oh, that scent, when the sensation inside you lasts for longer than a moment. It makes me want to draw things out, just to get a little more of it. To tease you, until there is nothing but that filling my senses."

"And by *that,* you mean—" she started to say, now so sunk into his every word that it seemed like a miracle she stopped herself, before she finished that terrible thought. But that was okay. That was fine.

He was happy to finish it for her.

"The sweet slickness between your legs, of course," he said.

Because apparently there was another level of explicit in him.

And this one made her squirm.

"But I never get that way."

"You are that way *now.*"

She shook her head. Like someone caught committing a crime.

Even though the crime was his and all the ways he was speaking. Not just soft now but earnest almost. Passionate. "Mina, you are so wet I could catch the scent of it from outside the school. I can actually hear it, every time you squirm or squeeze your legs together. It sounds so slick, like you already have someone licking you there. Kissing you. Making you come so hard you soak those little cotton panties I just *know* you are wearing. I know you are. And not simply because you're that sort of girl, sensible and sweet about things like that. No. No. It's because that sort of material makes a certain sound, when it strains over a swollen, slippery little cunt. When it turns transparent, because you're so excited you make a mess," he said, so fast he had to stop there and take a breath. She watched his chest heave, with a headful of the filthiest things she could imagine anyone saying.

And somehow, it made *her* take a step toward *him*.

She had to remind herself who he was, just to stop from going farther. "You're just trying to humiliate me now," she said, voice breaking in the middle. But he gave no quarter. He came for her, relentlessly.

"If I was, you wouldn't be enjoying this."

"I'm *not* enjoying it."

"Yes, you are. And you are because you know I'm not saying any of this to be cruel. I'm saying it because I want you to *feel* it. I want you to know what you actually like and explore it. I want you to hear the words that excite you and sound them out in your own head, until all you can feel is that sweet ache between your legs. And all you can do is *make magic*."

"But it will be your voice I hear saying them."

"So imagine someone else, then. Someone better than me."

Like who? she thought. But as soon as she did, it came to her. That face turned toward Lilibet. The being from the Underneath saying that Bram was the best of us. "Someone kinder. Someone sweeter. Someone more loving," she said, and as she did, she found her eyes closing. Just for this. Just so she could see someone like that a little better.

"Exactly so. He loves you so, so much. And everything he says is because he does. He tells you that you make him weak with desire, desperate to kiss you. That when you kissed him for the first time, he felt himself come apart."

"But it felt good, though."

"Oh god, yes."

"He loved it."

"He did. He moaned into your mouth, to feel it."

How do you know that? she wanted to ask him.

Despite how silly that was. This was just a deadly little game. A way to fantasize about something that couldn't possibly be real. If it seemed so clear she could almost touch it, that was just because he was convincing. And she wanted to be convinced. "I can almost make it out. The way it burned through him and into me."

"And can you make out other things, too? Can you feel other things?"

"His hand in my hair. The way he blushed after licking just a little."

God, she could actually see it. A million specific details she shouldn't know—like the fact that moonlight had made that flush look very deep against the paleness of his skin. How he had pulled back, how his lips had parted. The scent of cut grass in the air, and that same sweet scent on him.

Is this a flash of her memories, she found herself thinking.

Even though it couldn't be. He followed it too well.

"He thought he had gone too far," he said.

And she had to nod.

"He did. But he hadn't."

"You liked it. You liked it all."

"I did, oh god, help me, I did."

"Now tell me how you let him know that."

Don't, she thought. But resisting was far beyond her now.

She could feel her head had gone back. Her whole body was trembling.

And not just over this rolling wave of almost memories.

She could feel him standing so close to her. Right by her side, in a way that should have made her open her eyes. But she didn't, she didn't. Instead, she let herself sigh at the sense of his warm breath against the curve of her throat. She let herself think of him biting. Then of him always holding back.

And she answered as plain as that other girl would have, with her lovely Bram. "I told him he could do it between my legs, and I wouldn't care," she said, half ashamed of herself. Half sure she had never felt a thrill like those words created in all her life. And worse:

She wasn't sure he had, either.

His voice seemed actually breathless, when he spoke. Eager.

"And then what? Then what happened, after you did?"

"He said he wanted to."

"Yes."

"So I lifted my skirt. I worked it up over my thighs, slowly. To make sure he could say stop if he liked. But he didn't. He let me get it all the way up, right the way around my hips, in a way that let him see everything."

"And why could he see everything, exactly?"

The question hung in the air—deadlier even than the last ones.

But this time she didn't hesitate. She couldn't.

He had been right about the way she wanted the story to end.

Like this, like this, all sweet and tangled up in something like filth.

"Because I wasn't wearing any underwear," she said, and could have sworn she heard him make a sound. *He's too good at this game,* her mind moaned. Even as she leaned into his next words.

"Yes. Yes," he said. "Now tell me the reason for that."

"The tension between us that had simmered all day. Every brush of our hands, every look, every whispered word. It all just built and built until I could hardly stand to wear them. They rubbed against everywhere I was sensitive, everywhere I was slick, and so I slipped them off just before we sat out in the garden."

Outrageous, her real self said.

Delicious, this other her insisted.

And the other her was right. She could feel that exact thing between her own legs, the moment she visualized something so *lewd.* It made her moan, and he didn't make her regret it. "For that reason, but also so he could drink in all of that beautiful cunt," he said, and for the first time she let herself think:

The way he curls his tongue around that word is electrifying.

It urged her on, even as she blushed anew at what came next.

"I spread my legs to make sure he could."

"Then his reaction—"

"He fell on me like a starving man."

"But you liked it. You like that."

"God, I loved it. I loved him. All I want is to feel him again," she said, all of her knowing that she had been brought to that point by everything they had just shared. By his words, by her words, by the images in her head, like photos from a book she had never read.

Yet still, the way it made her feel to say the word *love.*

To be so full of desire for someone who didn't exist.

Where did this come from? she wanted to cry out.

But before she could, she felt him step away. Cold air hit where his inexplicable warmth had been, hard enough that she knew he had almost touched her. She knew that he had come so close.

And now he was back to where he had been.

She opened her eyes to see him with his hand near his wand, instead of on her.

"Good. Now defend yourself," he said, as he went for it. But in truth, he didn't even get close. Her hands seem to come up of their own accord, already so full of blazing bright magic she couldn't see through it to him. All she knew is where he was, and she aimed true.

There was an almighty crash, and when the dust settled, the only thing she could see was a hole in the stage. Dust billowing up, the splintering of wood. Followed by a hand on the edge of that damage she'd done, as he levered himself back out of it.

"There, you see," he said, as he shook debris out of his hair. "Once you make the connection, everything else is easy."

Chapter Twenty

She didn't know what to make of what had happened. It had felt like a dream—like before, when she had felt Lilibet's ghostly hand on her shoulder. Only so much more intense and vivid that it had almost seemed as if she was living it. She was still mired in it days later, and to the point where she could hardly concentrate.

All she could think about was the kiss from someone safer than him. The feel of her skirt sliding over her thighs. The freedom of doing something so lewd and knowing it would be accepted. And then that glorious sensation of someone's mouth on her. Soft and greedy, all at the same time. Good, good, good, and so much so that she found herself waking, with her hand between her legs.

She almost let herself go further.

And she only stopped when she realized something, in a great rush:

Her back wasn't on the bed, somehow.

It was on something harder. More solid. Like the stone of that table he'd put her on, it felt like, and she panicked a little. She tried to push herself up, thinking she'd sleepwalked to a dangerous place. But once she had, she could see where she actually was.

That was her bed, down there.

Her bed was *beneath* her. The *floor* was beneath her. She could see her shoes on the rug by the dresser, and the top of her chest of drawers, and her stack of books on her windowsill. Like everything had turned upside down.

Though of course she knew it hadn't.

She had done this. She had put herself on the ceiling, in the night, using magic she had barely been able to access before. It flowed through her now, so strongly that she had actually drifted up there. She had flown somehow. She had done what she had only looked up to the sky and dreamed about, before.

And more, there was more.

She made herself float down, with absolute ease. Like it had always been in her—and so deep she didn't even need some of the tools she saw others use. No broomstick, no vaulting pole, no tree branch or chair or upturned table. Just her body, so tightly controlled that she touched down on tiptoes. She stood like that, for a second, before dropping to the bottoms of her feet.

Then she saw her lamps, unlit for all these months, and snapped her fingers. She made fire spring to the tips and was able to flick it to where it should be, no problem at all. And once she had, a bluish glow filled the room.

For the first time, she was able to get dressed in something other than near darkness. She worked on a pair of woolen tights without snagging them, and found the exact clothes she wanted to wear with ease. Her black corduroy pinafore, the blouse with the neat little curved collar.

It filled her with a kind of peace she hadn't yet known in this place.

So of course she couldn't try to resolve the feelings that were making that possible. She had to simply endure the simmering beneath the surface of her body, as she made her way through the morning dorm bustle and out into the crisp November air. *This will cool me off,* she told herself.

But it didn't.

Her cheeks and throat and chest were still flushed when she got to the main building. Like he had mentioned, the day before. Like he had murmured to her, in between a million other things she really didn't want to be thinking about right now. She wanted to be cool and calm and collected.

But then she saw him, across the hall. Talking to a couple of older students she didn't recognize—most likely players on the Harrowhall Gauntlet team. And this time he didn't even pretend to not notice her.

He looked the moment she did. His eyes met hers, full of the same strange, unfathomable emotion she'd seen in them as he started talking her through that fantasy of how things could be. And once she saw, all those feelings pressed on her, even more fiercely. They stopped her breath. Her legs almost buckled.

It was all right, though.

He was there to catch her.

He crossed the hall and took hold of her arm—just her arm, nothing more than that. Yet the contact seemed to sear through her blouse. She yanked away like she'd brushed against an oven door. "I'm fine," she said. "I'm fine, fine."

Even though she knew she wasn't.

And she felt even less so when he urged her into the shadowy space under the east wing staircase and spelled the doors into disappearing. She watched them dissolve with dismay, heart hammering. Trapped with him now, in a way that should have been terrifying.

Yet somehow didn't seem it.

It seemed like something else.

Something thick with words she wished he hadn't said to her, and feelings she should have made go away that morning. *If I had just,* she thought. Only there was nothing that came after that *just.* She barely knew what she was doing on any level, when it came to sex and lust and all those kinds of things.

It was most likely why it was throwing her so much.

Why *he* was throwing her, even though he was barely doing anything at all.

He just stood there, looming over her with his big body. Chest going up and down like hers was—most likely because she had annoyed him. In fact, that was definitely what was in his eyes. They were like black sparks, like burning embers. Heavier than usual, but not beyond the bounds of how he usually looked while angry.

And he sounded it when he spoke, too.

"What happened? Did someone hurt you?"

Yes, she thought. *You did, somehow.*

But she couldn't say it. Because he hadn't, really.

"I just felt hot, that's all," she said. "I didn't sleep well."

"Tell me why. Tell me why right now."

"Calm down, the why is good. I woke up, and I was on the ceiling."

"So outside your bed? That doesn't seem positive to me. That seems like something that is going to get you eaten by wraiths or goblins or the hands that start sprouting under your bed the moment you sleep outside it."

"Hands? Are you *serious*? What do they do to you?"

"They drag you down to the City of Sudden Silence," he said, voice rough with exasperation. Just exasperation. And he definitely hadn't moved closer, she was sure. It just felt like it, as he cut her subject change dead. "But that is not the point."

"No, the point is that you are getting mad at me for doing exactly what we both wanted me to do. Magic put me up there. Without me even calling it or gathering it or anything. I just did it. I just flew," she protested.

It didn't really *feel* like a protest, however.

And had she gone up on tiptoe?

Maybe. Maybe.

Her face *was* suddenly closer to his.

"I'm not mad about that, Mina."

"But you're not happy. And you should be."

"Because you can avoid being flung out of a sky door?"

"No. Because now you probably don't need to give me lessons anymore."

There that settles it, she thought. Only somehow, he didn't pull away. Instead, his eyes seemed to search her face. They trailed all over it, as if trying to find a crack in her certainty. Before they met her gaze once more.

"*Really,*" he murmured.

So she lifted her chin. Tried to seem confident. "Yes."

"All right, then. Make a knife."

"What do you mean by that?"

"I mean make something that can kill me, before I kill you."

"So you still think you could just murder me in cold blood, then."

The light in his eyes shifted. Bright to dark.

Then they dropped to her throat. Her fluttering pulse.

"It isn't a matter of *could*. It's a matter of being unable to stop myself."

"Fine. Fine. Give me a second, and I will. I just need to concentrate," she said, only even as she did, she knew it wasn't going to happen. The second she tried to let it, her whole body just became so much more aware of him. Her skin bristled; she felt her back arch away from the wall he was coming close to pressing her against.

She had to stop.

So of course the magic didn't bloom.

"Nothing seems to be happening," he said. And not even smugly. His voice was soft; his gaze had drifted down between them. It made her think of him looking at other things—like the fact that her dress had ruffled just a little. She could see a lot of her own thigh, when she followed his eyes.

Which only added to the issue.

"Because you're distracting me," she burst out, as that gaze roamed back up to her face. While she kept her own on anything but him. The floor to their side, the door that wasn't there anymore. *Please, god, let him stop*, she thought.

But he didn't.

"Or you're still avoiding fully giving in to the feelings you need to."

"I'm doing nothing *but* give in. I'm barely anything other than that."

"And yet you still can't make a blade. So I hardly think stopping now would be a good idea. In fact, I think we should do the same thing we did yesterday; we should try to build on the foundation we made, explore things that you like slowly, more deeply, and in a way you could never deny—" he said, one seductive word tumbling after the other until she just couldn't take it.

She had to cut him off.

"*Stop*. No. I can't do any more of that, I can't. Please, I'm just not used to it. I'm not used to hearing things like that, and feeling things like this. I swear I don't want my magic to disappear, but god if all of this heat doesn't die down just a little. Just enough that I can *breathe*," she burst out, far louder and more frantic sounding than she really wanted to seem. It came out like a scream, in word form. And she couldn't help trying to get away from him, at the same time. She jammed her hands up, between their bodies, so close to shoving at his chest that she felt the cold heat from him radiating against her palms. In fact, the only reason she didn't go the whole way was that he got there first.

He saw those hands and stepped away.

Yet somehow, once he had, all she wanted to do was pull him back.

Even as he poured more sultry things into her ear. "Mina, your magic is not going to disappear if you stop giving in to desire. But at the same time, it's not likely to do you any harm if you simply explore. If you simply take what you need," he said, in a way that turned that one word—*take*—into something that almost made her moan.

She had to fight to stay reasonable.

"You don't know that. I could make such a hash of everything."

"I promise you, you won't. In fact, exploring what you desire, what makes you feel good—it will only deepen the connection between you and magic. It will make it second nature, the moment you understand completely whatever it is that gives you the most pleasure. All you have to do is just touch yourse—"

This time, he cut himself off. Though she knew exactly why.

She had blushed too deeply, over what he had definitely been about to suggest. Winced, just a little. And she saw the moment he caught it. His eyes widened; she heard an actual intake of breath.

She braced for the mockery that would follow.

Then didn't know what to do with the softening in his expression.

"You've never made yourself come," he said, hushed, unsettled.

It made it hard to know what to say, in response.

"Sex is just not a thing for me. I told you that."

"Yes, you did. But I thought you just meant . . . I didn't think you meant . . . "

"Well, now you know I did mean those things. So you can be quiet about it."

She kept her eyes away from his. But she could see him searching for an angle that would make her meet his. He ducked his head, tilted it—and then most wonderfully awful of all, his hand lifted. It moved too close to her face.

As if he wanted to touch her chin and urge it up.

But in the end, he couldn't seem to do it. He confined himself to words.

"How can I be? All the possible pleasure inside you, all the ways you are so obviously ripe and eager, and now you tell me you have never once allowed yourself to explore it, or give in to it, or even grasp that it's there. God, no wonder a dance and a bare body on a bed and a few words have you looking like this," he whispered, and oh lord, the sincerity in his voice. It sounded so *real.*

She slipped into asking about it before she could stop herself.

"Like what?" she asked, fool that she was.

Because *this* was his answer:

"So ready for someone to have you."

And after that, there was nothing but the beating heart between her legs.

An ache intense enough that she couldn't hold back her intake of breath. It was honestly a miracle she managed to tell him no. "I can't let myself do that with you," she said, half stumbling over the words, choking on them, sure he was going to laugh at her clumsy assumption the second it was out.

However, he didn't even give her that.

"But you *can* do it to yourself."

"No. Maybe. I barely even know where to—"

"Begin? Then let me help you. Let me tell you what feels good."

"How would you even *know* something like that?" she asked, aiming for incredulity. Only somehow it came out restless, impatient. Go on, she heard, in the back of her own voice, behind the actual words. And he leaned in close again, at the sound.

"I told you, darling. I can hear your body. I can see every time something brings you pleasure. I can catch the scent of it before you even know it's there. Just say the word, and I will take you to it. Give you everything you need. Make you feel so good you forget it's even me here with you," he said, every word like a caress against the lips he was now an inch from.

It took everything she had to not do something foolish.

To stick with at least some small resistance. "But I *will* see you."

"So close your eyes. Close your eyes, like last time. Think of him."

"All right. All right. Though you have to know I'll know it's you, the second you touch me."

Because your hands are colder, crueler, she thought and shivered just imagining it. The slide of them over every single place she ached—the curve of her breasts, her belly, that softness between her thighs. By the time he spoke again, it was almost a disappointment to hear him say he wouldn't. "There is no need for me to lay a finger on you," he whispered, before he dipped closer for the kicker. "When I can do everything you need just by saying this: Slip your hand under that pretty dress. Do it for me now, before you can even think about it. Before you can consider how terrible it is, to be doing this in front of me."

And it was terrible, too.

She thought of him seeing her like that, all spread and lewd. One hand working between her legs, in any way he liked. Then blushed so hard it almost felt like something else. She had to rush to put in guardrails, before it got worse.

"I will, if you—"

"If I what? Tell me, if I what?"

"I want you to close your eyes, too."

"They already are. Now tell me you've done what I told you to."

How could I not when you talk like that? she thought. And it wasn't even over that "told you to," either. It was the first thing. The first thing. That simple admission that he had stopped looking, before she even asked. The way it sounded, caught somewhere between the idea that seeing would be too much for him to stand, and the need to not look just to make her feel safe.

She couldn't decide which one it was.

She only knew that both of them were mad, completely mad.

And that they made her do it without even thinking. She had to, just to stem the sweet ache that happened the moment those two possibilities occurred. *He wants to and yet won't*, she thought, and suddenly her hand was beneath her dress. It slid there of its own accord, and cupped the soft curve it found there. Then it squeezed, gently.

Though god it felt like anything but.

She couldn't even tell him she had obeyed.

The only thing she could manage was a startled moan.

But naturally, he knew what it meant. He knew.

"Oh, *yes*. I bet it feels so sweet to cup that pretty cunt," he said, while she searched what to be staggered by first. The sigh buried in that *yes,* the word *pretty,* or that last one—oh, the way that last one kept unraveling her.

"*God*, when you use that word," she said.

And of course he set his mind to making it worse.

"Do you want me to use another? I could say sex, pussy, quim."

"Jesus, that's even worse. That's so much worse."

"Even though it's making you stroke yourself, before I've even told you to?"

She wasn't, exactly. She had just started rubbing a little. Only a little.

Yet still she felt like she had to explain. "Because I'm aching; god, I'm aching—oh, I've never felt anything like this in all my life. I can hardly take it; it feels like too much. Like I might not be able to stay on my feet."

"Then let me hold you."

No, she tried to say.

Then somehow nodded instead.

She let him slip a hand around her waist, like he was about to lift her and fuck against this wall. For one thrilling second it even felt like he might—and then that sudden touch stopped. It came to rest just above the curve of her ass. Hard enough to keep her on her feet, soft enough to be absolutely maddening. She moaned over it, hand tightening reflexively over that soft swollen place between her legs.

And that was *before* the words.

"Oh, that's it. That's it. Ease that ache."

"It won't ease anything; it's unbearable."

"Then go a little further, for me. Slide your hand inside your underwear."

She flushed at the suggestion. But only partly because of how rude it sounded, coming from him. There was another thing she had thought he knew. Only somehow he didn't, and now she had to explain. "I want to, but . . . but . . . " she said, then froze to hear a sound come out of him. A moan, caught somewhere between horror and desire.

Too close to either tell which one it was for sure.

Yet blistering to her, either way. She actually bucked into her hand.

While he talked, quick and faint.

"You *liked* that idea. Of going without anything on under your clothes," he said.

And what could she say? No?

"I didn't even realize I had done it, until this moment."

"And now you know; now you can feel your own bare cunt—"

She made a frustrated sound. "It feels unbearable. So terribly sensitive."

"Oh, I am sure it is. Almost agonizing to touch, I would imagine. Every single thing you do only seems to make it worse. So listen to me, just listen to me—stroke yourself softly, with just the tip of one finger. No pressure at all, simply let it glide over that seam between. Just slow and simple and careful, back and forth, back and forth. Like you're almost teasing yourself open. Like you're readying yourself for more," he said, and oh, how it felt when she listened. The sensation that rolled through her. She couldn't stop her soft gasp of shock and delight.

Or the way she squirmed in his arms.

And of course, he knew what it meant.

"Oh, does it feel that good?"

"Mmmm-hmm."

"Then go further for me. Let me hear how wet you are."

"So wet I can feel it now. I can really feel it, all slippery."

She could, too. Every time she stroked, that slickness eased the way. It made the contact sing, made her ashamed at the thought of him hearing. Even though hearing made him talk faster, hotter. "But it'll be better if you just ease down, down, into the swollen seam. If you sink right into that hot, wet cunt. Go on. Go on try for me; let me hear you finger yourself, just like you did for him."

Who? she thought wildly, *who?*

But then she realized: his better double.

The one she'd needed, the last time they'd done this.

Yet somehow she didn't need anymore. She hadn't thought of that safety net even once, all the way through this utter filth. And she didn't even want to now. She just did as he had said. She found where her body dipped and rubbed there just a little. Then when it sent a spike of pleasure through her, she couldn't resist sinking in.

Slowly, half of her wondering if it would hurt.

Only it didn't; it didn't at all. It made her twist in his arms, instead, over so intense a sensation.

While he held her fast. While he whispered in her ear. "Good girl. Good girl, that's it. Ease them in nice and slow."

"Oh, it feels really, it feels so, it feels almost like—"

"I know. I know, oh *god*, you're so close. I can *feel* how close you are. Are you going to come for me, just like that? Just those fingers working in your cunt—oh, you're so desperate for pleasure. So ready to feel it," he said, his own voice almost as breathless as hers now. As if it was actually exciting him, to hear her soft cries of surprise and pleasure. To get that rock of her body, almost against his. To know that she was fucking herself—desperate enough about it now that the sound filled the stairwell.

Though she would never have said for certain.

She would never have truly believed it.

If she hadn't opened her eyes, just as her pleasure seemed to reach its peak—just as it broke over her body in a great unstoppable wave—and seen his face. How lost in this it looked, as if nothing mattered but her pleasure and his delight in it. The way he'd leaned into her, so close to touching she could see him trembling with the effort to not. And just as she gave in entirely, she let her gaze drop down, between them. Over that tautly held body, that trembling live wire.

All the way to the place between his legs.

And the undeniable evidence of what this had done to him.

The heavy shape of it, so clear she just couldn't help it.

She said his name. She called it out desperately, as she shuddered through more bliss than she could ever have imagined her body contained. It seemed to claim her sex, before swelling through her belly, her chest, oh god, she could feel it in her *teeth*. It ran right up to the roots of her hair, leaving her boneless and shaking.

Half of her wanting to be embarrassed about what she'd done and said.

But the other half knowing she could never be.

The way he had behaved made it too easy to not.

She found herself laughing, hard to believe what it had been like. One hand coming up, to touch his face. To make him open his eyes and look at her. *I think maybe things are different to the way I thought*, she imagined saying. But before she could, he caught her wrist. He stopped her.

And when he met her gaze, he didn't seem pleased.

He seemed agonized. "Make a knife," he said. So coldly she almost couldn't. It shut down that lovely sense of being open to everything, right away. But then he saw her hesitation and snarled; he snapped at her, teeth so sharp that it just happened. As if all her instincts were aligned now.

She didn't have to relax and wait for desire.

It was just there, in the background. It let her form a blade, as bright and sharp as the one he had made, all that time ago. And when he snapped again, like something now barely leashed, she brought it up. She held it to his throat, just to show she could. *See*, she wanted to say. *See, it's okay now. I can defend myself.*

But somehow that didn't appear to matter.

It wasn't enough to him, it seemed.

Because he got hold of that wrist, too. He held it firmly, so firmly it almost hurt.

And he didn't use it to force her hand away. He used it to *draw her hand closer*. He pulled until that knife was so near to him, that the light from it backwashed over his skin. It bathed him in that shimmering blue glow, in a way that made him seem beautiful.

Yet so terrible at the same time.

And even more terrible than that, when she realized what he was doing. She felt that knife actually make contact, and let out a sound of horror. But still he kept forcing her hand. Still he kept pressing and pressing, until her arm was almost shaking with the effort of fighting him.

She actually screamed over it.

"Stop it. What are you *doing*?" she heard herself say. And still he wouldn't relent. In fact, he did the opposite of it. He doubled down, until there was blood, actual blood. She had to beg him with her eyes, but when she did, he *turned away*. He closed his own, so he couldn't see how frantic she was to not do this.

Because doing this was killing him.

He wanted her to kill him.

There was no way around it. No chance to redefine it.

He didn't care about anything, except the oblivion that knife represented.

All this time it wasn't me you wanted to hurt, she thought wildly, as she fought him. *It was you. It was you. It was always you.* "Just let it happen," he said, but god, how could she? She had to stop this. She had to snap the connection between herself, and her magic.

But of course the irony was: It was too in her to do it now.

It didn't want to go. He was going to die, because he had taught her too well.

That's the point, she thought frantically. *That's the point.* And then she did the only thing left to her: not moving away from her magic, but going *toward* it. Fully toward it, in a way she didn't think was possible. She pictured what she needed, bright and clear, and then just pushed herself right into its depths.

And the second she did, she felt it.

A doorway emerging between them, right through the handle of her blade.

Then all she had to do was push him through, to his room beyond. Just one little push, and he was on the other side. And just as he tried to get back to her, just as he launched himself off the ground and toward the doorway she had opened between them, she closed her fist. She made it seal him in, somewhere safe.

Though she didn't feel triumph when she did.

How could she, when she caught his look, just as the magic she had made winked out.

Nothing but despair, of a kind she knew she would never now be able to unsee.

Chapter Twenty-One

She tried not to think too much about him and everything they had done, over the holidays. But he sent no messages, and there were few opportunities to run into him, with no classes and no crowds of students around. She couldn't just find him talking about Gauntlet tactics with someone who sported a monocle.

Almost everyone returned home—including Anaya.

Her friend had hugged her at the gate, and told her to be careful, and then disappeared over the hill in her family's old, battered Beetle. While Mina remained, with nothing but letters from her mum telling her that they couldn't afford the gas, and could she perhaps fly home on a broom? Was flying a thing?

Even though her Mum knew that Mina wouldn't be able to tell her. And not just because she had only book learning and vague instructions and some wobbly practicing to go on, with regard to broom flying itself. Or even just lifting herself off the floor. There was also the fact that she couldn't tell either of her parents hardly anything now. If she tried, she knew the words would be stopped in her throat, and for the first time, she really found herself wishing that was not so.

There was just so much silence she longed to fill.

Two weeks of nothing but being alone with her thoughts.

And her thoughts were always racing, racing, racing. She did her best to make her room a cave of books. To surround herself on all sides and bury her brain in the pages. But somehow it just didn't work. She found herself wondering constantly about why he was so suddenly quiet, if he was all right, about what had happened.

Then hating that she cared.

So what if he's messed up, she told herself, in the middle of Boxing Day morning. One finger between the pages of *Mastering Practical Flight*, holding her place. Still in her nightgown. Hair a wild, tangled mess. *It's probably just disgust with himself, for wanting you for even a moment.*

But it was difficult to make that stick.

And even more so when she finally did see him again. On the morning of her first practical lesson, as she made her way to the hallway she had heard others call *the run up*. Fifth floor, and so long and narrow she couldn't see the end of it, when she joined the line of nervous students there.

All she could do was hear the whoops of joy, as someone succeeded.

Or the screams, as they plummeted.

"Let me see you float again," Anaya whispered, as one particularly bloodcurdling one rang out. But Mina couldn't answer her. She couldn't show her what she had practiced over Christmas: Some fumbled hovering, that her friend definitely didn't have faith would save her.

She was too busy realizing that it was him, ahead of her in the line.

Even though there was no reason for him to be there. He didn't need to come to any of these lessons. He already knew everything there was to know about the basics of flying. But that shape was unmistakable. That height, heads above everybody else. The shoulders, broad enough to almost fill the narrow passage.

And then he turned and looked right at her.

And god, the expression on his face.

It wasn't disgust or horror or disdain.

Instead, he seemed to jerk as if struck. Like he hadn't expected to see her, or have her see him, and now couldn't cope with it. She actually saw his intake of breath, followed by a flash of that same agony she'd seen that day, under the stairs. Then he looked away, whip quick.

Before it got any worse, she suspected.

And she didn't know what to do with that. "Have you had a falling out?" Anaya whispered, but all she could do in response was shrug. She couldn't let words emerge. She knew they would be terrible ones, like *I think it might be somehow the opposite, and he just doesn't know how to cope with that.*

Or even worse:

I don't know how to cope with it, either.

Despite the fact that she had this to deal with now. They were basically ten people from Professor Kirkpatrick, with his clipboard. Someone had just definitely hit the ground. They watched as he confirmed with the resident physicians that some healing spell hadn't taken. *We need a clean up box*, she heard him say, and knew that this meant *coffin*.

It was vital that she focused on this.

And not on Harker, up ahead. Not on the fact that he was now on the edge. *He can fly*, she told herself. *He can fly, he can fly, he isn't about to drop off a precipice to his doom*. Though she couldn't deny it looked like that. He didn't even sit astride the broom he had, the way some did. He just kind of stepped forward, in a way that made her stomach lurch. It made her think of words like *suicidal,* even though she'd done her best to suppress them.

And her heart only restarted when she saw him swoop back up.

He headed into the night sky, as if he could somehow go and never come back. She couldn't even see him by the time it got to her turn. There was just the huge drop and a dozen students still swooping around—including Anaya.

She waved from her own broomstick.

Ready, Mina thought, to catch her.

Even though catching was against the rules. "Don't you dare, Ms. Syal," Professor Kirkpatrick called out. And Mina tried to communicate the same. *Don't risk anything for me,* she had told her friend, way back at the beginning of the line. Now she made it as clear as she could with her eyes. She aimed for confident, for *I'm fine,* as she put one foot out over the abyss below. No broom, no object to help her, just her and her body. Letting herself feel fear, but everything else, too.

What it was to fly. How it felt to desire.

Bram, she thought, as she closed her eyes, and gave in.

Though she knew it wasn't him who filled her with everything she needed. It never had been. It was Harker, it was him, it was his face behind her eyes. It was everything he had done for her, and all the ways he'd disguised it. Because it had been a disguise, she could see that now. She understood it now. How could she not?

He wanted to die, rather than doom her.

"Oh *god,*" she said, as she felt her magic catch her.

Heartbroken, awestruck.

Consumed by these revelations.

But soaring into the sky, at the same time. Not trapped by

these feelings, not frightened by them, but freed—as if he had made himself a stone, so she could be the sun. So she could shine. And she did. She glided across the grounds, hands close to her body at first. But as her courage grew, she let them unfurl. She touched the air with them, felt it rush between her fingers. Used that to make herself turn, until she was on her back.

As if the sky was a body of water, and she was floating in it.

The stars above her. The sound of her friend calling to her in her ears.

"Mina," she heard, and opened her eyes to look.

But instead of Anaya, there was just one of the students who'd laughed, when Sebastian had tried to set her on her fire. His face loomed large: haughty brow, mean mouth, a sneer all over him. And then he struck her hard, with the hockey stick he was flying on, and suddenly she was spiraling. She caught a glimpse of the ground and then the sky, ground and then the sky. The former closer each time she spun.

Scarily close.

She had gone down fast—as if he'd applied some spell at the same time. *Sink*, she thought, and tried to countermand it immediately. She even knew how to do it instinctively. Reverse it by drawing your hands in, instead of out.

But it was too late.

She felt its grip dissolve, just as the path between the trees to her dorm became excruciatingly clear. Then all she could do was close her eyes and brace, as she hit that hard surface. As she waited for her bones to be pulverized to paste, and her skin shredded by the thin gravel that covered the ground.

And somehow got something soft, instead.

Why is it soft? she thought wildly.

But she couldn't follow it up.

She was too busy being whirled around again.

Over and over, and so violently, this time, that she couldn't breathe for a second. She couldn't right herself. She tried to put a hand out and found her arm barred somehow, like something had hold of her. And she only registered what it was, once the whirling stopped.

She came to rest on what felt like grass, with something over her and surrounding her. At which point, she knew. Even with her head spinning and her breath coming in gasps, she recognized all those little things. The winter scent, that strange mixture of coldness and fever, the way he held her.

The way he cradled her, in his arms.

Harker. Harker had saved her.

How had she not known that Harker had saved her? He always did. He always had. He still wanted to, even through his fear. And he *was* afraid, she could see that now. It was in his harsh breathing; the way he held himself over her body. That face of his, now so close that she could see all the ways in which that cold stoicism had given way.

His eyes were haunted holes in his face. There were furrows around his mouth, between his brows, across his forehead. And though it seemed like he wanted to spit some words out, he couldn't seem to do it. They hovered between his parted lips, full of a kind of ghostly tension.

It honestly tore her in two to see.

She wasn't surprised to find herself reaching up to him.

And *oh*, the way his expression shifted. It seemed to dissolve down from panic, to such a sweet softness she didn't know how to stand it. She wasn't sure how she couldn't have seen it. Even with everything he had clearly done to disguise it, to hide behind a mask of cruelty, it was all there. He wasn't a stalker, a shadow, some evil double.

It was just *him*.

Of *course* it was.

"How did I not guess?" she whispered. "How did I not see that it was you, that you are the one, that you are the man she loved. That she loved you. Somehow it was you all along."

But he didn't answer.

He went very still, instead.

And then his eyes snapped open, and all those lovely things were gone.

"So you know, then," he said.

"I think on some level I always have."

"If you did, you wouldn't have said that to me."

"But it's the truth. You loved her. You loved Lilibet. You *are* Bram."

"As you think so, perhaps it's time I showed you what my love did," he said, so dark and grave she knew it was going to be bad. She could tell she had misjudged something somehow, even before he yanked her to her feet.

However, it got much clearer when he started dragging her toward the water they had landed near. A murky pond it looked like, of the kind she knew would be full of horrors. The very sight of it made her struggle. But of course he was too strong for that. He was too strong for anything.

He held her wrists, like his own hands were a set of manacles.

And he hauled her to it, before she could think of a single thing to do. Her mind was a howling blank, when he forced her to her knees. “Hold your breath,” he said, and she had a second to do it, barely anything at all.

Then he just plunged her face into the water.

And after that there was only darkness.

Chapter Twenty-Two

She didn't know what she was looking at, when she opened her eyes. It seemed like the night sky, like stars, but they were filmy. Blurry. As if someone had streaked something over them. *A swipe of red paint*, she thought, because there was a definite crimson hue to it.

Then she registered the pain and realized.

It was blood. There was blood in her eyelashes. If she swiped it away, she would be able to see the North Star clearly, as it gleamed away up there. But the problem was, she couldn't seem to lift either of her hands. They laid there limp at her sides, unwilling to listen to her commands.

As did every other part of her.

Her legs were lead, her head heavier than the center of some terrible black hole. Even her chest didn't seem to want to rise and fall.

And that was bad.

That was really bad. That meant she wasn't breathing enough to keep her body alive, quite possibly. *More* than quite possibly, because there was something else stopping it, too. Something in her throat, it felt like. A thickness, a wetness, a thing that rattled whenever she tried to take a breath.

Not a thing at all, she realized, after a moment.

The *absence* of a thing. The absence of some vital part of her throat.

I lost it on the way to wherever this is, she thought wildly. Because she could tell now that she wasn't in the forest anymore. Or at least, not the forest as it was in her time. It looked similar—it looked almost the same—but the trees were definitely smaller. Things seemed greener, not barren like they should have been in winter.

And Harker was different, too.

She could really see it now, when it was this close up. All the subtle changes he had made—to his hair, from soft and falling too far over his forehead to that smoother look he sported now. Sideburns in her time, but none there, little no doubt magical touches to his nose, his eyes. *He made himself uglier*, she understood, with a start.

Though it was more than that.

In this past he'd plunged her into, he looked almost boyish.

Younger, even though he couldn't have been. He had to have stopped aging the second he hit full grown, and yet there were so many things that made him seem fresh-faced here. Open-hearted, easy to shock. *This version of him hadn't been ruined yet*, she thought. Then somehow got to watch, as that ruin happened in real time. His dazed confusion melted away and was slowly replaced, piece by piece, with other things. Realization, shock, horror. Then finally, oh, finally: the most harrowing agony she had ever had the misfortune to see on another person's face.

It was like watching a void open up where a man had once been.

He seemed to try to scream, and no sound came out.

And she knew why, too.

His mouth was as bloody as her throat was. It formed a beard beneath his bottom lip. It made a thick stripe down his neck. The collar of his T-shirt—absurdly colorful, striped with the name of some Gauntlet team she didn't know—was soaked. Like he'd spilled a lot of his food as he had eaten.

And of course Lilibet had been the meal.

She had been the meal. *She is me and I am her*, she thought, and wanted to laugh hysterically. But when she did, blood rushed more quickly into all the places it shouldn't have been. She choked on it, coughed it up, choked some more.

Then watched her murderer reach for her.

He put her hand over that ruined place.

Like maybe he could cover up what he had done, if he really tried. He could put back what he'd taken, or hold all the blood in, or something, anything to make this not be what it was. *She wore the dress made of blood because he tore her throat out*, she thought, the idea so obvious and so clear she wondered why she hadn't grasped it before. All those flashes of memory, all those whispers from the past, from the girl she had been. And she hadn't realized.

She had almost trusted him.

Almost *liked* him.

How could that have been? *Why did you not tell me the most important part, Lilibet*, she asked in her head. Desperately, as she looked up into that agonized face. As she heard him sobbing these great wrenching sobs, magic pouring out of him and into her. Screaming for someone to come, someone to help.

And in the middle of all that, Lilibet answered.

I did, she said. *I did, I did—I tried a thousand times.*

You didn't hear me. You still can't hear me.

Let yourself hear me.

Then somehow, Mina found herself sinking down, down. Into this other body, this other version of her. She saw not *through* those eyes but *with* them. She didn't watch as the girl she was touched his upper lip, kissed him under the moon on some rickety chairs, let him bring her more pleasure than she could stand.

She felt all those things.

She felt whatever she had before.

She became that girl, lying on the forest floor, slowly dying. And the moment she did, there was only one emotion she knew. A frantic one, a desperate one, she could feel herself trying to speak and failing so completely it was like being cursed. *It wasn't you*, she tried to tell him. *It wasn't you; you didn't do this.*

She even managed to lift a hand. She tried to grab him, to make him see.

But the most terrible part of that was: He seemed to think she was pushing him away. Her, the girl he loved and thought he had killed—he felt her touch him in one last attempt to stop all these events being set in motion, and saw it as fear, horror, revulsion. She watched him jerk back, utterly broken.

And there was nothing she could do.

She died in that place, in the sweet summer of '89.

Chapter Twenty-Three

She came back to life in a great rush, in her own bed. As if it had all been just a nightmare, and now she was waking up from it. All she had to do was take several calming breaths, and it would be a distant nothing. A vague imprint of something terrifying, of a sort that gradually faded into even less than this.

Though of course she couldn't believe anything of the kind.

He had dipped her directly into the past. And the past hung on. That other girl was in her now—not just outside, whispering. Not just one hand on her shoulder. She could feel her, beneath her own skin. A second heart beating with her own. A flood of memories that now belonged to her.

And they all said the same thing:

He loved you. He thinks he killed you.

He thinks he accidentally tore your throat out, in a frenzy.

But he didn't. He did not. More than that: You know he could never have.

Even if he doesn't.

So now she had to do something extremely difficult. Almost impossible, in fact. She had no idea how she was even going to manage, considering it involved undoing almost forty years of extreme trauma and self-loathing. But she knew she had to try. She had to do it, for the man who had felt affection from someone he loved for the first time in decades, who had seen a ghost of his beloved come back to him, and responded by trying to impress on her that he couldn't be trusted.

"I'm coming, Bram," she said. And only realized after she had that she had called him by his real name. That part of her now knew him only in that way, and not just when it came to horrors like this. She could see him laughing with abandon, in her mind's eye. She could feel him actually being joyful. Running from her spells across an empty Gauntlet square, in darkness. Arms around her waist, as she flew him across the lake on her broomstick.

Because he had been terrible at flying, she remembered now.

And the *books*. Dear god, the love of books.

She stopped dead in the middle of pulling her boots back on, struck to her core by this sudden understanding. It all just fell into place, like an incredibly simple jigsaw that had somehow still eluded her.

He had mocked her for her love of reading, *because reading was how it had all began.*

He saw me devouring a book he loved instead of listening to a lecture, she found herself recalling. *Secretly, under the table, frantic to turn the pages. The real version of Dracula, before the magical authorities made sure only the sanitized and more ordinary version was released. And he knew exactly the sort of person I was.*

One in love with the dream, over the dull reality.

One he could talk to. He could share with.

And then, she remembered, he had sent her a book. *From a fellow bookworm*, he had written on the inside. Right beneath the title, of another book that had started off as magic, trying to break through to ordinary people. Before finally ending up as something she knew very well: *The Velveteen Rabbit.*

God, *The Velveteen Rabbit.*

She had to finish putting on her boots with tears streaming over her cheeks. She couldn't even make them stop once she stepped outside her room. People stared; someone she barely knew actually asked her if she was all right. If she ran into Anaya, there were going to be a lot of questions she didn't know how to answer.

But she kept going.

She even knew where to go to.

He couldn't fool her, anymore. She remembered all his hiding places.

The bench beneath the willow tree, the couch at the bottom of the library, the hollow under the stairs. That portrait on the fourth floor that slid back when you touched it with magic, to reveal a little cubby. They had hidden there once, when Professor Hargreaves had been furious over a book they had stolen from her collection. Though she didn't remember reading it.

She remembered kissing.

She remembered his sighs of pleasure.

The memory of them made her heart flutter. It made her whole body flush hot, even in the middle of all of this. And it was in such a state—weak, thrown, half in love and half still her old self—that she found him. In that copse of trees by the lake, that you could only get to by seeing your way with magic.

Like putting a particular key in a certain lock.

Hard for her before. So easy now it was breathtaking.

She formed a shape with her hands like a heart, and the path opened up, and there he was. Sitting an only slightly safe distance from the water, with his arms around his knees. *Hoping something will eat you*, she thought and wanted to roll her eyes. But instead she found herself wondering how many times he'd tried to do something similar. Let himself fall off a roof, wandered into the library after dark, attempted to make some weapon that could be used against himself.

God, it was no wonder he'd wanted her to do it for him.

Constantly, all he had cared about was her doing it for him.

Make a knife, he had said. And now she was even more in her feelings than before. She almost buckled when he looked up, emotion so suddenly clear all over a face she was still used to being steely. He looked haunted, horrified. Before she could even say anything, he tried to stand up and back away.

She made him stay down with a spell.

Invisible wall—two hands flat and face down, together in the middle, then drawing outward just above his head as he rose. He clocked into it pretty hard, and thumped back to the ground with a sound of surprise and protest. Then after a second, he let out a weary sigh.

"Oh god, now you're remembering how to do everything," he said, with a shake of his head. "And you're not even going to use it to get revenge, clearly. You're just going to do stuff like make me stay here and listen to you probably being insufferably sympathetic toward the man who murdered you."

"So that's why you dumped me in my bed and ran away."

"I didn't run, all right? I just walked very fast. Then hid."

She looked back at the path she had easily found.

Then back to him. "You didn't pick a very good spot."

"Only because I had no idea that one memory would give you loads more."

"I think it's a little like poking a hole in a dam. Once you do it . . ."

"The deluge. Yes, I can see that. God, you even look more like her."

"Because I *am* her," she said, more insistently than she intended to. She didn't even know she believed it like that, until it came out of her with all the passion in the world. She put her hand to her chest but somehow ended up clutching it instead.

It made her feel silly.

Until she saw the way he reacted.

He jerked as if shot through the heart; the breath he let out seemed to break, in the middle. And the way his eyes searched her face, that hand on her chest, the curve of her shoulders, the dark tumbling waves of her hair. She knew he was letting it all sink in. That she wasn't just almost, but lacking the memories to be more.

She was *actually*.

And the acceptance made his expression sink.

It disappeared beneath waves of emotion she wouldn't have said he even knew how to feel, before now. Before it broke down entirely. She saw his face almost crumble, in so traumatic a way she took a step forward. She put out a hand, caught between what Mina would do if it was Harker, and what Lilibet would do for Bram.

But he held up his own hand before she could decide.

While the other covered his face as best it could.

To hide what it looked like to see him sob, she thought. Though she didn't know why. The sound he made broke through just fine. It made her think of something being wrenched out of a person. A hoarse and brutal thing, that hit her so hard she felt her eyes sting.

She almost swiped at them, before he could see.

Then she remembered. She didn't have to do things like that anymore.

He wouldn't mock her for it. He'd never even meant the mocking he'd done. It had all just been an act, a show, and now it was over. And he was simply this. "I'm sorry," he blurted out, from around that hand. "I'm sorry, I'm sorry, I didn't mean to do this. I didn't mean to drag you back to this hell. I thought it was just a myth, an old ordinary human tale, something to scare their children with. If you do this, a witch will return from the grave and come knocking at your door. But I should have known."

"You should have known what?"

"That the soul of a witch never dies. And so, if you call out her name enough times . . ." he said, trailing away into something he obviously found endlessly dark and awful. Even though she knew the end. She remembered it from her childhood, and her one much loved book full of fairy tales.

The picture in the middle, of the girl falling from the tower.

The bell of her dress, billowing up. Her prince with his hand reaching for her.

Then the last page, with her in his arms, once more.

"She will come back to you," she whispered.

And now he looked at her. Begging for understanding.

"Yes. Yes. But I *swear* I never intended it."

"Of course you didn't."

"It was an accident."

"I can see that."

"But *how* can you?"

She thought of her version of the story.

The one she'd drawn in her notebook, as a kid, of the prince being the one to fall.

"Because if you were gone, I would cry out for you all the time, too," she said, voice so thick with longing and unshed tears that every word came out strained. They split down the middle. She wasn't even sure he would understand her.

But as soon as he abruptly stood, she knew he had.

"For god's sake, Mina, you should *want* me away from you. Can you not at least see that now? Surely even you, who endured every misery I could throw at you and came back for seconds, can grasp that actually killing you is enough to want me gone? Or to be gone from me? You should *loathe* me," he said, so furious suddenly it should have been scary.

But of course she knew why that fury was there.

"How can I, when I know why you did all of it now? Like trying to force me to leave, repeatedly. Oh, that was horrible indeed. I hated you so much for doing it, I really did. Suggesting I didn't belong, mocking me for doing the wrong things, and going to the wrong places, and terrorizing me with tall tales of what would happen to me if I would stay," she said and knew he would seize on it.

He had spent too long doing it to stop using it as a prop.

"Yes. Precisely. I was hideous."

"You were. But you see, now I can understand every bit of the motivations behind it. I can grasp each step you tried to take. And the first one was targeting insecurities you knew I had, to make sure I didn't stay in a place I wasn't safe."

There, she thought. *Get out of that one.*

And it did seem to take him a second. He jolted on the last word, then simply stood there, flummoxed. Thrown, she thought, by the fact that she'd guessed. Before something seemed to click behind his gaze, and a brand-new argument jumped to the tip of his tongue.

"Does that somehow make it anything other than cruel?"

"Of course it does. Because now I can see every single way you couldn't *stand* to carry on. Like when you saw how much it hurt me in the hall of headmasters, and changed tactics there and then. Instead of insisting that I should go, you started doing things to help me stay. Like sending me back to the beginning of the maze, so I wouldn't end up in some terrifying tier I couldn't cope with."

"I only did that because I didn't mean to draw you to the middle," he said, the extra bit of confession bursting out of him before he could realize and drag it back. He even seemed to curse himself in the aftermath—eyes up to the heavens, a faint *fuck* on his lips. But it was too late for that.

"So you did that, too," she said. "You made the maze shift to spare me other dangers."

"You were just so—you couldn't remember how to do things."

"Like deflect a fireball."

"All I did there was give your friend a lift to the top of the maze. She did the rest."

Again, a confession he didn't need to make.

However, this time he didn't curse. It was her, instead.

"Holy shit. So even that was you? *Everything* was you? Did you let me drag you back to the beginning, too?" she asked, and didn't even have to wait for his answer. His face scrunched up on one side; he wouldn't meet her eyes. "You did. You actually fucking did—though I suppose I should have known that one, too. I mean, what better way to watch over me, right? Pass me notes in lectures. Clock anyone who might be a threat. Always be sure to see when I went to the library, to warn me before it closed."

She half expected him to deny it, when she was done.

Only somehow he didn't.

He let them all stand.

Then shook his head despairingly.

"While berating you for loving books."

"That's the worst you've got?"

"I don't know what worse there could be."

"Doing it again, after I told you how much it stung. After I said what it was like to feel so robbed of everything I longed for, how you were ruining my joy, my most loved things," she said. "But instead, you just shifted gears again."

"I turned up at your door, fangs bared."

"To scare me into agreeing to your terms."

"There were no terms. It was your idea to do the lessons."

Oh you little liar, she thought.

Mainly because she could see it all over his face.

That cocky certainty, now crumbled down, down, down, into a frantic attempt to convince.

"That *you* steered me toward. And always so carefully, too, so as to retain your air of threat. To make sure I was still too afraid to ever like you, or form any of the old attachment, even as you taught me how to survive." She half laughed, marveling. "You know I always wondered why the idea of me tattling worked so well, considering how hard it would have been to do it. I wondered a thousand things like that. Why you were so willing, why you never a found a way out of it. I should have known."

"Nobody would ever if someone was that rough with them."

"You mean because of the velvet curtain."

"Yes. Yes, that and—" he started to say. Only something seemed to hitch in his throat, before he could get to the rest. Like he was doing his best to hammer home just how awful he was, how untrustworthy, how cruel his measures had been. But his own horror over the very idea of them kept getting in the way.

So she helped make it clear.

"Pinning me down. Making me stab you. Throwing snakes, and spiders, and blades. Scaring me, scaring me, scaring me," she said, lingering on each one in a way that made him flinch. It made him feel it. Then just as he couldn't seem to stand it, she ripped it all away. "And yet at the same time, you know what I realize? Deep down, I was never really afraid at all. As if somehow, I understood. I saw without seeing. I felt it without letting myself feel. All the ways you looked after me, and loved me, while never being able to say a kind word, or hear a single one in return. My *god*, how unbearable it must have been for you to never hear a single one in return."

And oh, the look he gave her for those last words.

For that crack in her voice, in between every one.

It was agonized fire. "Stop thinking of me. Think of *yourself*," he begged her, in a voice more raw than her own. Horrible to hear, now that she understood it all. Now that the lengths he had gone to were clear. He had burned himself alive, just to let her warm herself with the glow.

"How can I? How can I, how can I?" she cried. "You made yourself the object of all my loathing, you endured all my loathing—while loving me so deeply it defies description. You did it out of love for me. Tell me you didn't do it out of love for me."

"I could have just told you. I should have."

"Oh, but we both know why you didn't."

"Don't say it. Please. Just let's stop now."

He did step forward, then. He put a trembling hand out, clearly trying to ask her to be gentle. She had to look away, over the lake, just to keep going. She *had* to keep going. "God knows I want to. But I can't. I can't. Because the idea is burned right into me. It's there like a brand on my heart—the reason you kept silent, even when you could have said. I see it more clearly than I can my own self: You just knew I would forgive you, if you did. You knew I would want to be by your side. That I would love you again. Instead of doing the final thing you were sure had to be done. Just one more thing to keep me safe, after all the others put in place. That knife at your throat, that I can still see whenever I close my eyes," she said, trying her best not to cry as she did.

And doubly so when he reacted.

His hand went up as if to take hold of her face. As if to draw her to him, hold her in his arms. But then he forced it to close, before he could. He made a fist and crushed it against his mouth.

She almost felt the agonized sound he made into it.

Before he made himself be calm. He took some soothing breaths, paced, put his hands in his hair. The same way he probably had every time she had turned her back, after he said or did something cruel. She even saw his face settle into something like that scathing stoicism, once the job was done. "It's what I deserved. You have to know it is. You saw what I did to you, all those years ago," he said, flat and cold. Face turned toward the lake, so he couldn't be moved.

It was all right, though. She knew how to undo that, too.

"Yes, I did. I saw. But the thing is, seeing isn't the only way to understand something," she said, and he scoffed. He shook his head.

"What else could there be?" he said.

Though she saw the way he went still. How he folded his arms across his chest. *He did that so frequently to protect his act*, her mind whispered. *Like with the cigarettes, too.* And it strengthened her resolve. "I heard my own voice in my head. I felt my own feelings. And I know one thing now for sure. If you speak to the murdered dead, they can say something that no one else is ever able to truly know in quite the same way: precisely what happened, when they died."

"Yes. I savaged you."

"So you remember doing it, then."

"When in that feral state, I am conscious of nothing."

"You were conscious enough in the library to lay me somewhere soft to sleep," she said, tone neutral but the meaning so clear it made him let out a shaky breath. And she could see his gaze turning inward. Considering what that meant, and what she might be suggesting by it.

Even though he tried his best to discard it.

"You don't know I did that."

"I didn't then—I thought I just managed to escape. But now it's obvious."

"Even so, it's not evidence of anything. I was younger then, I was less in control—when things happened, I just couldn't steady myself. You had to run from me all the time. Always the countdown. Always the hunt."

He made a sound of horror, thinking of his own terrible mistakes.

But all she could do was marvel over the sudden rush of memories.

And every one of them so different in feeling to that time after the ball. God, the *thrill* of them by comparison. The joy of them. How could he imagine she didn't know about the joy? "Even though they never actually ended badly, at all," she said, stunned and full of wonder. "You *never* hurt me. It truly was just a game. I ran through the long grass, through the trees, through the maze. And you would just catch me. In my nightdress, waiting in the middle, swooning for you on the very stone table you pretended to torment me on."

"I shouldn't have let that happen."

"But it says everything you need to know now, love. You sank those teeth in while between my legs, my whole self offered up so willingly you could have taken everything I had. And instead you did nothing but give me joy. Give me gentleness. Give me exactly what you knew I loved."

"That doesn't mean I didn't do this."

"Maybe not. But the fact that I recall being killed by magic certainly does."

Now he looked. Half broken and convinced already, quite clearly. But still trying to resist, until she delivered that kicker. Then after that, all he had left was one faint protest. "Why would you let me argue all of this if you *knew* it wasn't true," he said, as she closed the only ever so slight gap that still existed between them.

"Because I want you to feel it, darling. I want you to know it so deeply there is no way out of it. You did not just somehow hurt me by accident. You did not hurt me *at all*. You could never have, never ever, and do you know why? Because you are the kindest, gentlest, most loving soul I have ever known. And I am so sorry that I left you here, all alone," she said, then on the last word, she touched his hand. Just a little, most of her half expecting him to flinch.

But instead, he glanced down at that one small piece of comfort.

He saw it, and felt it, and let himself look back up at her earnest face.

And then he made a sound like someone finding sustenance, after a long starvation, and hauled her into the most desperate embrace.

Chapter Twenty-Four

There were a lot of things that still needed to be said, as they walked back side by side, to the school. But after what seemed like hours of intense emotional upheaval, and the sudden reversal of everything she thought she knew about him, it felt like kind of a lot to keep going.

She needed time to let things sink in.

To sift through what this all meant.

Not to mention coming to terms with all the new memories that were now jostling for attention in her head. She was able to remember a whole other set of parents. A high school experience that wasn't the same. And sometimes those things made her feel like a slightly different person.

Though she was surprised by how much of the other her felt the same.

The only real major difference seemed to be that Lilibet had known, utterly and completely, that the man now walking at her side loved her. That if she reached out and laced her fingers with his, he would welcome it.

But Mina didn't know how to process that at all.

She looked down at the space between his hand and hers, and it just seemed insurmountable, impossible, thick with tension. And not just because of the way he carefully held said hand, so it never moved closer than six inches away. He had also made a fist. A tightly clenched one, that *could* have meant nothing.

Even though she was doing the same.

She did it the second she felt the urge to touch him.

So she had to wonder if maybe, just maybe—

Yes that's why he's doing it, too, Lilibet said in her head. Though now it wasn't so much saying from outside, as hearing her own thoughts. And her own thoughts were very persuasive. They forced her to look up at his face, and when she did, she saw what she expected to. Harker St. James studiously trying to keep looking straight ahead, while an actual nervous, embarrassed blush spread over his face.

As if Harker St. James was capable of feeling such things.

But then of course, he wasn't really Harker St. James at all.

His actual name was Bram. Short for Bramhope, he'd told people.

Though it wasn't. It was short for Ambramin of Ember, the realm where the Areifen roam. If you said it right, it sounded like water running through rock. It was wonderful, and she wanted to speak it aloud.

But even that eluded her.

"I don't know what to call you now," she finally landed on. Spoken low, because they had just gotten to the courtyard. And he answered in kind, leaning down just a little so only she could hear him.

"You think *you* are having a hard time with that?"

"Yes, but you've had chance to get used to Mina. And I am still kind of her. I still love the mum and dad I have now and hate the people who were cruel to me in this life. I recall things that shaped me a little differently. But you . . ."

She trailed off, thinking of the strangeness of that.

Of how her life had doubled now. But his was a single line.

Even if he had drawn some of his own, between the past and now.

"I don't mind being Harker," he said, with a shrug.

"It's not the real you, though."

"In some ways, I want it to be. In fact, that's why I chose it."

She waited then, for him to add more. Let the silence spool out, as they pushed through the main doors. The entrance hall was empty—the absolute opposite of what had been that first day, when she'd seen him amid the crowd. And it sunk her deep into a series of complicated emotions.

But once they were at the stairs, she realized he wasn't talking on purpose. "I take it the choice was one you also now feel awkward explaining."

"I mean I think you will probably laugh at me for it."

"Even more reason to immediately tell me, before I figure it out on my own."

"Or you could just leave it alone. Let me just be humiliated in my head."

"Is it really that bad? Somehow, I don't think it is," she said, though she knew it wasn't her words that prompted him. It was the hand she let brush against his. The look she gave, of a kind that felt unfamiliar, on her face.

But was obviously not, to him.

He took in that quirk of a smile, and some of his wariness dropped.

"I did it because of Jonathan Harker," he said, and oh, the impact on her heart, when those words hit. Even after everything that had happened, she wasn't ready for it. She had to focus for a good thirty seconds on keeping it beating.

It took her an age to get words out.

"Because he's not the monster of the story."

"Something like that."

"He's the hero."

"Exactly."

"He treats her kindly. Takes care of her. Never hurts her."

"Yes. *Yes.* He is perfectly human and perfectly able to take care of Mina the way she deserves. So you know. It just felt right," he said, relaxed enough by her lack of scorn to run with it now. "And even more so when you turned up with that exact name, her name, from the book. Like a sign that I was doing the right thing. I was trying to be the kind of man I should have been—like re-writing the part of history I had ruined. In some other place I was him, and you were completely safe."

Then he nodded, satisfied.

He strode on, down the hall.

It took him about twenty seconds to realize she wasn't with him anymore and turned back, confused. And he stayed confused when he saw her standing still, fist clutched to her chest, agony all over face. "What on earth are you crying for?" he said. As if it was absolutely inexplicable that she was.

"Because it's *heartbreaking.*"

"Well, I don't see why. I just wanted to be less evil."

"But you aren't. You aren't, Harker. You aren't, darling Bram. Did you not hear a thing I said? You are the monster that isn't one at all. Dracula from the real story before they changed everything around," she said—much to his mingled frustration and shock. The former for her refusal to let him return to that way of seeing himself, she suspected.

And the latter for his name.

God, his name made him react like someone had knifed him in the chest. He jolted, hard enough that she thought she had done the wrong thing. But then he held out one of those tightly clenched fists. And as she watched, he let it unfurl. He did what he had held back from, a moment ago.

So she took it gladly.

Held it tight.

Went on, with one more piece of acceptance between them. One more step toward something else, something she wasn't even sure how to name. Though of course there were other things, still in the way.

"We should probably consider who *was* the monster, though," he said.

And it made her heart jump so hard, she couldn't help shaking her head.

"Or maybe we could just let it go. Whoever it was, they're probably gone."

"We don't know that. I don't even *feel* that. In fact, I suspect I haven't felt that for far longer than I knew. It's like I could somehow tell that there was something else, like a hand on my shoulder. Some sort of darkness, following me around."

"A shadow," she said, as his words made everything sink into place.

The being in the Underneath. His words, like a warning.

As Bram seized them and carried on.

"Exactly. And just because they haven't tried again, doesn't mean they won't. It may just mean that you look different enough that they weren't sure. Or that they haven't noticed you. Or even that they think you're not the same sort of problem to them anymore, so why risk murder a second time? Until you do something we can't know, that makes them think they should. Excelled in a way they couldn't, achieved something they wanted, challenged something they couldn't stand being challenged."

"I can be quiet and unassuming and not critical of a thing."

"And you really think that's the answer? That *you* should suffer?"

"No, but—"

"But nothing. Whoever they are, *they* are the ones that should. *They* are the ones that will, and in ways I don't want to say, in case you think less of me for it. I *will* have my revenge against the nightmare that stole our lives from us, Lil. So start thinking about how we can uncover who they are," he said, so fierce she was almost breathless, before he got to that one last thing.

Her name.

So casually said.

Just that one syllable, tripping off his tongue, like no time had passed at all. So perfectly her that her heart raised its hand and said present, before her head had even caught up. And it took her a second to recover from that. She almost teared up—but knew why she held it back.

She didn't want him to ever feel self-conscious and stop.

She had herself back now. And that meant staying the course.

"They must be a powerful magic wielder," she suggested.

"Making a wound look vampiric isn't exactly hard."

"True. But knocking out a well-fed vampire is."

That struck him. Or at least enough for him to concede, with a grim nod.

"All right. What else?"

"They knew what you are."

"That would narrow the field down considerably."

"Not necessarily. Maybe they never let on to you that they did.

Had some reason to keep quiet, while still wanting to kill me. And kill me in a way that kept them safe. I mean, throw me in a lake and you're going to know. You're going to hunt them down. They're suddenly in grave danger. But frame *you* for it—"

"Then the only person I want to kill is myself."

She felt the words sink, right through her heart.

And couldn't help asking. "How many times did you try?"

"Not that many. Cobble wouldn't let me."

She snapped her fingers. "Knew it was him who helped you."

"He did more than that. He covered everything up, while I was beside myself. Kept me fed, when I refused to eat. And when I went catatonic for all those years, when I slipped into the long sleep, he made sure I was safe. He made that room for me, at great personal risk."

"So at least we can rule him out."

"Oh god, yeah."

"Now we just need to do that with everybody else. And I know where to start: the same place I went to, when I was sure you were something you're not."

"The library, then?" he asked.

"The library, then," she agreed, so excited for a second that she wasn't sure what happened. One moment she was Mina, cautious and unsure of what all of this was. The next she was reacting like someone else. Bram said *let's do book things and solve problems,* and a new kind of glee overtook her.

It made her take hold of his sweater.

Two great fistfuls of it, until he was suddenly close. Very close. Closer than that even, because oh good god was that his mouth on hers? It was, and she had done it. She had made it happen. She had kissed him, all clumsy eager exuberance.

And Harker? Well, he was very not that.

He was cold. He was disdainful. He looked down on things like clashing teeth and explosive joy and passion. *Oh god,* she thought, as he made a sound of shock horror. Her face already heating, her excuses already lined up, her body leaning away from his.

And then his hand went to her waist.

And instead of letting her go, he hauled her closer.

It wasn't horror; it was delight, her brain informed her.

This isn't Harker, this is Bram, it tried to stress, Then for just one blissful moment, she let herself feel it. She sank into it, the same as he was doing, with one long groan of relief. At long last, that body language seemed to say.

Before he came back to his senses, and ripped himself away.

Chapter Twenty-Five

They sat opposite each other, at the same table she had been sat at when he had come to torment her, all that time ago. Annals of the right years piled up next to them. Both of them flicking through, studying pictures of students who looked suspiciously similar to anyone around now. Making lists of professors and patrons and members of the magical authorities in close proximity. Everything quiet and peaceful, until she found another picture of him.

And this one was something else.

It wasn't just a side profile. It was dead on, and close up, over a caption that said *Most Prolific Library Patron 1988*. Everything about it ridiculous, including the little placard he was holding, proclaiming his title. But his face—god, his face. For the first time, she didn't just accept that he was handsome.

She understood what it was to feel desire over the kind of handsome he had been. And it made her blurt very foolish things out, before she could think. "My *god*, you were gorgeous," she said. Then knew that he had snapped a look up at her. She practically felt it happen and cringed.

She couldn't look at him.

Even though he didn't laugh. He just stayed silent for a moment, then finally and rather carefully spoke, into the suddenly tense air. "So you think I was better the way I was then," he said. While she did her best not to meet his gaze.

"Not for most people. I mean you are probably more classically handsome now."

"Yes, but classically handsome isn't the least bit attractive to you."

"What does that matter?" she asked, confused enough that she looked up without thinking. But she wasn't confused once she had, because suddenly the man in the picture and the one sat with her were the same. *Exactly* the same. The softness, the sideburns, the messy hair. God, it was like seeing a ghost.

"I think you know why it does."

"You shouldn't do that. Someone else will see."

"They won't. This is just for you—if you want it to be."

She shook her head, almost angrily. "No, okay? No. It's not your exact features that matter, it's not your hair being a certain way. I just—I like when I can see you, underneath. The good stuff, inside."

"And now you can see it better."

"I could already. The second you let yourself be kind."

"Really warms up my face, doesn't it? I was surprised by that, honestly. How much I changed, whenever I made myself cold and cruel. I really didn't have to do much, to seem like a different person to anyone who saw me."

"And you don't have to do anything more for me. Honestly, I don't even know why you would think you need to, considering I looked like *that*. And now I look like me."

He leaned forward at that.

Put his elbow on the table, chin in one hand.

"Why don't you explain to me what you mean by that," he said.

But of course now she didn't really want to. She tried to pick up a book, instead. Then watched, as he used his wand to turn it into butterflies. They fluttered up to the rafters, while she fought the blush rising over her face. "Well that was better than spiders, at least."

"Don't try to change the subject. Come on. Tell me what you meant."

"You know what I meant. I was very beautiful, then."

"And you think you're not now."

"Of course I'm not. You even said—" she started to say, frustrated.

While he stayed calm and collected, as he cut her off.

"I don't remember ever saying anything about the way you look. Mainly because the more you lie, the harder it gets to keep track. Not to mention how shaky I know it would have sounded, if I'd tried."

"So what would have been the truth, then?"

"When I first saw you my heart stopped."

Her own did the same when he said it.

Though she tried not to let it show.

"Probably because you had just seen a ghost," she said, half-laughing. Then she took in his expression, and even that poor attempt died. It didn't waver, it didn't shift. He gave her no quarter at all, nowhere to hide. He was going to make her believe this, no matter how hard she tried to not.

"Yes, that's what I told myself at the time. It was the shock that made me stare when I first saw you, like someone hypnotized.

But then you must know it happened again, for the second. I looked so long I knew I was making it too obvious—and yet I simply could not stop. Like every facet of your face made me drunk, dragged me down, undid every bit of my resolve. All I wanted to do was drink more deeply, and not just then. In the corridor afterward, in the lecture hall. I used to force myself to face forward, and still I stole glances whenever I could. In the end I skipped lectures, made myself wait outside. And I didn't do anything because I was a fool, lost to something that wasn't there. I did it because in every single way, you are as lovely to me as the day we met. Whether by the beauty of your soul shining through, or the sweetness of it that just is anyway—I don't know. Or care. I only understand that this is the case," he said, so clear and direct and unembarrassed about it that she didn't know how to cope. She wanted to look away, midway through. To escape that impossible surety.

Though she knew why she didn't.

Because she didn't want to break the spell. The one not made by magic, but by a thousand feelings, falling over them both. *If we keep going then we might, we might*, she found herself thinking. Hardly able to imagine what *might* could be, and yet knowing so well, at the same time.

It made her move her hand close to his, on the table.

Not quite touching. But close to it. Their fingertips brushed; she felt his legs shift under the table, until it was barely a hair's breadth from hers. And just as she thought that was enough, he parted his lips. He let his tongue curl up, over the top one. While she tried to stay calm enough to ask what she needed to know.

"But she was more than that, though."

"What more is there to be but kind, funny, intelligent, beautiful?"

"The way she seemed in that picture. The way I can feel sometimes but don't know how to be in the same way. It's the thing I least understand but know that you liked. I know you *loved* it," she said, more breathless than she intended.

But she just couldn't help it. The flood of memories simply poured through her, the moment she started speaking about it. Kissing him so passionately he sprawled back, onto some old couch in a house she couldn't quite remember. Then the lust-stunned look on his face, when she pulled away.

Her hand underneath one of the desks, in a lecture hall. Sliding up his thigh, as he squirmed. As he passed her a scribbled note: *Stop it, before I stop being able to control myself.* But of course he hadn't been able to at all, anyway. She had undone him completely, in a thousand different ways. Persuaded him to make love to her in the sky, made him come using just a spell. Said his name, in such a manner that even that had made him lose it.

And he quite obviously saw all this, all over her face.

"So you mean she knew how to seduce me," he said, half-amused.

Even though it wasn't amusing at all. "Yes. *Exactly.* She could just do it. I can *feel* that she could. I can see the way it affected you, all the time. Constantly, god, just constantly, I swear sometimes I don't even know where to look now, in my own head. When I saw that picture, I didn't just think *beautiful.* I thought of you in that stairwell, that exact stairwell, *begging* her for more. One hand in your jeans, because you simply couldn't wait."

"You're right, I couldn't. But it wasn't because she had some secret skill."

"Then *how*? How did she manage to be like that? How was she that for you?"

She looked at him, utterly baffled. Able to see it all now, and feel it, but still struggling with how to fully grasp it. How to step into it, with such ease. It felt impossible, despite the look all over his face.

He seemed to find the question completely inexplicable.

"There's no great mystery," he said. "It's just the same thing you do, whenever something excites you. It shows on your face, no matter how much you try to repress it, or hide it. The shock of how pleasurable it is to feel it, the need for more, the eagerness. It used to drive me out of my mind—just as me feeling the same drove you out of yours. We loved the desire we inspired in each other, Lil. We loved it almost as much as we loved everything else. It was the sweetest sort of bliss."

"So you still feel that bliss now."

"Of course I do."

"In the stairwell. You wanted to."

"I came so close to having you up against that wall, it horrified me."

"And how does it feel now?"

She let the question hang in the air. And it did so easily, because said air seemed to have grown very heavy, suddenly. Much like his gaze had. It held onto hers, in a way she could hardly drag herself away from. She didn't *want* to drag herself away from it.

It was him who finally broke the deadlock.

"Like we should really focus on the problem we have," he said.

Only he didn't return to the books, their notes. He didn't completely look away. He dipped his eyes down, for just a second, at the thing they were sat at. Then he let himself look up at her, from underneath his lashes.

And she knew what he was saying, with that look.

She knew it better than she knew her own self.

"True. But it's hard to, when we're sat at the exact table you fucked me over."

"I didn't fuck you over this table. I fucked you up against those shelves."

"You did. And I loved every second of it."

Those eyes drifted closed.

His lips parted.

Even as he tried to wrestle himself under control.

Be calm, be reasonable, just think about what this meant.

"We need to slow down," he said.

And all she could think is: *Oh god, we are about to go so fast.*

"Honestly, I don't think you want to. I don't think you want to at all."

"Of *course* I don't. How can I, when even thinking that you might enjoy knowing what we did here makes my heart feel like it's beating out of my body. All of this conversation does. I should have stopped you when you started talking about still finding me attractive, and suggesting that you might want to hear me say that I still find you attractive, too, but god after all those years of being without you and months of being so close and yet so far, of thinking I could never express to you how out of my mind a single hint of your pleasure made me . . . I don't know how to say no. I don't know how to say turn back," he said, words stumbling over each other and fighting to get out, until everything was there.

All their cards on the table.

No need to ask anymore.

"Good. Because I don't want to."

"But we—but you—you haven't had time to really—"

"I think almost forty years is enough, Bram. Just make me feel again what I have only faded memories of. Show me what it was like. Show me all of it, before I die of longing for something I have missed all my life," she said, every bit of it so easy, now. Like riding a bike, for the first time in years.

Then getting to a perfect downward slope.

They didn't even have to pedal.

Though he didn't exactly do what she expected. She imagined him starting at what she could most clearly recall: him lifting her off the ground, his hand under her skirt. And instead, he leaned forward, slowly, hesitantly. Those dark eyes searching her face, as he did. Breathing rapid, faint, like he had forgotten how.

Then he got to within an inch of her, and she realized.

He meant to kiss her. This was going to be a kiss. Her mortal enemy, her immortal beloved—he intended to do something that tender, that innocent. He even reached up, and gently touched the side of her face, as he closed the gap. Still torturously slow, and yet somehow it seemed so fast now, at the same time.

Her whole body tensed.

She came close to telling him she hadn't prepared for this part.

And finally he pressed his lips against hers, as chaste as she could imagine anything being. It was barely contact. A breeze against her there might have felt as physical. Yet the moment it happened, everything in her seemed to stop. She couldn't breathe or hear her heartbeat or think of a single thing.

All she knew was the lightning strike of sensation that went through her.

And the desperate need to know it a second time. *If he had done this at any point while pretending to hate me, I would have lost myself to him without a word of protest,* she thought. And she knew it was true, because she didn't wait for him to do it again. She saw him draw back, gaze full of caution and questions.

Was that all right, she could almost hear him saying.

And she answered by darting forward, to capture his mouth again. She kissed him, and not with the same timidity he had extended to her. She *couldn't* extend it. He had filled her with desperate electricity, and now all she could do was push against him, part her lips, persuade him to part his.

Though it surprised her when he did.

Almost immediately, and with a sound that she felt to the roots of her hair. It spilled out of him and into her, rough with relief and desperation and something else, something she understood more between her legs, than in her head. He made it, and her cunt seemed to bloom. It grew heavy with arousal, in sympathy with that same feeling in him. She could feel her own slickness, over a moan and a kiss.

And she suspected he knew it, too.

His eyes flashed wide the second it happened. Then his hand went to the nape of her neck. So he could hold her there, she suspected, while he kissed her the way he always used to. Shivering with restraint but losing it anyway. Mouth helplessly greedy, rocking and rocking over hers, all hot and open and oh *god*.

That flicker of his tongue.

Barely anything, but so intense all the same.

It was all she could focus on—the way it sparked her desire, and then stopped short of satisfying it. The slide of it, the heat of it, the *lewdness*. It made her think of the things he had said, when she'd been pressed against that wall. How easy it had been to imagine his mouth between her legs.

Hell, she didn't even need to imagine, anymore.

She knew what it was like, to have him lick her in all the places she ached the most. How quickly he could make her come; how hard she used to go over for him. *Once I cried out so loudly he thought he had hurt me somehow*, she thought, and god, that made her frantic. *Everything* that had led to this made her frantic. The thought of then, the idea of what it would be like to experience it in this body now. Familiar longing, all the new layers to what he had done to her throughout their lessons.

He had turned the screws for months now.

And so she couldn't blame herself for being the one who pushed things further. For touching what she had thought she shouldn't want to. She slid her hands into his hair, down the back of his sweater, over his shoulders. Got closer, pushed harder, until he was almost on his side of the table again.

While she found herself nowhere close to her own.

She half-stood without knowing it. Her knee was almost on that smooth surface. Like a little more temptation might make her actually climb over it, to get at him. Mortifying, she tried to tell herself. Desperate, she tried to tell herself. Greedy, she tried to tell herself. But just as she did, he seemed to register where she was.

And the *sound* that came out of him.

The shock in it, the sheer heavy heat of helpless arousal. There was no way to doubt what he meant. Though even if she could have, his hands told the rest of the tale. They ran down over her body, immediately. They followed the line of everything they could now reach, from her throat to her waist and the curve of her hips.

Further, in fact.

Oh, she didn't know what to do when he went further.

When those big hands slid over the curve of her ass, all purposeful, and so obviously greedy about it she had to wonder how close he'd come to this before now. Had he almost at the ball? While between her legs? Was there a moment when she'd bent over, and he had looked without meaning to?

It certainly felt possible now.

He didn't seem to want to stop. She could see him watching himself getting great handfuls of her there, around her body. Then before she could catch her breath over that, he started ruffling her skirt up. Right up, in the fucking library, with someone talking about magical legislation, five sections away.

She heard them droning on, just as he bared her cotton underwear to the air. Another person hissed shush to them, when he slid his fingers underneath the elastic and over her plump curves. And then he suddenly looked up at her, eyes as black as she'd ever seen them, face almost slack with desire. Only the barest hint of question there, amid the sense that he was too far gone to even form one.

All she had to do was nod, and she knew what would happen.

Yet still it thrilled her to feel it, the second he started sliding them down. He just did it so feverishly, hands making as much contact with skin as he could. Half of him still wanting to see, and the other half so beside himself that for a moment he pressed his face into her body. He moaned into the soft curve of her breasts, as if he was losing his mind.

But all that did was make everything more intense.

Her legs were trembling before he even did a thing. She found herself sagging, barely standing, as he finished tugging her underwear down and started sliding a hand over her inner thigh. He had to hold her up with the other, and when that wasn't enough, he hauled her.

All in one go, right over the table and into his lap.

Breathtaking, impossible seeming. As if he no longer had to hide exactly how strong he was. But he was right about that—he didn't. The move made her thrill so hard that she gasped with delicious abandon. She said his name, like a prayer for something more, something sweeter.

And he gave it.

"Ohhhh *god*, do that again," he moaned—as if she was the one who had done something hot. She was spread around him, bare pussy pressed so tight to his groin she was sure she could feel something stiff, there.

Though she understood, once she realized what he meant.

His name tasted good on her lips, too.

She did it again as she rubbed at whatever she could feel, between her legs.

"Bram," she said. "Bram, Bram, Bram." And in response he sagged back against his seat. Eyes stuttering closed, teeth sunk deep into his lip. Body now almost shaking with desire and excitement.

And maybe also with some pleasure.

Every time she circled her hips, he shuddered harder.

Like he had that time in the kitchen. After everyone had gone to bed, at the place her brain called *the summerhouse*. That tension in the air, simmering away. His eyes all over the thin dress she'd worn, then trying to pretend that wasn't the case. *I should go to bed*, he had said.

But he hadn't gotten up.

He couldn't.

He had known that his hard cock would have been instantly visible, if he had. It had been anyway, the moment she got close. She remembered her heart pounding at the sight, him blushing to the roots of his hair. And then blushing even harder when his apology had prompted her to whisper, into his hair.

We don't have to take off our clothes; you don't have to touch me, she had said. *We can just make each other feel good. I can make you feel good. Make you come the way I know you must need to. All this time spent worrying about what would happen if you were close to someone. It must be agony.*

And then he had simply crumpled.

He had let her do what she was doing now.

Rutting against him until he looked like this: flushed, breathless, unable to stop himself running a hand over her body. In fact, he pushed her back against the table, so he could do it better. He spread her out in front of him like a feast, and stroked over her throat, her collarbone, her breasts.

Then couldn't seem to stay away.

He cupped those soft curves.

Let himself squeeze gently.

And when she let out a soft cry, he ran his thumb right over the stiff peak, at the center. More confident than his younger counterpart had been at that point. More skilled. As excited clearly, but able to hold himself back. In that kitchen, he had come hard and fast. Thrilling to her, at the time.

But god, when he made her go first.

He played with her, gently, one hand guiding her hips to get the best possible contact on her clit. Keeping her away from the hard and heavy shape of his cock, but making sure to let it show. As if he knew what seeing it would do.

And it did.

Pleasure rolled through her in one lovely long wave, the moment she let herself think about it. Then again, as she imagined all the times he must have hidden it. *You know he made himself come every night, thinking of every almost touch and heated glance and fight that he wanted to turn into a fuck*, she thought, and god, it just built and built. It filled her up, so intense she could hardly stand it.

She had to cry out, over the sensation.

Even in this silent, stifling space, she had to.

In fact, she did.

And was only saved by the hand he put over her mouth. Just one big hand, to hold some of that bliss in. Yet somehow, it only seemed to make it sweeter. She trembled and shuddered over the feel of it. Bucked against him, desperately, the sound of her orgasm screaming against his grip.

But the best part was: He didn't let go.

Of course he didn't—he knew.

There was no guessing with him, no awkwardness, no being unsure. He understood completely that his hand made her come harder for him, in a way she didn't need to be told. Though he did it anyway. "Ohhh, that's it my sweet girl," he moaned, as she rocked through the last delicious waves of her orgasm. "I love to see how much you love that."

Then he just cradled her.

That hand sliding round to cup her face.

Everything feeling like a long, slow caress, of something more than just comfort. There was a kind of marveling disbelief in it, over all they had just done. Over her body, still sprawled in his arms. Her total abandonment to this. And then finally to what she said, when she saw his expression turn to desperate hunger, for everything he had been starved of all these years.

"Take what you need," she murmured, against the brush of his fingers over her lips. "Let me see what you love, again."

And she knew what he would do, when she did.

She put her arms around him, before he picked her up. Then felt him push her against that wall of books. Like he'd said—only better. Because now she could *feel* how familiar it was, too. The way he had pushed her dress up her thigh—short then, longer now. How he'd lifted her leg, until it was hooked around his waist. Moved her hand until it was above her head, holding tight to the shelf.

And all the while that mouth on hers.

Moaning into her, so brokenly it made her want to cry.

It made her want to come all over again.

But nothing beat the sound of him unbuttoning his jeans.

The feel of his bare cock pressing between her legs—the thrill of that forbidden thing, of knowing he could fill her. And then the way he spread her slowly, with the thick, solid length of him. Almost too much, just the way she remembered. But made sweet by the steady way he went about it. The care he took, even though she could feel him losing that control now.

He shuddered, over the sensation of that slick give.

Then sobbed her name, too fast for her to silence him with a kiss or her hand. It rang out in that silent space, loud enough that she knew people must have heard. She knew, and knew that there would be more to come. Yet somehow, she just couldn't care.

How could she, when words followed?

And oh, the words were these. "Oh, I love you. I love you; god, forgive me, I do. No man has ever loved anyone the way I love you," he said, all in a great tumble, too sweet for her to ever want it to stop. Then he simply sank into the hilt, so deep and quick it made her gasp. It made her turn her head, still wanting to say those words back. But unable to, while so swamped in sensation and memory and a million other things.

She could feel him trembling against her. Expression completely broken open, that gaze locking with hers in a way she feared she would never untangle.

She wasn't even sure she wanted to try.

It felt too good to be looked on with those eyes, once more.

To look back, as that familiar body moved within hers. Forged paths it had before, stoked pleasure she knew well. Gave back what he had been waiting for, for so long. She knew he liked it when she kissed him, as he fucked her. So she did it. He loved the feel of her grabbing his bare backside, so she tried. She urged him into her, over and over, until she knew he was close.

His soft, short moans were always the tell.

But it was the last thing that really got him.

The thing he could never hold back over. The thing that made him lose his rhythm and fuck into her hard and frantic, fearful of doing something bloodthirsty at the point of total pleasure, she knew. But of course she also knew how to make it right. She saw how to stay all his fears.

"It's all right now," she said. "You don't have to be scared."

Then she bared her throat and let him bite.

And in response he let go, gratefully, into nothing but bliss.

Chapter Twenty-Six

It was strange to wake up in bed next to him. Especially when he didn't have to wake up at all. He was just staring at her, through the dim light cast by one magical flame. Face propped up on one hand, covers barely around his half-undressed body. Expression all love, and faint disbelief, and the sweetest hint of total contentment. Like he couldn't believe she'd let him do that and then come back with him to his room. But was very glad she had.

And she was glad, too.

She even tried to tell him, by touching her hand to the side of his face. A little caress that somehow ended up sliding down, down over his collarbone and past the sheets, and oh, he wasn't really wearing much at all. His chest was bare, and then further down, she could see—

"*Lil*," he blurted out, half shocked.

One hand catching hers, before it could go any further.

It made her face heat. "Sorry. Sorry. I just thought . . . I don't know. That this was okay now. I mean, it would have been okay before. But of course I understand that doesn't just give me permission to do what I like, you know? So if I overstep or go too fast—" she babbled, even without really knowing what she was babbling for.

"Fast? We just waited thirty years for that."

"I know but not really. Kind of. Honestly, I would understand."

"Love, there is nothing to. The speed is not the issue at all."

"Then what is?"

He rubbed the nape of his neck. Went to say something, then didn't. Looked away and then back. "Well, I was sort of hoping if you were willing to do those things with me again, that it could be a little more . . . or a little less . . . I mean not quite so . . ." he tried to say. But it was only when he saw her encouraging and wholly confused expression that he managed to blurt the rest out. "I just want to make love to you."

After which she had to laugh.

Partly with bafflement, but still.

"And do you not think that it felt that way?"

"I think it made my heart almost burst out my chest."

"Then it seems like it was as it should be."

"But was it for you?"

He thinks he was too rough and rude, her mind informed her. And in truth, she understood. He'd just spent months being everything but the sweet man he wanted to be with her. Of course he doubted what he had just done. Of course he craved something more, something gentler, something softer.

It was just that he didn't need to.

"I have never in my life felt so loved as I do at this moment. In fact, I know now that my life has been spent longing for some missing thing, because it knew that you were not in it. That there was no you to love me this way, to make me feel good like this, to know me so effortlessly. I think I shut myself off to desire because I knew what really inspiring it is like. And it was always you, only you. You wake me up, you make feel beloved, and to a such a degree you could do it with anything. Fuck me, and it will still fill my heart more than anyone else's softest touch," she said, as plainly as he had always done for her, when telling her the most remarkable things.

And she could tell it had almost the same effect.

His expression was the mirror of hers, every time he'd done it. Eyes like moons, the light in them lost to feelings. Unable to stop staring, not knowing how to speak. Though he managed a lot faster than she had done.

"Did I say I loved you, in the library?" he asked, in a voice hoarse with enough emotion that she knew why he did. She knew what was coming.

Though she was happy to play innocent anyway.

"You did. You did several times."

"Then perhaps I should say it again, when you know I have all my senses."

"I don't need you to. I know you do. And I hope you know it, too."

"But if I say no, you might let me hear it from your own lips."

"Sweetheart, there is no might, there is no let. I love you, and as endlessly as you love me. You call and my sleeping feet will march to where you are. I call for you, and I have no fear that you will come. And I am not afraid to say it. You've stripped me of every single worry about doing anything like it," she said.

Then he didn't wait.

He took her in his arms, in his bed, under the painted stars.

SHE WANTED TO wait until he returned with food, before she raised the things they really needed to talk about. But even the food itself was a distraction. For some reason he brought her an entire wheel of cheese, and a huge still-steaming round of crusty bread, and all kinds of pickles and meats and salad items. Fat little tomatoes that popped under the pressure of her teeth. Sliced strips of cucumber that somehow produced the same amount of juice.

She ate ravenously, sitting up in his bed.

Bare from the waist up but uncaring.

"I'll never get used to just being able to get whatever food I want," she said, in between bites. "Growing up, we were lucky to get cheese at all. And if we did have it, it never tasted like this."

Because it was salty and sweet. It filled her mouth with flavor.

She didn't even need to slice it. You could scoop some out and almost spread it onto the bread. Truly, she thought, this place was the land of excess. A dragon's horde kept from everyone else. She even said as much, after she'd finished, and he made the rubble vanish with a wave of his wand.

But his response was just a thoughtful look.

Like he was going over something, in his head.

It seemed like a good point to say something. "All right. That's twice we've had sex instead of tackling the elephant in the room. And because the elephant in the room could, at any point, decide to murder us, I think we should at least try to make some more headway on talking about it," she said, as she brushed crumbs from the bed and made space for him to sit back down.

He didn't, however.

He took a second to hoist his sweater over his head. He bared his entire torso, from his shoulders to the line of dark hair just about the waistband of his jeans. And even though she'd just spent the last two hours exploring every inch of that broad, heavy chest, it almost distracted her again anyway. She found herself mooning over the glow of his skin in the low light. The steep curve of his back into the bloom of his ass. Then he started on his belt, the button on his jeans, and oh, she knew he was doing it on purpose. She knew.

"I don't even remember where we got up to," he said, as he let them drop.

She came very, very close to reaching for everything she could now see.

Those thick thighs, the slant of muscle either side of his groin, that heavy thing he'd used to make her beg him for more, barely half an hour ago. *Oh god, don't stop*, she'd said, as he held himself over her. Waiting, just like he used to, until the peak she'd almost reached died down.

Before starting all over again.

Partly, she thought, so he could savor everything.

But mostly because it made her come so hard she almost couldn't take it. It echoed in her now, as she watched him sprawl across the bed. One arm over his head, gaze just a little too knowing. A little teasing.

"You're not going to win doing that," she said, and his expression immediately shifted to exasperation. But he settled in to listen when she plucked her notebook from her bag, by the bed, and flicked to the right page. "Okay, so. We couldn't find any evidence of students who look suspiciously like any of the ones who currently want to kill me. No Sebastian Silly Hair, no Oliver Chinless, no whoever tried to make me plunge to my death. Which leaves us with these professors, patrons, and members of the magical authorities."

"I am *certain* it's the headmaster."

"You only think so because of past events."

"So you mean like that time when the one before Dodson tried to feed the entire school to an abyssal monster," he said, so deadpan about it that she couldn't help laughing. She had to cut it off and replace it with a withering look.

"That doesn't mean Dodson is the same way. You barely hear from him. He might as well not exist. In fact, honestly, I don't even think he does. The last announcement he made, it sounded like Kirkpatrick to me. So who else?"

"There's got to be at least some chance that answer actually *is* Kirkpatrick."

"He had every chance to murder me at the sky door. That seems unlikely."

He touched his finger to his lip. "All right. Yates was around."

"Somehow, I don't think a professor of magical medicine is the culprit."

"Probably not. And Gibbons is out, too. He couldn't organize a fen ring if he was made of mushrooms. I once saw him fall asleep in his soup. Same with Cottingly-Smythe, just old even then. Old and useless. Not to mention completely motiveless. None of them hated you."

"So maybe we should think about that more. Who did?"

"I've been trying to think, but I'm coming up blank. You were a good student; you didn't do anything wrong. Or even anything they might just see as wrong. I mean, you were different, like you are now, and you were a little outspoken sometimes about how unfair things—"

He stopped dead there. Like he'd finished the thought he'd had a moment ago, after she'd said something about the food. And it made him go very still. Very unsettled looking. It even seemed like he was holding his breath for a second, gaze far away and focused on the disturbing idea.

She had to prompt him, in the end. "You just thought of something."

"Yes. Maybe. I don't know, I don't know."

"Well, just tell me. It could be I will."

He hesitated. This time, however, she didn't need to give him a push. "But it's not anything. I just had this feeling. I had this feeling every time you started talking about reading books people disapprove of and not liking how this system works and things. It would make me panic, somehow. And I didn't know why; it made no sense. It still doesn't, because I had no idea anyone but me hurt you. Yet somehow . . . somehow, I think . . ." he said, his words trailing into nothing when he got to the disturbing part. The one that made him reflexively put a hand next to hers, and then when he seemed to register that he could, he touched it. He put his own over it.

Held it gently at first, then tighter.

As if to reassure himself that she was still here.

That she wouldn't just suddenly disappear.

While she finished his sentence. "You think I said something that unsettled someone," she said and could see him trying to resist, even as something he himself had known and raised.

"You never did, though. You only ever told me that kind of thing."

"What kind of thing? What specifically did I say, even if it was just to you?"

"Nothing much. You mostly just wanted to find a way that I could go back to Calabaraia—I think because you felt responsible for me getting stuck. Even though you weren't at all. I just couldn't stay away from you. I didn't want to leave your side. It was never there that I missed, it was you; god, I missed you even when you were alive, all the time."

He shook his head at himself, half amused.

While her heart rose and sank, in the same instance.

"Oh," she said. "Oh, now I'm remembering that."

"It wasn't your fault, Lil. You just felt like it was. Plus, you know, you always wanted to do whatever you could to make things better. It's one of the reasons I fell so hard for you. I was different and clumsier at hiding it, and you were so kind. You were so welcoming, even when you realized what I was."

"It must have made it heartbreaking when I wasn't this time."

"It was heartbreaking to make that happen. And then again, when I knew that somehow you still cared. When you tried to stop me falling into the long sleep, I almost broke and told you everything, there and then."

She tried not to cry, at the end of that. But blinking tears back and holding her breath and looking at the ceiling did nothing. They spilled down her cheeks anyway, so freely he noticed right away. He put his hand on her face and swiped one with his thumb. Then when that just made it worse, he pulled her to him.

She wound up curled in his arms, cheek against his chest.

Soothed by the slow sound of his strange heart.

"It's all right," he said, as he stroked her hair. "Everything's all right now."

"But it's not, though. We're still in danger. We're no closer to the truth than we were a day ago. And for all we know, the clock is ticking. Whoever it was could have twigged and started plotting our demise as we speak."

"I'll protect you."

"It's not just me I'm worried about, Bram."

"You should be—they let me live. Clearly, they can't let me go."

"And has them not letting you go been a barrel of laughs for you? Maybe this was just meant as *your* punishment. Leaving you here all alone, in hell. Or maybe not alone exactly, I mean you must have—" she said, embarrassed by what she had just suggested. By the presumption of it. But he didn't even wait for her to finish.

"There's never been anyone else but you," he said, calm as you like.

And in the ringing silence that followed, she tried to take it a different way.

Because you couldn't risk it, she told herself. *Because you didn't have a chance*, she told herself. *Because they would never know the real you*, she told herself. But really, she knew the truth. Thirty years of torment and torturous sleep and pretending to be someone he wasn't.

And he just couldn't be with anyone else.

He couldn't allow himself even a moment of it.

"Not even someone putting their arms around you?" she asked, thinking of at least some comfort for him. But even that made him shake his head.

"Sometimes it happens when we win a match. Although to be fair most of the time I've numbed myself so hard to get through any possible bloodshed that I don't really feel it. And even if I did, it's not as if I particularly like the people who do it."

"Yeah the game sure does attract a lot of arseholes."

"Because the goal is to hurt other people."

She heard him swallow thickly, when he said it.

Though she would have known anyway how he felt about that.

"God, you must fucking *hate* it. How do you even do it? You used to save spiders from drowning. Sometimes you half starved because you'd try to sustain yourself with slices of black pudding, from the cafeteria. I remember you being horrified when you thought saying my dress seemed very tight was a compliment, then discovered it wasn't."

"I'm still agonized about that now, honestly," he said, with enough of a laugh in his voice that she felt a little better. Or at least, felt relieved that he was feeling so. And to the point where she could laugh, too.

"The explanation was very good, though. In fact, I think that's why—"

"You kissed me, that first time. Yes. Yes, it was. I fumbled through trying not to say what I meant, and you knew. You knew it was more than books and kindness and affection between us. That I wanted you."

"Lord, you did. And god knows, I wanted you."

"We couldn't keep our hands off each other."

"Not even in lectures. Do you remember that time when Hargreaves caught us canoodling and called us a disgrac—"

She stopped cold, the word half unsaid.

Both of them knew what the word was, though.

And they knew what it meant. "Oh my god. It's her. Of course it's her," he said, while she was still sat there, frozen. Mind going back over a million snide comments and pinched looks. Before finally, fury thawed her enough to burst out with words of her own.

"Honestly, I have no idea why we've been wasting our time thinking of anyone else," she said, caught between punching the air and putting her face in her hands. "She hated us. She hated me then. She hates me *now*—oh my *god* the other day she told me that I was fraternizing too much with you! You need to consider where such things lead, she said."

"You *cannot* be serious. Why didn't you tell me that?"

"Because she was kind of *right*, at the time. I thought I was in the middle of a horny toxic spiral with a psychopath. I've never wanted to fuck someone so much in my life, despite the incredible threat of murder. What she said almost sounded wise. Instead of what it is now: an intense flashing warning sign."

She made said "intense flashing warning sign" with her hands.

It made sparks fly from the ends of her fingertips.

She had to take breaths, to stop herself setting something on fire. But it was all right—so did he. He went to stand up, on the bed still, then sat back down. Put his hands in his hair, and made two fists, and couldn't seem to get them back out.

And she could see his teeth.

He snapped them together, as she watched.

Like he was thinking of a certain throat between them.

Though that did seem to bring him back down to earth. Now was not the time for biting. It was the time for thinking this thing through. "So she knows what I am. And she thinks it's disgusting," he started to theorize.

But something about that didn't seem complete to her.

"It can't just be that. It isn't just that. There are other things—"

"The way she used to shut you down. Like that time you said the beings who lived in Calabaraia should be the ones to decide. That they should be able to welcome who they want to their world, not the other way around. Not based on some test that some stuffy authority designed, to let who they approved of see. You said it should be dismantled, that it *could* be," he rushed out, voice thick with passion and fury. Then he seemed to remember one last thing, one final touch that put it all into place. And he went to tell her that, too. "And when you did, she replied—"

"People have been beheaded for less, Miss Langley," she finished for him.

Then Bram was on his feet. Already pulling on his jeans.

He did it so fast he put them on backward and had to start again.

But she stopped him, before he could. She clicked her fingers. And when that didn't work, she clapped her hands, as close to his face as she could get. "Hey hothead, we need *proof* before we go to someone with this."

"And who exactly do you think we're going to?"

"I don't know. Anyone who will listen to us."

"Darling, I'm not doing this so we can plead our case with a magical justice system that doesn't exist. I'm doing it so I can unearth who murdered you and then murder them. Maybe after some light torture. Or heavy torture, depending on how much they beg for their lives," he said, so matter-of-factly she couldn't help looking a little aghast. She went to say something, too, something about his soul and stains and if that was okay. But he got there first. "Don't look at me like that, Lil. There's no other choice. This is what we will have to do, and you need to understand that. And understand something else, too: that me being willing to find proof first is all the magnanimity either you or I owe."

And after that, she had to say: He had a pretty good point.

"All right," she told him. "I'm in."

Chapter Twenty-Seven

She knew he hated the idea as soon as she said it. But she had no idea how much he hated it until Anaya burst into her dorm room at ten past midnight, ready to murder her for the crime of never telling best friends what perilous danger you are secretly in, and instead of Bram immediately lying his ass off about everything that had happened, he told her it all in great and explicit detail.

Then demanded Anaya order her to see sense.

"Go on. Tell her that breaking into Hargreaves's office in the dead of night is foolhardy and strictly forbidden by me. And by you, a person she might actually listen to," he said. And somehow instead of collapsing under the weight of the most unhinged story to ever exist, Anaya gave her a *look*.

"He's right, you know. You'll get into her office, and it'll eat you."

She had to throw up her hands. "Oh, come *on*. All you're going to do after he spills that great mess of nonsense is gang up on me?"

"Well, that great mess of nonsense is you not being murdered by a secretly evil Professor Hargreaves. Or not so secretly to be honest, because, well, she did just let a werewolf eat a student right in front of us," Anaya said. Then seemed to process a bunch of stuff all at once, and turned to Bram in a rush of glee and shock. "Oh my *god*, is that why you got yourself bumped to the remedial classes? So you could make sure a werewolf didn't eat her? It is, isn't it? That's why you threw her into a tree! You know, I thought that was weird at the time."

But Mina had to make an incredulous noise for that. "You did not."

"Did so. Why did you think I've been so accepting of you and him having some kind of weird thing? It was obvious you had freaky soulmate-bond nonsense going on. I have totally read this book before."

"If you had, could you not have just clued me in a little?"

"I did try. In fact, sometimes it felt as if I could almost tell that you wer—" Anaya started to say. But just as she got to the point, the delighted light in her eyes seemed to darken. It turned inward, slowly, and her breath caught in her throat.

It was like seeing her own expression in a mirror, when she'd realized.

And sure enough, sure enough, a moment later Anaya spoke the confirmation into the suddenly brimming-with-tense-energy air. "I'm someone else, too, aren't I? Somehow, *I'm* someone else, too," she said, and now the air fairly near crackled.

She practically saw the understanding pass between them.

And the name was on her lips before it was even all the way through.

"Jyoti. You were Jyoti, and I was your friend Lili. And Frank—"

"He was my guy. He was *Will.* And we spent all our time in the secret house, the summerhouse under the stairs. The north wing stairs, the invisible door, oh my god. Is that why I kept thinking there was a door there when I couldn't see one? Is that how I knew how the dining hall worked, how I knew that it was *relief* that sparked me?" Anaya met her eyes, dazed. "We were all friends."

"We were."

"Then you both disappeared, and I don't know what happened after that. I don't know what happened. I think I left the school; I think I was frightened—I don't know," she said, looking from Bram to her and back, as if they had the answers. But of course, that part was beyond them. *I was dead and he was asleep, most likely sure he was a danger to you, too*, Mina thought, even as Anaya had more to ask. "Did someone call me back as well? It can't have been Will—he's such a dope. I adore him, but he's a dope. Oh, Will, were you okay being a dope somewhere, on your own?"

It didn't surprise Mina to hear the break in Anaya's voice then.

Or to see her suddenly sit down, hard, on the edge of the bed. Face in her hands, body trembling minutely. It made her go to her friend before she'd even thought about it, a gentle touch on her shoulder. And words spilled out, before she could stop them. "You are the friend my heart has been crying out for all my life. The one I knew was there but didn't know how to find. Bram, I knew how to get to him, but you . . . oh god, Anaya, I'm so sorry; I'm sorry I've dragged you into all of this. I didn't know what I was doing," she said, words descending into a babble and then finally a break in her own voice.

It made Bram step forward.

Just like he would have done in the past, when his friends were troubled. *Once we hugged each other, in the garden of the summerhouse under the stairs. We formed a circle, an unbreakable circle, full of comfort for all our hurt*, she thought, and just as she did, Anaya turned and threw her arms around her. She spoke into her hair, voice thick with tears.

"Friend, what are you sorry for? You brought me back from being probably murdered by Professor Hargreaves. And now I get to avenge my own most likely terrible death. And Frank's most likely terrible death. Oh my god, *do you think I brought back Frank*? Do you think I brought back my big daft Will?"

She pulled away then, searched Mina's face.

She didn't have to, though, now. The answer was clear.

"I think we might have all brought back each other. For love. And for this. To finish what we started. To make things fair," Mina said, and that energy boiled. It bloomed. It became a bracelet of memories and understanding between them, bright as a new star in the Calabaraian sky.

"I think I've changed my mind about going to that office," Anaya said.

And this time, Bram did not protest.

She could tell he was still nervous about the plan. But it felt as if he was a little less so, knowing that Anaya and Frank were watching Hargreaves's sleeping quarters, while they tackled the office. Or not Anaya and Frank, exactly. Jyoti and Will. Jyoti, who loved to dye her hair pink with magic, and made huge pots of keema for them to all eat in the breaks between terms, and had a bicycle that flew because she loved the movie *E.T.* Will, with his dimples and his obsession with televisions and his tendency to blurt out the strangest things.

"I think someone dropped me down a well," he said, as they stood between the staff quarters and the offices. And then Anaya dragged him away, half giggling over the absurdity, half thrown by the existential horror of remembering your own death. Just as they all were. Or at least all but Bram.

He was just unsettled that they were all so fragile, and might leave him again at any moment. She gathered magic and pushed it into uncovering whether Hargreaves's door had any kinds of alarms or protections on it, and came up with nothing. Yet he still made her check and check again. And after she had, and she had sprung the lock, he didn't want her to go in. He put a hand out to stop her. Tried to maneuver her behind himself.

"Please, Lil," he said. "At least let me protect you a little."

It was his expression that convinced her, however.

She could see how tense and haunted it was, even in the near darkness of three in the morning, in the east wing office hallway. His eyes seemed enormous, liquid. That soft mouth was now a tense line again. And when he heard a sound from somewhere down the hall—just wood settling, nothing more—he seemed to choke while trying to breathe. One hand went out to her, to shield her.

She had to let him go first.

But she kept hold of him. She prepared herself to yank him back or maybe even throw him through a portal, if she could make it in time. *Draw a circle; that will be fastest,* she told herself. *Or make a glass wall again, of the sort that stops things getting to him.*

And it helped.

But she still held her breath as they stepped inside. Her heart still hammered so hard she could see her own skin jumping, when she caught a glimpse underneath the V of the shirt of his she had on. She was sweating, trembling. She jerked at the first shadow she saw and almost flung a fireball.

Only to find a completely empty room.

Quite literally—Hargreaves apparently had almost no furniture. Just a punishing-looking chair, and a tiny table, and a stunted little shelf with nothing on it. "No books," she whispered to him and was heartened to see him look just as mystified and disgusted by this as her. *I now have a partner in crime for all my weird concerns*, she thought.

Then squeezed his hand tightly.

And he squeezed back.

Even though this whole thing was clearly a bust.

"Yeah, we're not going to find a single thing in here. She doesn't seem to believe in secret drawers. Or keeping records. Or even having a place to hide the heads of her untold amount of victims, so she could rub them all over herself when she feels sad," he whispered back, through the hollow silence.

Much to her horror.

"Jesus. Is that really the sort of thing you thought we might uncover?"

"Maybe. I mean, if she killed you, then purposefully left me to suffer for thirty years, and possibly murdered Jyoti, too, and maybe Will, she has to be capable of a lot. Who knows what other horrifying things she's done over the years—and to whom."

"I did wonder if it was worse than just wanting you to suffer. She wrote a paper once about some vampire blood. People using it for weird purposes, doing things with it they shouldn't. And the tone was so . . ."

"So what?"

"Stilted. Strained. I don't even know how to explain. It was like looking into something that had been hollowed out. Completely terrifying," she said, so far into her thoughts about it that she didn't see the look on Bram's face. She didn't notice that he was looking past her, at the door. Body suddenly so tense, it was trembling, like a plucked wire. One hand slowly reaching for her waist, to surreptitiously urge her behind him. She even carried on speaking. "Though, of course, not as terrifying as doing something like this."

Then she looked up and saw.

His still face, the tremor running through him. How almost behind him she was now. And she didn't hesitate. She was already drawing the line with her hands before she'd finished turning. She threw the glass up between them, without even seeing what was there.

But what was there just batted it away.

One swish of a wand, and there was nothing between them again.

It was just her, and Bram, and then outlined in the doorway.

Professor Hargreaves.

Fully clothed at three in the morning, in one of her pinched, practically Victorian dresses. Every iron-gray hair just so, not a lick of tiredness in her steely eyes. Like she was always just waiting for things like this—and powerful enough that she could definitely rise to the occasion.

Though the latter was a given.

After all, she'd done this. And casually, too. *Dear god, Jyoti*, she thought and only managed not to lose it entirely because of the thing Jyoti had done before they parted. The light she'd pressed into her skin, just above the wrist. *If it goes out*, she had said, *then I'm in trouble.*

But still it glowed.

Most likely it was going to be hers that winked out.

"I should hope it isn't, Ms. Morrow. When a little meddler and her fool of a boyfriend and her two little friends make a mess like this, being that terrified is the very least they should feel, don't you think? After all, who knows what is going to happen to them now," she said, in the brusque, withering tone of someone talking about an exam her students had failed.

Yet somehow that just made everything worse.

Mina watched the woman tidily step into the room, and shut the door, and felt her insides clench, then try to shrink back. As if they could get away from this horrible threat, even as the rest of her refused to.

Of *course*, it refused to—Bram was here.

Bram was in front of her, already snarling. "The only thing that's going to happen here is you being torn apart," he said, teeth bared. So razor-sharp looking that even she felt a trickle of fear over them.

But Hargreaves didn't seem fazed at all. She waved one thin hand.

"Goodness me. Do put those fangs away, Mr. St. James. Or should I address you by your given name? Of Ember, is it not? The Areifen sect that hails from the endless stairs? Though of course I know *sect* and *endless stairs* are such clumsy words for the where and who and what of Calabaraia. I try my best, but I am only human," she said, then spread her hands.

As if to say: It is what it is.

And even stranger, she went to her desk. She passed right by them both and went to the one drawer in it. Took out what looked like a pipe, small and neat as a pin, and clamped it between her teeth, to light. And she did light it, too. She puffed on it and leaned back against the windowsill behind her.

As if they were just here for a friendly chat.

Which was still deeply unsettling to Lili. But now it seemed unsettling in a slightly different way. And she knew Bram was feeling the same thing. He didn't lunge again, despite how close

Hargreaves now was. Just a narrow desk between them, nothing at all really.

It should have been easy.

Instead, it seemed suddenly absurd.

"Now," Hargreaves said, as she settled with her pipe. "Are you going to tell me what this little escapade is about? I would assume Ms. Morrow is once more the self I suspected she was and set on her usual nonsense. But I can assure you, you will not find any help in breaking any barriers here. And I would advise you, as I tried to before, to not seek them. Somehow, I doubt the only thing that happened to you was you mysteriously disappeared."

After which, the unsettling feeling shifted again.

Now it was only 20 percent terror and 80 percent something else. Something that felt like dawning realization. Though Bram still tried to protest. "Of course she didn't. She was killed. By you," he said, furious enough that she let her hand close around his arm, as calmly as she could manage.

Though her voice sounded tense when she spoke. Tense and faintly despairing, as if everything was falling apart in ways she just couldn't fully fathom yet. "No, I wasn't, Bram," she said, and now he turned his head, eyes flashing.

"But she *knows*."

"It doesn't matter. She didn't do it."

"What? Just because she's talking like this?"

He gestured at Hargreaves—but it was a half-hearted thing now. And she could see the conviction was gone from his eyes.

He let it sink in, long before Hargreaves cut through their argument. "So that's why you're here. You think *I* killed you," she said, so amused sounding about it that it made Bram blush. Even in this shadowy room, she could see it all over his face, and knew it was on hers, too.

"No," Lili said. "No we don't think that anymore. I'm sorry."

"You should be. What a silly thing to think, when I spent so much of my time trying to keep you safe. It never pays to try the patience of the sort of people who want to keep magic all to themselves here."

So that's what all her meanness was about, she thought, heart sinking even further than it already had. Trying to say without directly saying, warn without directly warning, show regard for Calabaraia without directly showing it. Instill in all of us a deep respect, at all costs.

"You love them. The beings who live there," she said, and suddenly those stern gray eyes were soft and kind. Relieved, it seemed, that she could finally say.

"Of course I do, dear one."

"It's what the magical authorities do that you hate."

"Always. Always." She looked away, as if seeing all the words she had long wanted to say. Before turning back, resolved. "It is not for our good that I say what I do. It is for theirs. It is for his. It is for yours. Every place the authorities govern, they make a mockery of the gifts Calabaraia offers. Of the welcome Calabaraia alone should be able to decide to confer or not. They have made it a thin thing that only the rich and powerful may access, in lands such as ours."

"So when it's someone like me, like Anaya, like Frank."

"You are mistakes. Statistical errors. Drawn here by others."

Hargreaves let her eyes rest on Bram, on that last word.

And there was admiration in them. It made him rub the back of his neck and stop being able to look her in the face. Partly, Lili suspected, because he felt embarrassed about the accusations. But there was something else in there, too.

He just didn't know how to handle someone else seeing him.

Then liking what they saw.

She had to be the one who kept trying to figure this out.

"But if it wasn't you, then who?" she asked, sure that Hargreaves must have some idea. And judging by the *do catch up* look on her face, it seemed that was a safe bet. A safe but wholly terrifying bet.

"Why, whoever has the easiest and only access to the vampire they framed for all of this, of course. Because someone did frame you for it, did they not? And then suddenly here was your savior, who seemed *so* helpful when you needed to cover this terrible accident up. So keen for conversation about things you could never have shared with anyone else," Hargreaves said, in an almost cheery sort of way.

While Bram's face sank like a stone.

Everything sank like a stone.

It made her think of being on an elevator, then suddenly discovering the destination was hell. "No," Bram said. "He's my friend."

"If he was your friend, he would not have used you like a resource."

"But he didn't. I *wanted* to tell him about Calabaraia. I was glad to."

"And were you glad when he published those things in papers?" She raised one arched eyebrow. "Somehow, I suspect you were not. But, well—he *had* saved you, had he not? It only seemed right. Then when he suggested you sleep, I'm sure that seemed right, too. A good rest, away from all of this."

"It was the best thing for me."

"And the best thing for him, too. A perfectly oblivious vampire body for him to exploit and steal from. All that blood in your veins, full of magic and power, ready for the taking. I cannot imagine a more tempting prize for a greedy little man," she said, face suddenly as sour as it usually was.

Lili couldn't help thinking what hell it must have been for her, in this place.

Even as she swam in the horror that Bram was currently going through.

"But he seemed so kind," he moaned. "So good."

"Good is not in manner, Bram of Ember, but in deed. As I fear Professor Cobble is about to show both of you, quite at my expense," she said, the words barely out, before everything went very wrong. Lili saw Hargreaves move, her wand out whip quick. And then there was a sound like a gong being struck, loud enough that it actually seemed to have a physical presence.

She felt herself pushed back into Bram.

He caught her, yet somehow, he was pushed back, too. They both hit the wall, too stunned at first to take stock. But she did have some idea of what had happened anyway. When two powerful spells struck, they could make a kind of reverberation, in the middle. Nothing to the spell casters, of course. But enough to do damage.

And not just to them.

There was a crack now, in the wall on the other side of the room.

She registered it, about a second before a second set of spells were cast. Lightning tried to emerge from the end of Hargreaves's wand, blinding in the shadowy room and incredible enough that

Lili was sure she had it. But then she saw him, illuminated by that light.

Professor Cobble, now in the room.

And she knew. She knew.

Hell, Bram knew, too. It had most likely sunk in just what kind of man his old mentor was, the moment Hargreaves had explained. *Impossibly powerful*, she thought, and he thought the same. It was the reason he didn't wait to see if that lightning landed. He just reached out and tried to grab Hargreaves's arm.

To pull her out of the way, quite clearly.

But it was too late. She looked at Lili one last time. All the regret and sorrow plain all over her face, for things she had not been brave enough to do or say. Then suddenly she was jerked back, as if yanked by invisible strings. And the strings didn't stop there. They seemed to almost fold her in two, so brutally Lili thought she heard bones snap and crunch. It set her teeth on edge, made her make a sound of horror.

Though the rest was worse.

Because the folding kept on.

In half again, her body buckling in ways no body every should. A third time, and now she was the size of a bird box. A whole person somehow reduced down and down and down, faster and faster, until there was nothing left. She simply winked out of existence, in the end.

And then they were left with the man who had done such a thing.

This tidy chap, looking as absent-minded and affable as ever.

"Now," he said. "Who's next?"

Chapter Twenty-Eight

She knew the only thing to do was act fast. No waiting around to chat about how he went about his evil plan. No stopping to find out how he had known they were here and that they knew. The only plan was to get her and Bram out of there immediately, before they ended up as origami, too.

But unfortunately, Bram had other ideas.

He lunged. And with such speed—there was nothing she could do. It didn't even seem like Cobble was going to be able to. A vampire at the full height of his power was a fearsome thing to behold—he became a blur. She felt as if she blinked and missed him moving somehow. One second he was with her, the next he had hold of Cobble.

Or at least, it *looked* like he had hold.

She saw him curl his fist around the collar of that tweedy little jacket, and a wave of vicious relief ran through her. Now it would end. Of course it would—Bram had a foot on the man. He loomed over Cobble, so young and vigorous and healthy looking by comparison. Cobble doddered, he needed a cane; he frequently sat during lectures, as though worn-out. It almost looked as if he needed support, when he clutched at Bram's chest.

Until his entire face changed.

It seemed to split into a sort of grin.

Although really it was more like a grimace. A ghoulish thing that made her think of graves, of horrors. She got a glimpse of teeth that were definitely not normal, and tried to warn Bram. But of course, Bram already knew. He made his own sound of shock, about a second before Cobble drew him close briefly.

As if for a kiss.

And then he simply wound back his arm and threw Bram into the darkness of the hall beyond. She heard a crash, distinctive enough that she knew what it meant. He hadn't just hurled him against a wall. He had hurled him *through* it. *Into Professor Sullivan's office most likely*, she thought. Though it could have conceivably been farther. It could have been through to next week.

Because Cobble was not weak, he was not old, he was not feeble.

He wasn't even *human*.

He was a vampire.

Or at least, whatever sort of vampire he'd made himself, by stealing whatever he could from the man he had claimed to care for. *What ghastly experiments did you do to turn yourself into this?* she thought. But of course, she couldn't say. Terror and fear for Bram had seized her throat.

And they seized it harder when Cobble casually turned his gaze on her.

Mouth closing, face relaxing into that old familiar absent-mindedness. He even took his little glasses off and gave them a polish. As if to really rub in just how wonderful his act was. To show off a little, maybe, after years of having to pretend he was nothing at all.

"Well, my dear. It seems it is just you and I now again," he said, almost chuckling as he did. "So much the same as it was all those years ago. And this time with an advantage—oh, dear me, yes, a *wonderful* advantage. That cretin suddenly smart enough to keep you a secret, to not say a word even to me, to sneak you around and share with you and give you a chance to shock him with the truth," he said, then laughed and clapped his hands, delighted. "And yet somehow still, you prove too pathetic and weak to really do a thing about it. I am to win the day for stability and decency once more. Delicious, indeed."

"*That* is what you think you're doing? Defending stability and decency?"

"Of course. Though naturally, I would never expect such a corroded soul as yours to understand such a concept. Consorting with creatures and lowlifes and the like. That little friend of yours, my goodness. And her disgusting little boyfriend, too. You can tell the cracks are showing when the barrier is letting their kind through. Though not to worry—after this, I think I shall pay them a little visit, as well."

He shook his head and sort of looked down.

As if to say, *Well, it's all very regrettable, but what can you do?*

When of course what he was talking about was *murdering* her *friend*. He was talking about *killing her*, once he had *killed them*. And after he had, two things became absolutely clear to her: He had done this many times before. To many people. That he had definitely done it to Anaya, to Jyoti. To Frank, to Will.

And that she would make her chest a cannon and fire her heart at him before she would let him get anyone else. Not Bram, most likely unconscious and waiting for whatever fate was coming. Not Anaya, still alight but in so much danger. No one, not one person more, sacrificed to some ridiculous idea that a few old rich men should get to decide who was worthy, and who wasn't.

Though she didn't quite have to sacrifice her own body for it.

She just had to understand exactly the kind of person he was.

And the kind of person she seemed like.

"Please don't hurt me," she said. "I don't have any of Lilibet's power."

At which, his face lit up. He took a step forward, almost rubbing his hands together with glee. "Oh, I know, I know. Such a pale imitation of her, really. Not even able to mount a defense against fire or so I hear. Yes, very unfortunate, all things considered," he said, tongue curling up to lick over one ugly, bastardized fang.

Just like she had hoped.

He didn't want to use his wand this time.

He wanted to see what the real thing was like, now that he had the means. *Stealing and hoarding for yourself what you would condemn and curse and keep from everyone else, how fitting, how very English*, she thought. But she kept the seething fury that produced off her face. She crumpled it and stepped back. She cringed against the wall of the office. Covered her eyes, so it seemed that she couldn't even see to do a single thing, to let even a bit of her desire in and her magic out.

And true to form, he went for her.

He surged forward as fast as Bram had done, one clawed hand reaching out to grab her. She actually felt it brush the back of her hand, scary enough that she thought she hadn't managed the trick. But then it fell away, fast as anything, as he let out a sound of shock.

And she moved her hand in time to see it.

Professor Cobble plummeting through the door she had made in the floor.

Down, down, down he went and not just through to the classroom below. She had made sure it went farther, far beyond, all the way to the place where real Areifen roamed. In fact, she could see said place now, when she managed to steady herself enough to look over the rim. There was that gleam of grayish blue, a hint of dunes. And Professor Cobble falling into it all.

She heard him scream as he went through the upside-down sky.

As he hit a staircase some ways up and went silent.

After which, she didn't quite know what to do with herself. She had been holding her breath; now everything in her body wanted to breathe. She had to stand there for a second, shuddering and gasping, hardly able to believe what she had just managed. *I tricked the man who murdered me, with magic I barely thought I could do*, she tried to tell herself, as she started toward the door.

Though that wasn't her concern now.

Bram was. Bram, who still wasn't around. *He killed him*, she thought wildly and couldn't stop herself screaming his name. No thought of anyone hearing, no idea if that was the right thing to do. She just did it—and then again, as she stumbled around the door and out of the office.

But this time, he answered back.

"Oh, you're alive, you're alive," she heard him say, just before she saw his trembling hand reach the jagged mess of plaster he'd been thrown through. He got hold and hauled himself up—with difficulty, it seemed to her. But once he fully appeared, framed by that hole, she could see why.

His other arm was not attached to his body right.

And his head looked very odd. It tilted at a strange angle, and—

"Oh my god, your neck is broken. Your neck is broken. He's broken your neck," she babbled, mind already riffling through for a spell to heal something like that. *Hands clasped*, she thought. *Hands clasped and then turn them inside out somehow, sort of.*

But he got there first.

"It's fine, love; it's all right, look," he said, one hand already on the grisly lump she could see on one side. The other hand on the side that looked fine. And before she could beg him not to, he just pushed with both.

It made a sound like detaching a wing from the body of a bird.

Bile rose in her throat to hear it. The world seemed to sway a bit.

Though it at least meant he managed to come to her. She sagged against the office doorway, as he scrambled his way out. One hand reaching out for her—and god, she reached back. She went to slip her hand into his, at last, at last.

Their fingertips even brushed.

She honestly didn't know how she ended up on her back.

All she knew was how it felt: like slipping on something, without moving at all. Followed by the horrible sense of having the breath punched out of her. She tried to breathe again and couldn't quite do it. Her body had that winded wedge jammed into it, just below the ribs.

And just as she got it out and gobbled down some air, something yanked on her leg, hard. She found herself hauled across the floor to the door she had created, fast enough that she couldn't grab a thing. She scrabbled over floorboards, and the rim of that hole in the middle of them, and for the hand Bram tried to grab her with.

But she went down anyway. She plummeted, like Alice in the old story.

Skirt billowing up, hair a tunnel around her face.

Bram screaming, screaming, screaming after her.

Because of course he couldn't follow her through. He could only watch through that barrier between him and his once was world, as she plunged through the upside-down sky. Clouds that weren't clouds suddenly parting, the air beneath awaiting her. *You're going to end up slamming into a staircase, too*, she told herself frantically. And for a second, she sought to solve this by scrabbling to grab fistfuls of that silver sandlike stuff.

It was only thinking of Cobble that saved her.

She got a flash of him falling, and the reason he had done so hit her.

He doesn't care to really understand how this place works, she thought. *He only thinks from his stolid, superior, old posh perspective.* And just like that, she flipped. She found her feet on the clouds, and the clouds became the ground.

Because of course there was no up and down here.

There was only what you made of it.

And she made it easy.

Now she could look above her at Cobble. Crouched on that staircase, with his wand out, still furiously trying to use it to drag her to him. He tapped it against the stone as she watched. As if he thought it had gone faulty maybe. After which, she had to laugh. She was exhausted, and still winded, and worried about what would happen here. But somehow it just came out.

Though naturally, Cobble was not pleased.

"You nasty little thing pulling that trick," he hollered down at her.

Then he scrambled to the edge and attempted to fly his way down.

Even though she knew he didn't have to. If you stepped confidently off the end of one staircase, it would set you on another that hadn't seemed to be there—another unrule he simply did not understand. *All this time spent keeping this place for people like you, and you don't even know that*, she thought with some bitterness.

But it was all right.

It meant something else, too.

Something she could use, despite his sputtering protests.

"Let's see you fool me twice," he said as he wobbled down to what he probably thought was the ground. Then he advanced. He jabbed his wand at her menacingly. As if he had great power over her. As if he had the same power as he did in the human world. And was seen in exactly the same way.

"Do you know how the Aerifen were made, Professor?" she asked as conversationally as she imagined he'd once started in on Bram. *If someone were to have just a little sip of your blood, now and then, what would happen?* she pictured him asking. Over cups of tea and crumpets.

The idea made her rage.

But she kept it off her face.

She waited, for the second time, for him to do only what he knew.

"Why would I care about a thing like that?" he spat.

And she smiled. She carried on, with one of her much-loved tales of old.

"People think they are fen gone wrong. That the name means literally that. But what I found strange about this is fen do not understand anything being inherently *wrong*. They do not think of each other, or of us, in those terms. They only think of *deeds*. Of whatever has been *done*. Of whatever has been felt, in a way that they feel, too. Their language is all in emotion, all in love speaking to love, pain speaking to whatever soothes it. So I looked into it a little more, and you know what I found? *Arei* means 'life.' It means to give life, where grief for its absence burned. No Areifen come from this place. There are no skin suit vampires. They are all human, almost lost to terrible tragedies, made able to endure. Don't you think that's beautiful? They heard our grief, they found children wandering alone and in pain, and they tried to make them all right again. They exulted them. Gifted them with names if they had none, places if there was nothing left for them, tried to return them to families whole, unknowing that we would scorn their gift," she said, unsurprised that he barely listened to her meandering through her own memories, and all the unapproved accounts she'd read. All the things she'd opened her heart to fully.

And that he of course had not.

"We scorned their gift because the gift was foul demons," he said, creeping forward as he did. That wand trembling just a little now, as he realized it wasn't quite working the same. But still he came.

He walked right into her carefully chosen words.

"And yet you stole it for yourself."

"To even the field of battle."

"So for terrible reasons, too. Not to honor them or ease misery. But to create it, in their name. A perversion of their gift. As terrible as the terrible meaning people like you attributed to the word *Areifen*. To everything here, really. All the times the books claim that fen—and every other thing here—will tear you apart, the moment you set foot on the upside-down sky. When really, it's nothing of the kind. They tear people apart for one reason and one reason alone: because someone does what I have just said that *you* did," she informed him, and as she did, she heard that music.

The one that sounded like the old song.

About it being hard to dance with the devil on your back.

They just want everyone to be able to dance, she thought.

And now the professor was very close.

"I have done nothing wrong," he said, as he tossed his wand away.

He bared his teeth instead, ready to sink in. But she didn't flinch. She didn't back away. She tilted her head and listened instead, for the great horn of the hunt. The endless hunt that drove trespassers mad. Or at least, trespassers who scorned and sullied and spoke only in hope of harm.

"Yes, but, Professor, the thing is," she said, "I don't think they quite agree."

Then she watched as nothingness became shapes, in the dim light. A hand of sorts where none was, the blade of a kind of face. Glittering skeins of something that wasn't silk—and all of it reaching for him.

It was only when they touched him, however, that they became like mouths.

Like rows and rows of tiny biting teeth, sinking in wherever they found purchase. Horrifying in one way. And yet at the same time, she didn't think she had ever looked upon anything so beautiful. It was like seeing the feeling *finally there is justice*. Like hearing in her heart that something was fair.

As he screamed, amid the maelstrom.

And was carried away into darkness.

Chapter Twenty-Nine

She walked back to the place where the door was, once the last glimmers of the man who had murdered her were gone. And she did it as quick as her weary legs could carry her, because she could hear him calling her name. She could feel the sky beneath her feet shaking and knew it was him, casting spells.

She got to the doorway and found him with his hands flat on the invisible barrier. Magic pouring out of him and into it, to the point where that surface had turned into a swirl of white-hot colors. Blue bloomed into red bloomed into purple, and all of it edged in a shimmer of the sort she'd only ever seen when fire hit glass.

She could hardly glimpse him through it.

And what she could glimpse blazed like the sun.

It reminded her of that night in the maze. The way he had looked dueling every person there at once—like a dragon breathing magical fire. Like Calabaraia ran through his veins. Beautiful beyond anything she could ever have imagined. And made more so now by all her knowledge of what he had done it for.

What he was doing this for now.

For love, for me, she thought, as she knelt by the edge of the door. As she put her hands against the places where his were. And watched his magic dissolve, the second she did. It turned into a glow all over his skin, shot through his dark eyes—like the aftereffects of something white-hot.

Then it was gone, and it was just Bram again.

Panting, shaking with exhaustion, so full of feeling he couldn't speak for a moment. He couldn't do anything. He just let out a sob of relief and sagged against that invisible glass. Hands over his head, forehead pressed to the place where her hands were. Unable to feel her, of course.

But she could feel him.

There was no barrier there for her.

She simply slipped through and sank her hands into his hair. "It's all right, love," she said. "I'm all right. Everything we ever read together looked after me. Calabaraia looked after me. Your love looked after me."

"I thought I'd lost you again."

"You know you never could now. Call for me, and I will come."

"Yes, but if you call me, I can't," he said, as he sat up. Eyes on the barrier between them. Between him and the place that had taken him in, as a child. She even remembered now what he had once told her about it. The picture he had painted of a skinny seven-year-old, more eyes than face, half starved, driven away by a cruel father, made whole again by a world called chaotic instead of kind. Instead of all the most loving feelings, over anything else.

"Because you've spent too long abiding by authority rules instead of remembering that they hold no sway here. All you have to do to cross a line made arbitrarily by us is not listen to it. Let it go. Everything Cobble ever impressed upon you, every bit of fear you have of what you are, every effort you made to fit in—leave it behind, live inside your heart. Come to me, my love, and we will dance again among the stars," she said.

Then he met her gaze.

He reached forward, breath held.

Hesitating—but only for a moment. She knew he could feel it thrumming through him, the second he touched where her fingertips were, on the other side. The sound of that music, the call of such wonders.

He smiled as easy as the sun rising.

And slipped through, to take her hand.

To dance forever with her, in a world made of magic.

Chapter Thirty

They walked to the top of the hill together. Her, and Bram, and Anaya, and Frank. The plan all settled in their minds, but still each of them wondering, worrying, looking to one another for strength. "What if this was the wrong decision? What if people freak out?" Frank said once they were there, the barrier between the school and the ordinary world visible now to his wary eyes.

It looked like a sickly storm cloud over a sunny day.

Like something that was ailing, anyway. Of *course* it was ailing. It wasn't the natural order to hoard magic. To insist that the beings within Calabaraia shouldn't be the ones to decide who was welcome to see.

"It will only be those who welcome it in return," Anaya reassured him.

Though of course he already knew. They all did. They had spent the whole of last term scouring the library for all the secrets they needed. The hidden histories of other places who had already made things fair. Shared magic with all who were meant to have it, who were worthy of it, in the only way that mattered.

If you do no harm, Lilibet thought.

If you tread lightly, live kindly.

See a skinny little boy and think, *How can I lessen his grief?*

"So how do we begin again?" Bram asked, but as he did, he was already taking her hand. And she took Anaya's, and Anaya took Frank's. And then they let themselves open to the place they were about to call out to. *Calabaraia, we have come to you to say these rules are not the wishes of this land*, she thought. *We believe in more. We believe we can be more; we only lack your light to guide the way.*

And she knew the others thought the same.

She felt their voices in her head.

All of them reaching out to show Calabaraia the truth instead of a hundred years of lies. *This is who we are; this is who exists in this land and asks of you with the same weight as an authority who told you otherwise*, she thought. And for just a moment, it seemed nothing was heard. She held her breath, answered only by silence.

It's been too long like this, she despaired.

They have decided we have withered.

That we should be left behind by the dance.

But then she felt Bram's hand squeeze hers, as impossible as the moon replacing the sun in the sky. Her love returned to her, after all this time. And she had no choice not to believe. She would always believe now.

Everything is possible now, she thought.

Then in the distance, she heard the horn of the great hunt.

As the barriers between worlds were the thing to wither, and finally melt away.

Epilogue

Outside, she could hear Anaya and Frank chasing each other around. Or maybe it was Jyoti and Will—they hadn't fully settled on who they wanted to be yet. People from the past, people from the now, some combination of both. "They'll figure it out," Bram said, as he listened to the sound of delighted love coming in through their bedroom window.

The bedroom in the summer house beneath the stairs, where they made their own. "Draw," he said, and instead of snakes and spiders and knives through the heart, whoever won filled the other's head with lines from stories they had once loved. That they still loved. *I am all in a sea of wonders,* he sent to her. *I am longing to be with you and build our castles in the air,* she sent to him.

They built them.

In Calabaraia. In this world.

In the home they made within each other.

"You know I meant you, don't you, when we danced. That when I said I wanted to return somewhere desperately, it was to you," he said in between kisses to her throat, the side of her face, into her hair. But he didn't need to hear her answer. Desire made her magic bloom so deeply she drifted above him.

And love made his so intense she didn't even need his touch.

The pleasure he wanted her to feel was already thrumming

through her body, filling her senses. "I thought you were so powerful, so much a master of the emotion that makes your magic," she said, as she let it take her. "But really it was just a shadow of what you can do when it consumes you," she said, and he replied as she lost herself to bliss.

"I am at my very best when I have you by my side, when I can see you happy, when I can give, give, give," he said, and oh, she gave right back.

Acknowledgments

First of all, thank you to the 1992 adaptation of *Dracula*. Without that film, Harrowhall would not exist. The oceans of time, Lucy's red veils, and the stone slab the beast ravishes her on have haunted my dreams ever since I first saw it as a teenager, and they inspired so much of this.

I'd like to thank Tessa Woodward, who made my life by approaching me to write this book. It was a huge dream of mine to get to write dark academia, and sex magic, and vampires. And she made it come true. I'm so grateful.

I'd also like to thank everyone at Avon for everything they did to bring this book to life. My agent, for facilitating all of this. My friends, for being the only ones in my industry I could tell while this was a secret for about a year. My husband, for holding my hand and making me many dinners when the stress of trying to get exactly what this was in my head onto the page. This book meant a lot to me, and I loved writing every bit of it, but phew, sometimes the anxiety was *high*.

And finally, my mum, who still cares for me enough that I have the space to do this.

The only reason I am a writer is because you made sure I could be.

About the Author

CHARLOTTE STEIN is the *Romantic Times*- and DABWAHA-nominated author of over fifty short stories, novellas, and novels, including the *New York Times*–reviewed *When Grumpy Met Sunshine*. When not writing deeply emotional and intensely sexy books, she can be found eating jelly turtles, getting way too excited over a million movies and TV shows, and occasionally lusting after mustaches. She lives in Leeds with her family.